Success Has No Place Here

JACLYN PARKER

DEDICATION

To those who are always admiring the "greener side,"
don't. Walking on grass is a bitch in heels.

CONTENTS

Intermission

ACKNOWLEDGMENTS

I want to say a huge thank you to my parents who've supported me every step of the way while I spent time writing this thing. It's because of you that I've been able to follow my dreams. Thank you Ira and Caleb for always being there to answer any and all of my questions. You guys are my role models in life! Thank you Bubbie for being the first person who said you were excited to read my book. Daniella, Sarah, I'm so lucky to have you both in my life. Aaron, I love you! Soda, I miss you.

And finally, thank you to all those I've encountered over the years who've made me think, who've made me feel, and who've helped me breathe life into this once lifeless work. I may have written this book alone surrounded by nothing but the four walls of my studio, but it was those years of random exchanges at bars and years of exploring the unknown with those who will always remain unknown to me, that really influenced Ray's journey…and mine.

1 ENTER THE MAP

I felt nothing just seconds before he choked the light out of me. When I woke up, I was in unfamiliar territory. The air was more polluted, but also more invigorating. Like a bird born with no wings in a paradise of blue skies, I took a breath in and out just like you, but fell from the sky with a force that only I could feel. I stared up at those who spread their wings and flew so effortlessly while I took those small, misguided steps to a place no one wanted to go. I was given something so generously and so cruelly all at the same time. I was a welcomed guest who wasn't given a key. I was asked to play the game of chess, but when I tried to make my first move I was already in checkmate.

I've chosen to live passionately or not at all. I fell in love then moved away. I fell in love then he fell in love with someone else. I fell in love and then I fell out of love with myself and forgot what it felt like to feel loved by anyone else.

My friends, my enemies, fellow readers, fellow wanderers, this may be the most honest fictional work you'll ever read. You might at some points lose yourself because you'll blur the lines between you and me. The pieces are sewn together with cheap thread, but perhaps they'll provide you with the warmth that they didn't give me. The words are real because you can feel them. If you let yourself, you can feel them all over like an ocean wave that consumes your entire body.

I was born with a threshold for happiness that was too high for ninety-nine percent of the world's population to meet. I am at the mercy of the mechanisms that control the mind. I remember sitting in that man's office when he told me that I wasn't suffering. I remember him using the fact that I was sitting before him as an indication that I wasn't really that sick. I remember wanting to reach across the table and throttle him. Too bad he didn't know I spent the night before driving around the city at four-thirty in the morning waiting for the coffee shops to open. Too bad he didn't know my worst enemy was my mind, and this train I was on had already been off the tracks for miles.

INTERMISSION

It's that time of night again. I sit here looking out the window knowing that the darkness of sundown is approaching when all I'll feel is euphoria because I'm filled with almost more red wine than blood. There's no one in my vicinity. There's no one on the other end of the phone line or waiting for me to step off the bus. I see so many cars rush by as I stare out the window wondering how the coldness from the glass hasn't made me shiver yet. I wonder how my naked body hasn't garnered any attention. It's all that stares back at me when I look in the mirror. Being five floors up doesn't make me feel any lighter; it's just a longer way to fall. In this moment I am content. In this moment, I've consumed more alcohol than any woman ever should, but I don't feel a thing. I guess that's the point. I lay my head down on the pillow and watch the ceiling spin until I close my eyes and forget that falling asleep only means waking up sober.

2 BETWEEN THESE WALLS

I've been a ferocious reader my entire life, until I took a few English courses in college. I learned that literary interpretations were subjective, and despite being a self-destructive person, I still wanted to protect myself from the cruel and insensitive judgment that English professors unsparingly disseminated to their subordinates. I finally realized that I'd never be able to gain control until I had the courage to do and say what I wanted, no rules to impede those misguided masterful thoughts.

If I could choose my last dying words it would be a fragment sentence with a preposition at the end. One final line to finally feel in control before I slipped away into a fairyland created to remedy the anxiety of being surrounded by nothing but a box and soil for the rest of eternity.

I write now because it's the only way I can create a world that will never exist outside of my imagination. I write because my real life is not exciting enough to keep me entertained. I put the blade down and picked up a pen.

I live with four walls surrounding me, probably very much like you, but my walls are a lot thicker. I've gotten to know them, memorize their defects, their marks, and their damages. I've learned to rely on the comfort they provide, like a parasite holding onto its host for dear life.

The words on a page that once spoke to me as a child, shielding me from the real world, are now the words that lie dormant on my nightstand covered in dust. I've transformed from consumer to creator.

I've thrown away my classic novels because I don't have the patience to decipher old English garble and I can never relate to the characters. I can't feel how a woman in the nineteenth century felt when she was heartbroken over a man who didn't ask her to the grand ball. I can't feel the same kind of loneliness they felt because I am living in a world of technology where everyone is only a click away, where people are bottled down into nothing but a username and a picture. We are who our profile says we are. I'd rather interact with a complete stranger behind my computer screen than talk to a person in the flesh. I'm happy having five thousand followers and five best friends.

There's a thin layer surrounding my daily activities. I've grown accustomed to the confines of my comfort zone and learned to love my limitations more than hate the world I've yet to experience. Every once in a while I peek outside, grab a man, or at least a cupcake, and bring him or it into the layer I've grown to love and loathe. This world has four walls that are ever changing.

3 A DREAM AT THE OCEAN

I live in Los Angeles, in the crazy and vibrant beach side neighborhood, Venice. I grew up in Rutland, Vermont. My family stayed there, and I moved to the West Coast alone. Desperate to click the refresh button, I needed to erase the history from my profile and learn a new method of surviving. I felt alienated in a culture that didn't know how to celebrate life the way I had always yearned.

I was given opportunities to go after my dreams, but achieved nothing. My family loved me almost as much as I loved them. I wandered aimlessly from one activity to the next. I failed each endeavor worse and worse as I tried to tackle more.

At the age of three I embarked on a career in acting. I landed one television commercial in New York City, but never made it any further. By the age of six, I started dancing.

That same year my parents took me to the Pacific

Ocean. I remember my mom telling me not to let go of her hand. We were walking along the boardwalk, just steps away from the sand. I heard the unfamiliar noise of the waves crashing. I couldn't stop watching the waves form and then disappear again and again. There was no specific pattern; they were all different sizes, some so small like little hiccups and some so large and fascinating like big, live water monsters.

I had touched rivers and lakes, but I had only ever seen pictures of the ocean. The endless waves, the rays of sun making the water sparkle, and the gorgeous sky in the background only made up half of the ocean's beauty. I learned that there were three reasons why pictures of the ocean would always fall short of explaining its true beauty. With a picture I couldn't hear the sound of the waves crashing up against the shore. I couldn't smell that fresh summer air mixing with the salt from the ocean to create a scent lovelier than a campfire. I couldn't feel the sand in between my toes or the exhilarating force of the waves pushing against my body filling it with life and a revitalizing sense of passion and hope.

The ocean was my first love. Dancing was my second.

I danced for twelve years until I was eighteen and landed myself in the hospital suffering from exhaustion and anorexia. Despite my meager frame, every time I stepped on the dance floor my goal was to inspire a feeling so deep in others that they could experience at least an ounce of the feelings that ran through my body every time I moved a muscle to the beat.

When I wasn't on the dance floor, in the gym, or at school, I was playing soccer with my friends or by myself. I played in a recreational league until I was twenty-one. At that point I realized that my passion for soccer wasn't taking me anywhere in life, just like the twelve years I had spent dancing. All of my aspirations as a child ended with no outlook for the future. At twenty-one I had to embark on a new journey. I decided to follow my first love, and so I moved to the ocean.

I slowly learned that being passionate about something in life always meant having to sacrifice something else. As a five foot seven dancer, I weighed a mere hundred pounds. While kids my age were having sleepovers and practicing kissing their pillows, I was working towards a perfection that took me twelve years to realize didn't exist.

People asked me how I did it, how I became so skinny. I said I ate less, I shrunk my stomach, cried myself to sleep for several months, and it all got easier from there. Dancing was my motivation at the beginning. Self-perfection became my motivation by the end. It wasn't just easy; it was fun. The numbers on the scale were all part of the game, the strategy. Watching the numbers decrease gave me the same feeling I had after smoking. My body relaxed and tensed at the same time. I rose so high but let my skin sink so deep.

I worked on my body like a person works on their home. I was methodical, strategic, and thoughtful. Every day I studied the changes in the mirror, took pictures, and admired that fresh invigorating feeling every morning.

I am now twenty-eight years old and have learned to love my body. It is my home whether or not it protects me. I'm sexiest when I have bags under my eyes, messy post-fuck hair, and bruises on my hipbones. The scar on my wrist is the only tattoo I'll ever need. It's the mark of beauty that reminds me of the ugliness I felt.

4 NO CAREER FOR YOUNG WOMEN

I play piano, but not the kind of piano you may think. My piano looks a lot different than the one you have sitting in your living room. It doesn't involve sound or notes, but it does have keys, a different set of keys: my laptop keyboard. When I press down on the keys, music doesn't come out, silent words do. I am a writer. I have no important initials in front of my name. I've done no Ph.D. I'm nobody's wife. I'm not even anybody's girlfriend. I'm Miss Raya Rivers. Most people call my Ray.

In middle school, a boy named Adam asked me if I was a pirate. There we were sitting on top of the monkey bars where I spent all my recesses. He sat there with his oversized black concert t-shirt and waited for my response. I sat there in my pink "I'll honk for Jesus" t-shirt. I stared at him blankly. When he carved our initials in a tree, I wondered how they'd look on our wedding cake.

Finally I said no, then smiled awkwardly.

"Really? Cause your initials spell, "RRRR," he said closing one eye like a pirate and bending his pointer finger into a hook-like shape.

I'm sad to report my dating pool hasn't improved much since then, but my name is no longer the center of attention or a cause for an awkwardly timed joke. It's just the words I sign on my receipts and the words I use to introduce myself. Ray. Just Ray: simple to write, simple to pronounce, and the simplicity ends there.

I have a laundry bin stacked high with piles of journals dating back from when I first learned how to write. When my pen hits paper or my hands hover above the keyboard, it's like another force takes over. I use my hands, but it's my mind that propels the engine. At the age of fourteen, I began writing my first manuscript. I discarded it because it was immature, superficial, uninformed, and unoriginal.

Since then I have matured. I've grown into a woman that still has no stable bearing, but I have less fear of the unknown. A failed manuscript isn't new to me. It can't lower my self-esteem any more than it already has. My words are like the extended fingers of my body; they represent who I was in the very moment I wrote them down, and they'll stay a part of me for as long as I can keep the project alive.

The reread that gets me every time. The words grow foreign. Immature. Lifeless. My name tarnishes on the same page as words with no authenticity. I'm never the same person twice. I'm never who I was five minutes ago, five hours ago, or five days ago. And I am definitely not who I was five years ago.

I have no stable career. I jump from internship to internship that pays for my lunch and sends me home at the end of the day with not even enough money to pay for the gas it takes me to get there.

I work to gain experience in a variety of fields so that I can narrow down what I like to do by experiencing everything that I don't. I want to be a writer, I've tried to be a writer, my friends and family call me a writer, but like the tree falling in the forest analogy, am I really a writer if no one reads my words? I've ended up in bartending, public relations, and entertainment, with very few opportunities to increase my likelihood of breaking into a career as a novelist.

Growing up I was told that I was a very sexy dancer. One guy pointed out that I would never have to worry about money because if I ever got stuck, I would make a great stripper. I would never admit it, but when I received rejection after rejection the thought of taking my clothes off for money seemed scarier and scarier as it became more and more likely to be my fate.

Currently my nights are spent making cocktails. I work at a local bar called Skinty's. I wear a skin-tight short black dress that pushes up my C-cup boobs and makes my Pilates-toned ass look delicious enough for drunk men to mistake for a sandwich. When I'm serving at the bar, I tell myself I'm working for my future. I'm working to figure out what I don't want, thereby clarifying what I do.

I've discovered that looks mean nothing. Pictures are worth less than the paper used to print them. A smile is not a signal of endearment or sincerity; it is a means to an end. It is a clever way to forge a superficial bond with the opposite sex for purposes of pleasure. I get smiled at all the time, especially when I'm wearing five-inch heels carrying a tray of drinks above my head and delivering them to horny men in button-down shirts hitting on vulnerable young women. I debated whether it's better than the alternative of not being noticed at all, wandering around being a servant and nothing more.

"Hey sweet cheeks. Another round," an over-cologned man winked at me.

"Sure thing," I said. "Numnuts," I muttered under my breath.

"What?"

"Four more appletinis coming right up," I said with lips turned upwards, teeth showing, and cheekbones raised just like a smile.

I'd be a hypocrite if I said I've never acted one way to ensure a satisfying result. I've smiled, winked, swallowed; the only difference is my actions didn't hurt anyone else but myself.

I brushed up on my acting skills last summer when I interned for a talent management company. I saw firsthand how celebrity images are manufactured. You start as yourself, but after a couple years of managers telling you what to do, how to act, and how to dress, you notice yourself becoming more and more diluted. You're less an image of you and more a collage of other people. You begin to see yourself as only a reflection of others. The portrait of yourself that you've spent your whole life painting becomes out of date, erroneous and inconsequential.

I spent my days corresponding with celebrity managers. We'd go over details like how many bottles of champagne should be in the celebrity's hotel room and whether one box of condoms would be enough. One time I was told to buy ten overripe cantaloupes, but every grocery store had cantaloupes that still needed time to ripen. I eventually checked out the sale rack of a big box food department and found four overripe cantaloupes. I needed six more. So I drove to the next town's grocery store, but they didn't have any. I traveled even further away, until I eventually located a few more. Five hours and thirteen stores later, I tracked down all ten overripe cantaloupes. I smelled each and every one of them to make sure that they were indeed overripe.

The smell was death. I watched a woman in a pantsuit pass by me with her cell phone glued to her ear. She was clearly in the middle of a conference call, discussing an investment.

"There is no way I'm investing more than half a mil in the company. I'm willing to take a flyer on this one, but half a mil is as high as I'll go. You tell them that. Tell them to be in my office in one hour if they expect to land any kind of deal," said the strong and powerful woman.

I wish I had that kind of conviction.

I watched as she put her phone away into her Gucci

handbag.

"Garden salad with light balsamic dressing on the side and no croutons," she told the man behind the prepared food counter.

Figures.

I stood there in my black polyester body-con dress I paid $6.80 for and watched as my cantaloupes rolled from one side of the cart to the other.

When I arrived back at the office I was told that the cantaloupes were for a client's son who loved cantaloupe. His mom had a meeting with my bosses and I had to babysit. I asked why I needed to get ten cantaloupes. How much can a little kid really eat?

"It's just in case some of them aren't ripe enough. Her son loves them extra sweet."

I stared at my boss, mouth falling open just a bit. I've learned not to ask questions; I do what I'm told. I'm the assistant. Not much surprises me anymore.

Ninety-five percent of what I do involves following orders that have been filtered down to me, with only five percent wiggle room to breathe and think like a functioning human being…in clearly defined parameters of course. When that summer internship ended, I grew a bit bolder and applied for a publishing internship.

In my brief time interning for a publishing house, I managed to get one of the assistant editors to read one of my manuscripts. Although I wrote the whole novel when I was drunk, it's more sobering than the bread and water I consume at the end of a bender.

The assistant editor rejected it because it didn't have

a complete storyline. He wanted a rise and a fall, and a happy conclusion he could jerk off to while lying on his single bed in his bachelor apartment. A happy ending would have ruined my main character. Her life was complicated and real, and I exposed her character perfectly up until the very last breath she took before she killed herself.

The assistant editor told me that the only good thing about my book was that the heroine died. I told him that she didn't die; she made the decision not to live anymore.

"How is that different?" he asked me.

"It was the first decision she made for herself in a really long time. It may not have been a good one, but she finally took initiative."

He stared at me blankly with that stupid look on his face. His messy blonde hair was annoying me; it was greasy enough to drown a fly. I could tell he was secretly wondering if I was suicidal.

"It's a fictional story," I told him. "They don't always have a happy ending. My character was flawed, but she learned, and she grew, and then she took her life. Readers should be able to witness such beautiful growth followed by such thoughtful destruction."

"Readers don't want destruction, they want peace."

I think his four happy hour pear ciders were going straight to his head; his words were hardly sensible.

I asked him to at the very least pass the manuscript onto his bosses so I could get a second opinion, but he refused. I'm pretty sure it's because his ego was bruised after I turned down his rather aggressive advances in the coat closet at the last book launch party we hosted. At first I was somewhat willing to turn up the heat, but when he stared me in the eyes and promised he'd get my book published if I fucked him, I decided to fuck him in the non-literal sense instead. And so I walked away, but before I did I promised him that I would get this book published one day and on that day I would fuck the first guy that hit on me at the bar. I'd do it in his honor. Because I'm all about giving credit where credit is due.

He never really liked me much since then.

I like to think of writing as making music. My fingers hover above the keyboard, yearning for inspiration from my mind to make my hands take on a solo performance of their own. Each word is strung together in perfect harmony with the one that preceded it. Music is the best form of escapism. It allows the mind to be transported into a different world within mere seconds of turning on the perfect song. I had to be in the right kind of mood when my fingertips lingered on the keyboard. No word can be out of tune in a masterpiece.

I spent over an hour last night searching for the right song before I could start writing. I used music to help nurture mental control. I used speakers to adjust focus; I turned them up when I needed to drown out the noise from my life and turned them down when my mind needed multiple stimulations at once. A single song could take me back to another year, a different time zone, and a different season.

I never write about myself, but I impose my emotions onto my character, the leading lady in my novel, the one that lives and breathes this lifeless air that I have passed on to her. She is the one that can't determine her own destiny because it is determined by me, the writer, the one jerking the string until it snaps.

As a kid, I filled my journals with words that depicted a life so imperfect I couldn't believe I was living it. At night, when I was alone in the dark, my mind raced a mile a minute, almost quicker than my hands could type. My character grew in the darkness, as I drowned out in the light.

My first novel portrayed a deeply disturbed woman who's main nemesis was herself. She was successfully defeated when she ended her life. I called the novel, *A Lifeless Dream* because every plot point was tainted with an unexplainable darkness. The heroine blew out her own light and chose darkness.

Six months after completing that manuscript, I was drunk one night and got a sudden burst of confidence that inspired me to submit it to several publishing houses. I sent it to ten before I passed out from the twelve drinks I had consumed earlier that night. And then I woke up sober, and never pursued any of my submissions.

INTERMISSION

That burning sensation, I feel it all the way down my throat into my esophagus. That feeling I yearn for so much I can almost taste the alcohol before it touches my tongue. It brings me comfort. It brings me hope. Hope that in a few minutes I'll be feeling more exquisite than I do now. It's the only sensation I can feel in my entire body. It starts when I open my mouth and let that pure substance change the firing of my neurons for the better.

I feel the excitement in my fingers, my heart beats quicker, I struggle to breathe, but I soak up all the goodness in that feeling. I dip my head back like I'm soaking up the rays of the sun. I feel every muscle in my body relax. I reach out and touch the sun.

5 ENTER THE OASIS

I live in a two-bedroom apartment with a guy I knew
from college, my best friend, Maksim. We lived on the
same floor in one of Columbia's residences. One night I
came home to my dorm with my dress torn and a scratch
on my cheekbone, and instead of asking questions he just
put his arm around me and asked if I wanted to watch a
movie. That's when we became friends. He had a
girlfriend at the time. She was a sweet girl, fairly smart,
and moderately pretty, but best of all she understood that
her boyfriend and I were simply friends. I didn't have to
worry about getting caught in the middle of a bitch-fight.
I didn't have to explain our bond. It just was.

About a year ago he moved to Los Angeles for a new
job as an assistant music producer. He found this two-
bedroom apartment in Venice and asked me if I wanted
to ditch the studio dump I was living in and share it with
him. I said yes as long as I could get a lock on my
bedroom door. I remembered the type of guys he made

friends with back in college and there was no way I'd want any of his football-playing, frat wannabes slipping into my room unexpectedly when I was sleeping at night. He agreed.

Luckily, I have a bathroom in my room, which allows me to isolate myself from the outside world for extended periods of time. I can go a long time without food, so my trips to the kitchen can be reduced to a couple times a day if necessary.

I've set up my space in a way that maximizes the ease at which I can perform my hedonistic tendencies and minimize the effort I have to put forth to indulge in my luxuries. My bed doubles as my desk, my workspace, my kitchen table, my exercise mat, and of course, the area in which I sleep. It's been two years since I've let a guy into my bed. I much prefer being in theirs.

Unfortunately, I was blessed with a great memory. My brain automatically records my experiences and rarely writes over the same tape. The tape grows larger and larger, and the worst moments seem to take up the most amount of space. The more I replay the moments however, the more they change and mutate into an event I've concocted to protect myself from what actually happened.

If I allowed men into my bed, it would break the sanctity that my bedroom represents. I'd have to buy new sheets after every encounter. I'd have to paint my walls a different color after each relationship because the color would ignite those memories of waking up the next morning with a guy who thinks I'm worth less than the money he spent on drinks to get me to the state of being willing enough to sleep with him in the first place. Afterwards, I'd waste my time lying on my bed listening to soundtracks only suitable for cutting your wrists to, while sobbing over the relationship prototypes that Hollywood movies have taught me to think are normal. And then after taking the last sip from the bottle of wine I devoured myself, I'd fall asleep and wake up not feeling better, but feeling slightly further away from the self I knew before him.

My fridge contains more alcohol than food. I've designed it to be this way because I have a fear of being trapped in my own mind with no way to get out of it.

A mother's haven is filled with bandages for their children and soup for the soul. A daughter's hell is a fridge full of liver damage. At any given time, I have at least three drugs to change the firing of my neurons. In the a.m., it's all about the coffee. In the p.m. it's about the alcohol. And when all else fails I blow smoke. Maksim helps me keep the fridge fully stocked. He goes through way more than I ever could, even on my best days.

If I arrive home after seven in the evening, I'm guaranteed to walk into a full apartment. Maksim has friends over almost every night. He's one of the most social guys I know. I've always been skeptical of social people; I never really understood what kind of person would want to make friends with everyone. How can you actually like that many people?

I have zero desire to spit out forced dialogue with

someone who's last name I hardly know. Time is as precious as money. Wasting words is just as bad as wasting money.

I let minimal reasons pull me away from my oasis, my home, my bedroom, my laptop, where I find the most solace and freedom. My job at the bar, my various internships, and my closest friends are amongst these very few reasons that make me want to venture out from the four walls that hide my dying light.

INTERMISSION

It's not until I see the ceiling spin that I can completely relax and relish in the opportunities that I've been given. I can't fully appreciate all that I have until I see it through the goggles of a bottle of wine, a pitcher of whiskey sours, and a handful of shots. I may not be twenty-one anymore, but only my liver knows that. Songs sound so clear and crisp. Words fade away less, and the world seems less scary.

Feelings, beliefs, and emotions will be as sporadic as the ocean breeze. Every sour memory is like a rock beneath a bare foot, but somehow now it doesn't hurt.

It's three o'clock in the morning and I've reached that special place that drives ambition, fuels the fire, and inspires me to be the dazzling creature I appear to be to friends. I plan next steps like the sky is the limit, I think like the world is an oyster between my fingertips. I promise myself I'll follow through when I'm sober. I was born with a deficiency, but I make up for it almost every night. On the coldest nights of the year, I warm up with a bottle of whiskey that I keep stored in my bedside table.

6 THE PUPPET MASTER

It's Saturday night. I can vaguely hear the sound of the DJ as he raps something over the loud techno beats that consume the club. All I can feel are his hands on me, touching my thigh, grazing it at first then fully grasping it with his overly zealous hands. The only benefit of grinding my back up against a guy is not having to see his face. I know he's behind me. I can feel him sharp and erect up against the back of my jean miniskirt.

I can sense his breath on my bare neck. I can sense his gaze over my shoulder, peering down into my cleavage. I stare straight ahead, my wavy blonde hair cascading down my shoulders. I notice the short, skinny pimply guy shoving his tongue down the throat of a girl whose first mistake that night was getting trashed enough not to notice that she was getting it on with a guy who can only get lucky when the lights are turned off and his victim is drunk or incapacitated.

The guy grinding on me turns me around so that I'm facing him. I know what he wants. I pull him closer to me so that our bodies are touching. My head rests on his shoulder, looking past him. He tries to pull me back so our faces will meet. I resist. He tries harder; this time I can't resist his strength. He puts his mouth on mine, his tongue prying my lips apart. My gag reflex kicks in and I plant my hands firmly on his chest trying to push him off me. After what feels like an eternity of letting his tongue devour mine, he eventually lets me go. A grin is plastered across his face: that frat boy I'm-going-to-be-jerking-off-to-you-later-in-my-bed kind of look. He looks at me; I'm one of his accomplishments, another checkmark to add to his nearly empty list of life goals.

My eyes race back and forth as I search for one of my friends I came to the club with that night. All I see are women in short dresses and men in plaid shirts. There are no faces. I see hands, I see boobs, and hands feeling those boobs. I see asses being grazed and grabbed. I see sweat dripping and pelvises grinding, but I feel nothing. I want to crawl into my bed in the comforts of my apartment, but all I hear is sound and all I feel is hollowness.

By the time I get home I'm soaked in sweat, covered in beer, and my face is flush from heat and exhaustion. I have a post-party ritual. I shower. I take one last shot of whiskey, provided I haven't already blacked out from the whiskey I've had earlier that night. I crawl into my bed, put on my headphones, and fall asleep to blaring music drowning out the tears that stain my pillow.

The next morning my cell buzzes. It's a text from a guy I've been casually seeing. His name is David or Michael, or something like that. With the live band only steps away, I couldn't hear him when he told me his name at the bar, nor was I really listening. I have him in my phone as "green shirt" because all I remember from the night I met him was that he was wearing a green shirt. It was covered in beer. Later on in the night when I took it off him I remember how wet it felt. I also remember how wet I felt two minutes later.

His look is his best asset. The conversations we have are just enough to keep me from blowing my brains out, but luckily we don't do much talking. He actually wasn't horribly offensive or pushy when we met. He didn't try forcing drinks down my throat, although I accepted them willingly. He didn't manhandle me in public as if I was automatically his property. I don't know whether it was his beard, his shaggy brown hair, or his subtle shyness that made me want to rip his clothes off.

He texted me this morning.

Hey, my place tonight? 10pm?

I guess we've gotten to the stage of our hook-up where we only converse in 140 characters or less.

While contemplating my answer, I couldn't help but remember lying in his bed last Thursday night. His bed sheets were so soft. Probably a very high thread count. He's got a studio apartment. I like not having to run into any guy roommates at the end of the night. I like that he texts me early in the day to arrange a hook-up for that night. It gives me time to contemplate, but not enough time to ruminate and talk myself out of it.

For a moment I think back to our last Thursday night. I remember my hands grabbing the sheets with such fierce determination as he methodically covered every inch of my body. I remember lying nearly lifeless unable to feel my own body; the alcohol had become a numbing agent. I texted him back.

I work 'til 1:30am tonight.

Two seconds later he replied.

That's fine, I'll be up late.

Ok, see you then.

I responded instantaneously. I knew both managers were on duty tonight at Skinty's, which meant that I would have to be very discreet as I consumed enough shots throughout my shift to get me pumped for the private after party I had planned.

My strict no sleepover policy is why I tend to go back to the guy's house. I also have a policy against how quickly we're allowed to get down to the main event. We must exchange pleasant niceties for at least two minutes before one or more of us are completely naked. Sex is too impersonal without at least a civil introduction. At least that's what my dance coach taught me, as he guided my hips through gyration.

When a guy asks me how my day went, I usually stick with a lunch anecdote like, "It was good; I had the best grilled cheese for lunch." Or, "Great, I had an extra-long lunch break." It's quick, it's positive, and it doesn't encourage any lingering conversation. And if I get a guy who asks more questions, I know I've got a dud.

When the night is done, the clothes have come off, and I've benefitted from the oxytocin boost that comes from physical contact, I get myself home as quickly as possible hoping that the inspiration from the night will not wear off before I get my hands on my laptop to work on my novel in progress.

Tonight when I got there he was already in his boxers. I thought it was a bit casual; I was just starting to get used to guys wearing jeans and a ratty t-shirt on dates, but I accepted it.

Five minutes later I found myself embracing his soft sheets. They were even more delightful than I had remembered. I'd been meaning to ask him if he uses a laundry softener. My sheets always lose their freshly washed feeling after a night of sleeping in them. He let out a cry. That was fast. And once again I ended up finishing myself while he went to sleep.

Although I didn't get back to my place until three-thirty in the morning, tonight's rendezvous gave me the much-needed inspiration to continue writing my novel. I tucked away my first manuscript for the time being and started a new project.

I'm depicting the life of a young woman, but this

time, my character is fighting for a happy ending. My character has seen both the light and the dark, and she's decided to do whatever it takes to survive. I learned from the woman in my first novel that only the strong survive. My character was weak. She fell victim to her mortality because she stopped fighting and I let her stop. She broke out of her childhood shell before she finished cooking.

My new character will be everything that I'm not and only the best parts of me will survive in her. She will be my access into the world I couldn't create for myself.

When I sit down to write, the first song I choose to play is very important. The first note sends either a positive boost of energy through my veins or leaves me frustrated and unfulfilled like an unsatisfying sexual encounter.

Halfway through writing, the delete button broke; it kept getting stuck. It broke because I made liberal use of it. No word could be a waste of space. Each letter had to propel the next with a fierce and unforgiving force. My heroine made every word count. Every sound reverberated through the receiver's body. Every orgasm made her scream.

The man of my dreams is the man in the book. His words are my words. I control his every move, his every touch, his every word, and his every breath. But the woman next to him is not me. She is also a figment of my imagination. She is the woman that gets the man of my dreams. The man I created. The man I trained to be with my female heroine. I'm like a puppet master, except my pawns exist only in my head.

There I was sitting alone in my apartment creating this man I've yet to meet, and detailing this woman I've yet to embody. I was a student impersonating a professor. I was an actress portraying the role, but I've never felt the part.

7 UNDER THE INFLUENCE

I was born unable to live. My world's made up of contradictions. Like a bird I fly high and low. I feel alive just as much as I feel lifeless. I push people away just as much as I crave human contact. I love to surround myself with endless drinks in the midst of a dimly lit room with all my friends, but only when I'm not suffocating between these purple sheets. You could say I love the wildest parties, that is on the nights I don't hate them. On a binge of extreme partying, I take one step further and fall into withdrawal. I enjoy the withdrawal just as much as I crave the wild nights. I need them both.

I lie awake almost every night until the early hours of the morning, drinking tea on good nights and sipping bourbon on the bad ones, just waiting to fall asleep as the sun rises.

Half my friends are real; the other half are just a figment of the imagination. They consist of the characters I write. Sadly the best people in my life don't make it past the delete button, but the ones that caused the most anguish and take up the most time and space in my mind, are the inspirations that lie deeply embedded in whatever manuscript I'm currently writing.

My characters fill holes that no needle and thread could accomplish. These personalities and personas fill a void too big to fill in real life. My heroines have the opportunity to meet and interact with people I could only dream of meeting. Not knowing whether I'll be able to experience emotions or feel nothing is what keeps me searching for nothing beyond my obligation to remain healthy and robust for the pretty picture in the eyes and minds of those around me.

When my mind goes to that dark place, where the neurons in my head stop firing the nourishment and life that I need to be the person I vaguely remember being, I fall off the face of the earth and land in my apartment drinking my wine from the bottle and crying myself to sleep. My tribulations lie hidden beneath the surface, within the dark hallways of the mind, and that's where I will them to stay.

When the scenes in my favorite movies start feeling more and more realistic, the gap between my wildest dreams and reality start to approach. When I see myself done-up to look like my favorite actress starring in my favorite movie, I begin to see why I haven't pulled the last piece of the puzzle apart.

You reading this right now will know what I don't tell others, but that's okay because you'll never really know me. I stay hidden behind the page; I lay dormant behind my hardworking words. But look in the mirror, and you may just see a bit of me in you. When I look in the mirror I see someone different every time.

I am never the same person twice. My desire to change is the catalyst that keeps my mind running and my heart beating. I'm always working towards a goal. As I approach success, I panic and start spiraling backwards. The thought of attaining that goal is what keeps me above ground, while my self-esteem plummets into another world.

In middle school I won a public speaking contest and tried to convince my family why I shouldn't have won. When I lost I expected it, and when I won I wondered why.

The day one of my suitors told me I was insecure, high maintenance, and nothing special, I gave him the best blowjob of his life.

Then I cried myself to sleep.

I live in a world of hypocrisy. I unfailingly contribute to this mass market of people who cannot explain their actions. I wish I was drunk the day I wielded the knife above my wrist and made an incision. I wish I could forget the coldness that I felt in the kitchen as I slid down to the floor with my back against the cupboards holding my head in my hands and letting the tears plummet to the wooden tiles. I wish I could have seen how selfish I was being. I wish the filters in my life would have let in a little more light so I could see that what I was suffering was only half as bad as what others had to endure.

My coping mechanisms are simple and effective for the time being. I drink. I party when I feel like it. I listen to music and escape into the sunlight that beams through my apartment windows. I reach for the phone, but call no one. I perform at my own vendor with no one but the fruit fly hovering over the week-old box of wine to watch.

At times I feel untouchable, like the world is beneath my feet and everywhere I look there's only bright skies ahead of me and clouds beside me that don't block my view. Other days, I force myself to get out of bed, or force myself to eat or stop eating. I'm never hungry, but I crave. When I satisfy that desire I let out that sigh where I feel my brain functioning normally again. For a few moments I feel inspired. And then I drop lower than the tectonic plate crumbling beneath my feet.

My cravings go far beyond food. I crave love. I crave to meet that one guy who makes my life worth living. I crave waking up in the morning with a man beside me, and the one-night-stands don't count. They're the pylons on my route to finding my way onto the yellow-brick road lined with palm trees.

I didn't think it was possible to be so high and drop so low. I was smart, competent, and bound for greatness. I remember desperately driving around the city at five o'clock in the morning looking for a café that was open so that I could get some coffee. I was an early riser. There's nothing weird about that, right? But when I started picturing what it would be like to ram my car into the brick railing surrounding the road, I began to wonder if my feelings were abnormal.

When I arrived home I looked around me and saw that I was alone, alone in that second with no one to talk to but myself. An empty apartment was all that greeted me after a long day. The dead Ficus in my apartment wasn't just a sign that I didn't have a green thumb; it was an insight into the direction my life was moving. I was dying slowly, and instead of finding the light I was blinded by it.

INTERMISSION

It's sunny out. I'm more than a quarter of a whiskey bottle deep. I can't imagine what my night will be like, but at this very moment that I'm staring out the window watching the sunshine reflect off a building and back into my eyes, I can't help but feel liberated.

I enjoy this moment now, knowing that one day every sip I take will just be a hindrance to the next AA chip I'll receive. When I reach that age when drinking is no longer young mischief, I'll be waiting for the intervention that I'll have to plan for myself.

When I hit the fork in the road that leads to perseverance or failure, I'll let the tears fall down my face and the anger seep through my entire body until I get angry. And when I get angry, I'll get determined. And when I get determined, I'll do everything I can to fight the odds. And then I'll stumble drunk towards the signs leading to failure, not because I enjoy a challenge, but because the successful side doesn't have a bar.

8 THE SPACE IN BETWEEN

"Ray! Perfect timing! We're playing strip poker," Maksim gestured for me to come sit next to him.

It was a Monday night. I just got home from working the night shift at Skinty's. It was another painfully slow night. Monday's usually are, but tonight was particularly boring.

I surveyed the living room. Maksim sat beside a brunette girl, Maksim's friend Johnny had his arm around a blonde girl, and another guy I've never seen before were all sitting on the floor in a circle. The blonde was clearly losing; she was minus a shirt. For her sake, I hoped she didn't lose again. She didn't seem like the type to wear underwear. Johnny was missing a sock.

I walked in. They were all sitting there looking up at me.

"I'll pass thanks," I said.

I was already tipsy from the shots I stole at work. The weeknights are sometimes the hardest ones to get through but luckily my workplace is always fully stocked.

"Awe, c'mon," Johnny begged. "What else would

you rather do than spend time with us sans clothes?"

His puppy dog face and the way his whole face lit up when he smiled was almost kind of adorable.

"That's a tempting offer, but no," I said with conviction. "I'll be in my room if you need anything…like a shirt, maybe?"

"Awe, you've disappointed me," Johnny said half joking, half whining.

I walked into my room and shut the door behind me, blocking out the noise.

I took off all my clothes one by one as quickly as I could and slid into my favorite black concert t-shirt. I slipped beneath my freshly laundered duvet and my bed sheets and propped my laptop on a pillow in front of me. It was time to write.

Tuesday went by pretty quickly. I went to a pole fitness class and arrived home, starving. Having a roommate wasn't always amazing, but tonight when I walked into an apartment smelling of roasted chicken, I was delighted. Maksim sat on the couch watching a hockey game.

"Yo baby Ray."

I turned around, slightly horrified and gave Johnny my "what the fuck" stare as he came out of the bathroom.

"Cute nickname, no?" He asked.

"No," I said.

I waited for him to speak, but while waiting I couldn't help but admire the blue plaid shirt he wore over a simple white t-shirt, and the way he was sporting a pair of dark navy jeans with a rugged brown belt. And that hair. That thick head of brown hair lying perfectly messy on top of his head.

"Another one of my buddies is on his way," said Maksim.

"Great. I'm gunna jump in the shower before dinner," I said.

"Need some help?" Johnny responded coyly.

"Johnny, stop flirting with Ray," said Maksim.

Maksim's my protector.

When I finished my shower I got dressed into my casual navy sweatpants and threw on an old white t-shirt. I went into the kitchen and found a busty redhead girl sitting on our bar stools.

"Hi," I said a bit surprised.

"Hey," she responded.

"Ray, this is Jordana," said Maksim. "One of Johnny's friends."

Of course.

"Hi Jordana. I love that shirt," I said.

"Thanks," she smiled pleasantly as she stared back at my sweatpants and t-shirt clearly searching for a compliment but not having one.

"So are we ready to eat or what?" I asked.

The room was awkwardly silent. I was starving.

"Yes, let's eat!" said Johnny with such sweet enthusiasm in his voice.

After dinner, the four of them left to go to a bar nearby. They invited me to come, but I just wanted to stay in with my comfy clothes, my movies, and my bed. I wasn't in the mood to be social, but I also knew that staying in probably wouldn't be much better.

The worst nights are the ones when I have nothing to dream about: no guy, no event, nothing. My mind goes beige. Not black, but beige. Beige is the most boring color. It's brown that has been stripped of its interesting pigments. It's white that's been dirtied by contaminants. It's the color of puke that your bulimic friend empties into the restaurant bathroom when you're not looking.

Tonight, I had Johnny on my mind. I wondered what he thought about the fact that I stayed in by myself so often. I wondered whether he thought I actually worked on my novel or whether I just used that as an excuse to be alone. Johnny probably didn't have time to think about that; he was too busy sleeping with half the women in LA.

The only thing people fuck more than each other is their own mind. We penetrate our thoughts and rationalize them to our own liking before we wholeheartedly support and endorse what we've pounded into our consciousness.

The more I tried to forge my own path, the more that path became crowded with foreign objects. I came home from night shifts at the bar and found my voice becoming more and more diluted every time I sat at my laptop willing myself to write. In one shift I'd encounter so many different kinds of people, different personalities, different attitudes, and different styles. Each one seemed to fit and not fit in its own way.

I could identify to some degree with everyone and no one at the same time. My characters could be inspired from someone whose first name I didn't even know. While sometimes I could spend a whole night serving people and not remember a single one of them. Other times I've waited on people that I'll never be able to erase.

The next night I served a table of freshly legal guys. There was a tall, dark and handsome man with strong arms and a smile so powerful it was impossible to look away. His flirty quips were pathetic but I'd accept any form of self-esteem booster. If he hadn't of flirted with me in front of his table of friends, I most likely would have accepted his overwhelmingly strong advances. But from where I was standing, the best I could do was smile and reject his request for my number.

Seconds later I came back to their table with their drinks. I served them first even though there were other orders before them. As I leaned over the table to pass the drinks along, the blonde at my left smiled and stared at my rack. As I walked away I heard whispering at the table.

I turned to a table just meters away and heard the blonde guy say, "She's going to get fucked by two guys tonight." Laughter at their table ensued, followed by a few high fives.

Unfortunately as a waiter, I didn't have the luxury of ignoring them. I had to return and ask them if they wanted another round. As their waitress I had to keep the smile plastered across my face. Too bad I wasn't living in London.

Luckily, I was in a "playful I'm going to fuck you harder" kind of mood. So I returned with pleasure and overheard one of the polo shirt-wearing guys bragging about how many girls he had.

"Can I get you guys anything else?" I asked, interrupting their locker room talk.

"You sure can honey."

Vomit.

"I'll have a whiskey," said the blonde douche.

"How do you like it?" I asked.

"Neat." He grinned.

"Hmm. Okay."

"What?" he asked.

"Nothing, it's just that I wouldn't have taken you as a neat guy," I winked.

"No? Why don't I take you home tonight and show you what kind of guy I am?"

I smiled. The vomit hadn't formed yet, but I could taste its essence.

"Which brand would satisfy you the most?" I asked, disregarding his question.

Blonde douche smiled while polo pimp with all the female connections finished his drink.

"The cheapest one you got, sexy."

"Petroleum it is," I said.

"Hah, this chick's funny," said blonde douche. Polo pimp was too drunk to notice my hilarity.

As the night went on, their ability to catch my sexual innuendos diminished. Their laughter became louder and their words became more obnoxious, but surprisingly my job got easier. I let myself turn into this judgmental monster that all the shots of tequila in the bar couldn't fix.

9 MARRIED TO HEDONISM

I laid on my bed, arms resting in front of me, hands by my lips, legs curled up beside me. I felt the ribs of my meager frame melt into the bed. I thought back to kindergarten, my first lunch box, the time spent sitting on top of the monkey bars, but I couldn't feel it.

I wanted to feel something, anything. I wanted to be scared that the ocean waves were going to swallow me entirely. I wanted to feel the coldness against my naked skin. I wanted nothing but darkness to surround me at night and nothing but sunshine to intoxicate me during the day. I wanted to feel the rush of coldness embrace my body as I plunged into the wide open ocean, alone with nothing but the scar on my wrist and the memories of longing for a lifestyle that supported only hedonistic activities.

I wanted to feel the electricity beaming from the body of the male counterpart feeding me drinks all night. I wanted to do something stupid and irresponsible, and get away with it. I wanted to do a strip tease without being labeled the slut. I wanted to feel his hands on me, touching, grabbing, squeezing, and invigorating. And then I wanted to wake up by myself, snap my fingers and turn on and off the best relationship I've never known, or alternate between being wanted then left alone to dream and breathe in peace.

I wanted each breath to be better than the last, each memory to be more vivid than the one preceding it. But I was suddenly awakened by the harsh realization that no matter how many words I spewed on the page of whichever book I was writing on any given day, I couldn't turn the silent written word into a fully functioning reality. I strung words together, hoping that they'd form a coherent whole that told a story worth knowing. Even more so, I wondered whether anyone would ever get to read these words.

I opened the top drawer of my nightstand and sat up to take a large swig of whiskey. It did nothing to me. I took another swig. Still nothing changed. I squinted my eyes again; I tried to cry but I couldn't. I focused on my breathing to remind myself that I was still alive.

Two seconds later my phone buzzed and it nearly made me jump. I looked at the screen, afraid to let the outside world drag me further down this hole. I had a date tonight. I wanted to cancel.

Instead, I got dressed in a red cocktail dress, put on my diamond earrings, and let another guy lead me to the bar where we drank a beer. The whole date I prayed he wouldn't rape me on the way back to the car. He wanted to go for a walk by the water. I was warned not to do that; I've watched enough crime shows to know that pretty girls always wash up ashore, beaten, bruised, and raped. I said no. He didn't care.

Making out by the water was exhilarating. When we occasionally came up for air, I'd stare out at the ocean, picturing myself on a boat all alone far out in the distance. I wondered if I'd die of starvation or give my body to the sharks.

I felt his hand on the inside of my thigh. He was teasing me, but I liked it. My attention span lasts about two seconds, so in no time we were back to locking lips. I ran my hand through his short brown hair. I pulled him close to me, and moaned just slightly. That seemed to rile him. For a second I thought that he was going to throw me onto the sidewalk and have his way with me in front of all the pedestrians.

I slowed the pace. I didn't want to instigate. It's fun to tease just a bit. Sometimes I'll pull away just to see his reaction. Sometimes I'll hover, with my lips just millimeters away from his. And then I'll let out a noticeable exhale so he can feel my breath on his lips. By this point I'm taunting myself just as much, if not more, than I'm teasing him.

It was pitch dark outside, and no person had walked by us in at least twenty minutes. We walked a few minutes along the sand to a little secluded area underneath the pier. I dreamed of my bed. I wanted to be in my car driving home but I didn't know how to leave. He kissed me again, pulling my body to the sand. I worried the sand would wreck my dress. I could feel sand underneath it, touching my skin. I felt his hand slowly move down my stomach, on my thigh, down to my knee, then back up a few inches.

I pushed his hand away and he moved it to my cheek, then down to my neck. He put more weight on my body and that's when I let my eyes catch sight of the lake and drift away.

I was a lifeless body lying there waiting to be impregnated with a feeling. I could hardly feel him but I knew he was there. My dead weight rocked back and forth. I waited for the motion sickness to end. I watched the clouds spin. I felt his body on top of mine, but all I could focus on were the drops of sweat our bodies had created, heavy and dirty like the water from an overflowed swamp.

10 ABUSE ME TILL I LIKE IT

It was Wednesday night. I walked down the street, warm wind in my hair as I headed to a costume party. I didn't dress up; my appearance was already fake. My mask may not be tangible, but it was there and it was thick. I couldn't take it off, but I could change it when I pleased.

Tonight's costume party was all about hide our identity and making a fool of our self. That's why I dressed sexy. While everyone else would be in their pig costume or their bunny suits, I'd be wearing my red and black skintight dress with unassuming three quarter length sleeves and material that wrapped around my body.

I walked through the doors and encountered not one or two, but nine people that I recognized. One by one I said hello, hoping that at least one of them would pretend to be happy to see me and would want to carry on a conversation for more than two minutes. But eighteen minutes later I was leaning against the wall, staring at the drink in my hand hoping that no one would notice I was alone.

It was time for round two. My mind was spinning faster than the wheels of a car going full speed as I tried to think of something to say that would result in a conversation longer than two minutes. I stood only inches away from a girl I called my friend, but nothing came out of my mouth. My mind went blank and all I could feel was the skin on top of my bones grow harder and thicker. She stepped in front of the flash and I felt myself held up still against the wall, not wanting the camera to break through the layers I'd built out of necessity to survive.

Many become motivated and inspired when they're surrounded by friends and have invites to the coolest parties or the biggest ones, but not me. I was motivated by exclusion. Being at the bottom of the totem pole was where I thrived. Like phytoplankton, waiting for the bigger fish to swallow me whole, I reveled in the power I knew I possessed. If I stored all the pity invites away between those four walls I knew so well, there'd be no air left for me to breathe.

Someone once told me that I was not the exception; I was the rule. My reasoning and actions were just like millions of others who saw the world the same way as me. I was not unique. Any uniqueness I thought I exhibited was all brought on but my ignorance of the rest of the female race. Or so he said.

I thrived on the criticism. I think I might have encouraged it. It gave me the strength to work hard so one day I could negate all the assumptions that I fell victim to by other people's unwillingness to read between the lines.

Needless to say that costume party ended with me in no costume at all. I remembered every step I took to rip off my dress, untie my hair, and collapse into bed…alone.

Lying there in my empty bed, my mind took a trip back to my hometown, Rutland, Vermont. It was a cold night in November, about seven years ago. Butterflies slowly annihilated my stomach, eating at the inner core of its lining. I tried on almost every single dress that I owned until I came to the one that disgusted me the least. I stared at the mirror, absorbing every black zebra stripe and admiring the sexy zippers. It was seven-thirty at night and he was late. We had dinner reservations but when we arrived at the dive, we just had a snack. It was supposed to be an outing but it turned into a half-naked rendezvous at his apartment. I could feel every grab, every scratch, and every shove against the wall as if it were yesterday. I remembered the feeling of wondering whether tonight would be the night I'd be raped. I remember telling him to remove his hands from around my neck. I remember telling him that I was still a virgin, but he didn't believe me. I was the slut he met just a few weeks ago. I was the one who compromised her morals and went home with him on the first night.

Our first night was like no other. He told me that I was too sheltered. I needed to explore, but he knew that

I wouldn't. I told him my dream of living in California. He was from Toronto. He was the first Canadian I'd ever dated.

He dreamed of leaving just as much as I did.

"I've been wanting to go to Canada. I've never been," I said.

"Let's go," he said nonchalantly.

"Sure, when?" I said, going with the flow knowing that there was only about a thirty percent chance I'd ever see this guy again.

"Tonight."

"Yes!" I said with exuberance.

"Great. You have your passport?"

"Not on me."

"Okay let's grab it. We can get to Montreal probably by three or three-thirty. Bars will be closed, but we'll figure shit out."

"I have an exam this Tuesday," I said, not completely sure whether saying that was relevant but plans were progressing rather abruptly and it was about time I stepped on the brakes.

"I thought you said yes."

"Right, yes…sure. I mean," I paused. For some reason I was reminded of the salad I ate last night for dinner. I remembered sitting in front of my laptop with my bag of salad, my canned tuna, and my sliced olives. I was happy. I was so happy.

"Fuck it," I said. "Let's do it. I live close by, but if my parents wake up when I go home, you're my gay friend from scientology class, got it?"

"Perfect," he smiled and grabbed my ass, his big strong hand firmly cupping both butt cheeks in one like a magic trick. "Wait, your parents think you're a scientologist?"

"Yeah, I needed an alibi while I was at my stripper pole dancing classes."

"I think I'd rather my kid be a stripper."

"First of all, you're a dick. Second, I'm not a stripper. It's just a sexier fitness class. I care about my health."

"And I fully support that," he laughed.

"Shut up and drive," I said.

There we were on the road, driving to Montreal. I could feel every muscle in my body contract then relax. I could feel my breath as my chest moved in and out. I was free. I was moving forward. I was sitting next to someone I knew nothing about and we were going somewhere I'd never been. Surprisingly, I was enjoying it.

We were still hours away. I was already stressing about studying for my upcoming exam. We drove on a highway so dark, the only light we saw was from the other few cars on the road. I pictured my books sitting on my desk. I mentally scanned through all the chapters I had to read and memorize before the exam.

I didn't want to be the one to break, but this new crazy sense of adventure I had suddenly developed was coming to an end. And so I broke the chain.

"Are you sure you want to go all the way tonight? I was just thinking, I have a lot to get done this weekend and I didn't bring any of my books," I said.

He looked at me again, this time with relieved eyes, but he did his best to cover it up. "Ugh," he sighed. "Fine."

"Let's at least pull over for a second and take a picture," he said.

"In the dark? We won't be able to see anything?" I said.

"We'll use the flash. Let's try."

"Okay."

He exited the highway and pulled over to the side of the road. No cars were passing us; the road was practically dead. There was no light. We proceeded to make-out in the darkness.

He pulled away abruptly.

"A car's coming," he said. "Let's take the picture right when we have the light from his headlights passing by."

He pulled out his phone, handed it to me and said, "Here, can you stand there and get me plus the car and the sign in the background?"

I paused for a moment, somewhat shocked.

I guess there's no place for me in this picture.

I did as I was told. I held his phone, followed his directions and took the picture before the fleeting light disappeared. The picture still looked pretty dark to me.

"Damn it, it's dark. Oh well. I'll just lighten it up afterwards with effects," he said.

"Great." I walked back to the car, got in, and shut up.

That midnight trip was the first of our many

adventures. I'm proud of every move I made. Every touch was propelled by years of loneliness and longing. I rejoiced with pleasure when I thought of the rules I had broken. He made the best omelets. He knew exactly how I liked them, but he never made them that way. I didn't mind; I learned a long time ago that my life's mission was making others' lives more enjoyable. I gave, and I kept giving, but I received nothing in return: nothing but the satisfaction of knowing that my phone would ring. But when it did, I'd pick it up in utter fear, wondering what method of pain he would choose to inflict on me that night. Would it be the slow, searing burn or the sharp and intense knife to the gut, quick and efficient? Neither of them were preferable over the other and yet somehow I kept answering the phone.

"Hello?"

"Hey, I'm in your hood, you hungry?"

"Yes. Always," I said.

It was as easy as that. I liked it that way. Or at least I thought I did.

It was like my lips, my tongue, my words blurred with the voices I heard around me. I preferred to surround myself with others who did all the talking, so I could just sit back, listen and reflect, ruminate and destroy. Talking was work; talking took effort. Talking could get me into trouble. Writing was a pleasure and listening was a comfort, but initiating dialogue was my deficiency. I could memorize and regurgitate, I could listen and respond, but when I was left to create the conversation I ended up in an endless rant, repeating myself until I finally had enough smarts to shut the fuck up.

Lying in my bed seven years later, I thought about everything that gave me comfort now. My favorite sound is the noise my front door makes when I close it shut. I attribute that loud screeching sound to the feeling of being home safe. Only my door makes that distinct noise. Our apartment may be in need of some renovations, but I'll keep the door just the way it is, making that sound and letting me know I'm just moments away from being between those four walls.

INTERMISSION

I'm perched over a mountain, watching my feet dangling over the edge. I feel the wind in my hair and the energy flaring in my veins. I lift my arm to touch a star, but they all collide. My vision blurs, my heart stops pounding, I lay my head on no one's shoulders. I fall until I am awake.

I'm unarmed on a battlefield. My only salvation lies in those fleeting moments when I tell the world to go fuck itself, and then guzzle down a pint. I have no preferences. The cheapest beer tastes exactly the same as the most expensive glass of champagne. They both instill faith in me that this world has more to offer than just an endless struggle towards something I'll never get. I try to believe that mercy exists when I'm six drinks deep into the night and I'm blinded by the road lights leading me nowhere.

11 INTO THE SILK

After a long day of writing and working the nightshift at Skinty's, I arrived home at two-thirty in the morning. I jammed my key into the apartment door, counting the seconds it would take for me to get from the outside to under my duvet cover. I couldn't wait to wash off the mascara, eye-liner, lipstick, and blush, and the rest of the day while I was at it.

"Well hello there beautiful," Maksim hollered from the living room couch. He was sitting there with two other girls. Johnny had his hand lying particularly close to one of the girl's boobs as he draped his arm around her shoulder and across her chest.

She had long blonde hair that had been perfectly curled. She must have used spray. The locks were too perfect. Her eye makeup was a bit much, but I assumed she did that to hide the scars on her self-esteem.

"I'm going to bed," I said.

"Why so early?" Maksim yelled.

"It's almost three in the morning."

I woke up the next day to find Johnny sitting alone on the couch, eating a bowl of cereal and milk. I went to the kitchen, still in my polka dot pajamas that a grandmother would wear. I was afraid to look in the mirror to see my hair misbehaving. I made myself some tea and politely returned Johnny's morning salutation.

"There you are baby. I woke up and you weren't there, I thought maybe you abandoned me," the blonde girl from last night said as she walked over to Johnny on the couch with nothing but Johnny's white t-shirt on.

A little too see-through if you ask me.

"Sorry babe, just getting some breakfast," he responded obviously not very interested.

A couple hours later I peeped outside of my room a second time to go make myself another cup of coffee. Johnny was still there. I couldn't see the girl though.

"Where is everyone?" I asked him.

"Mak's still sleeping…that lazy fuck. Everyone else left."

"You had a fun night?" I winked, then instantly regretted it.

"Yeah, it was a shit-show. Just a haze of beer and tequila shots."

"Beer, shots, and women…sounds like an epic night," I said.

"How was your night?" he asked, changing the subject.

"Well, I served bozos like you beer and tequila shots

all night at Skinty's, so you know I'm just livin' the dream."

I walked towards my room.

"What do you do in there all day?" Johnny yelled after me. "I swear I've never met anyone who spends as much time in their bedroom with the door closed. You making meth or something?"

"I've never met someone who spends more time sleeping on the couch in someone else's place when he's got his own empty studio apartment just ten miles away."

"It's your pretty face that keeps reeling me back in."

"Really, cause I thought it was my sunny demeanor that's just so irresistible?"

"Yeah, about as irresistible as sucking on a piece of glass," he said so harshly. "Sorry, too far?"

I poured myself a cup of instant coffee. "Anyone ever told you how much you suck?" I asked.

"Yes, you. A number of times."

"Wonderful. I'm ahead of schedule," I said just before shutting my bedroom door.

The day was productive and the night shift was long, but surprisingly I still felt ready to work. Every time I tried to shut my eyes I got another thought, one that was too good to let slip away and be forgotten by morning. The cycle ensued and before I knew it I was watching the sunrise through my window, caged between these silky sheets. It was the only good part of staying up all night. The sunrise introduced me to a beauty I could only dream to create on the page.

INTERMISSION

I feel it. It's working it's magic within me right now. I can't help myself. My head flies back in ecstasy. As a kid I jumped up and down on a trampoline for hours, enjoying every pure second of being jolted up into the sky. Now every second I enjoy is impeded by that loaded substance that enters my body in its most pure form. I am free. Maybe only for a couple hours, but I'll take it. My body is in another zone, one that is too far away to grasp. I feel nothing when the whiskey rolls down my throat. I picture my hips moving; my mind stands still, while a stranger's hands invade my space and I wait for it to be over.

12 PURSUIT OF EXOTIC LOVE

The words. They were there on the tip of my tongue, but not in the air. They lay dormant like a butterfly in its cocoon.

His words seemed so clear to me. Every word. His accent. His short black hair. The way the mere presence of his body made my whole body tremble. I had never wanted to get to know someone more from his favorite childhood memory to his favorite way to be touched. I had always been good at patience, waiting until I knew him intellectually before I got to know him physically. This time was different; I wanted to get to know everything about him all at once. Like a kid on her birthday, I couldn't wait to blow out the candles and embrace the soft touch of the sweet icing between my lips.

Our chemistry was undeniable. My hesitancy towards public displays of affection disappeared; the general timeline of dating milestones and dating rules became irrelevant to me. Even in my wildest dreams, I had no idea that this kind of chemistry existed. I was on a wild roller coaster and my biggest fear was it breaking down in the middle of the ride.

He made me feel things I never knew were possible. I would have climbed Mount Everest to have one more second to savor that deliciously satisfying stomach clench I felt every time we kissed. I would have never taken the headphones off if I'd known that would be our last dance. I would have never put my clothes back on if I'd known we'd never be naked together again.

He was the first guy I knew I'd never forget. By our first date, I felt like I'd known him for years. Too bad it took me more than a few screw-ups to learn that I wanted years more to keep learning about him, years that I'd never get.

I sat alone in bed, listening, feeling, and wanting, but not receiving. I heard the sound of the ocean playing in my head, I felt his touch on my skin, and then I felt nothing. Nothing but the hard metal beneath my fingertips as I typed these explosive words that no one would read but me. I felt comfort in knowing I could express my emotions, but then felt nothing when I touched no one and no one touched me.

Then I remembered sitting in my apartment alone on a Sunday morning, staring into a bowl of tomato soup, and tasting nothing but blood in every spoonful. The memory of him shoving himself so far down, it felt like he ripped my vocal cords, made me appreciate every bite

I took in peace before this day.

He touched me in so many ways. He got into my soul and left his heaviest mark there. I began to understand how an addict felt trying to give up their habit. If something or someone can make you feel that good, how could it be so bad?

I stared at my phone, checking it every two seconds like a little kid, but the screen kept letting me down. You felt nothing and I felt like an electric orgasm shot through my body every time you grazed my skin.

A year later it still stung. Two years later it didn't sting any less. I wrote him into my novel. I returned to the same scene so many times, deleting and rewriting over and over until I found the words that could provide at least the smallest amount of authenticity.

I gave my character a pierced soul and a pierced voice. I gave her painful memories that would help her grow strong. I gave her everything that I couldn't handle. I gave her the courage to confront him with kindness and love on the streets in front of the vast ocean with all eyes on her. Round two didn't hurt. But his rejection of me months later pierced deeper than the physical, and strained my voice worse than ever with the taste of blood still accenting the flavor of every bite I took. The most heartbreaking part was when I found out he wanted someone else. I was stuck coping with the thought that I'd never feel that same unexplainable bolt of electricity run through my entire body like I did when our bodies were close enough to kiss.

His words seemed so far away now. I wrote them

down in my journal to preserve their life, yet now when I read them I begin to doubt their authenticity. He said them, I felt them, I wrote them down and now I read them like a lifeless object feeling nothing, believing nothing, and creating nothing.

I hoped I would get the chance to hear him say those words again. It was this belief, or lack thereof that stained every one of my goals and motivations with failure because I couldn't believe in my own success. I searched for a meaningful life but couldn't find the meaning in anything.

When I embraced the ocean as my home, I knew I'd never see him again. His fear was poignant and our desires were opposite.

I was left with the endless sense of longing that wouldn't go away. Every once in a while we meet someone who has an immense impact on us; one that we can't explain. Sometimes we don't realize it until it's too late. For those lucky few, they marry the ones that change their life. So far all I've done is push them away.

I've made so many mistakes along the way. Most of the time the effects of these mistakes lingered no longer than a few days. Once in a while they lingered longer, so long that I wondered if the pain would ever go away. Before you know it your left with nothing but faded memories; so faded that you're not even sure if there's any truth left in them.

When we tell ourselves we're over someone, we don't actually fall out of love or lust with him. We just let ourselves forget how much we cared. Now that I know what passion feels like, I can't settle for anything less.

The moment I decided to move on was the moment he came back into my life in the smallest yet most meaningful way. It was the two-year anniversary of our first date. I was hoping it wasn't just a coincidence that this was the day he decided to reach out to me with just one click.

The moment I started to think that the male sex couldn't be as sentimental as the female sex was the moment when every ounce of my childhood innocence abandoned me forever.

I found hope in the oddest forms, but I relished in it as much as I could. Tonight I played a game of soccer underneath the lights of a deserted park. It was me, Maksim, and the other guys. I loved being the only girl. I ran my heart out every time I got my feet on the ball. For an hour my only goal was getting the ball in the net, and I loved the simplicity in that. I loved the way the grass stained my knees when I slid to make the game winning shot.

We didn't have any real jerseys so we played shirts and skins. I was always asked to be a skin. A few times after consuming several glasses of wine, being a skin didn't seem so bad. The guys would tease me and say that if I decided to be a skin, my team would win for sure because the shirts would all be too distracted. I liked that feeling: that feeling of power, like my actions had influence over others, even if it was just my body and not my brain that was the influential tool. One day maybe my voice would be the thing making an impact. For now however, I ran my body to the extreme using up all of its resources to let this drunk person run, and using every soccer goal as a signal of what I could accomplish in any state. I tried to run myself into an oblivion, but my legs started burning before my heart stopped hurting.

INTERMISSION

I hardly feel it anymore, that substance that used to change the firing of my neurons for the better after just a couple glasses. Now all I feel is sick. Every glass gets me no closer to that feeling I used to champion in my mind. Every minute I spend with my hand wrapped around the glass is just another minute that I won't remember tomorrow. My magic number used to be eight. Tonight, even twelve glasses didn't do the trick.

13 AN EXCLUSIVE PAJAMAS PARTY

I arrived home from my day shift at Skinty's to find the apartment full of Maksim's friends. The cologne barometer was at an all-time high. Every step I took through the kitchen, the living room, and the bathroom, a new vicious smell overwhelmed my senses.

"What could be more fun than coming out with us?" Maksim had been trying to get me to come out to the bar with him and his buddies all night.

I paused. "Oh sorry, I thought that was rhetorical."

"Seriously, what are you doing tonight?" Johnny chimed in.

"Stuff!"

"Like?" Johnny stared right at me. His phone was out of sight, no drink in his hand, no girl by his side, just Johnny standing there in dark blue faded jeans and a blue and white plaid button down shirt with a black and silver belt peeping through in the front.

I wanted to be alone tonight, like most nights.

"I'll let you have one of my Cold Breath beers if you come out with us tonight," said Johnny.

"You'd let me have one of your favorite beers whether or not I come out with you?" I asked.

"Yup, and I order that shit all the way from Canada. It's the best fucking beer you'll ever taste. And trust me when I say I don't let just anyone drink one," he said in all seriousness.

I chuckled. "Well I feel honored," I said. "But I'm still staying in tonight."

Johnny came over to me and put his arm around me and his hand on my lower back then whispered in my ear, "Okay darlin'," he said.

He snapped open a beer and handed it to me. I could smell the alcohol on his breath, but even more so I could smell the scent of his cologne, like the ocean wind mixed with a touch of cinnamon. His arm around me was the only chemical boost I needed.

"I feel like our relationship is a little one-sided though," he said.

"How do you mean?" I asked.

"I invite you to come out with us, but you never invite me to stay in with you," he said grazing my arm with his fingers.

Johnny is one of the biggest flirts I know, but despite his assiduous attempts to woo me for a night, I couldn't help but see him like a little kid demanding a ride on the Ferris wheel, and the parents being like, 'Go ride yourself you little shit fuck.'

"Ride's here," one of Maksim's buddies was halfway out the door yelling back at the others to follow. The guys headed out, but Johnny lingered behind still holding onto me.

I put my hand on the side of his face and smiled.

"I'll come out with you guys and party soon."

He smiled, and like a magic trick, the curvature of his lips made my vagina tingle.

Shit. Should I have said yes?

"Okay, I'm going to hold you to that," he said before kissing me on the cheek. "Don't have too much fun without me," he said.

"Oh I won't. Just going to write, binge watch *The West Wing*, drink some tea, masturbate, then go to bed."

I watched as his eyes softened and his dick got hard.

"Huh." Johnny's eyes lit up like the Fourth of July.

I kind of hoped he assumed I was kidding, even though I knew that was actually what was most likely going to happen.

He put his hand on my shoulder and whispered into my ear: "I'd rather watch *The West Wing* with you than hang out with this group of losers," he pulled away and winked his left eye at me noticeably leaving out any mention of my plan to masturbate.

I found myself smiling on the inside and out. And then it happened. I found myself speaking before thinking. I found myself speaking from this weird place somewhere above my abdomen and below my neck. Then again, these words were probably just emanating from my vagina.

"Hey!" I said just before he shut the front door. He paused, leaning against the door.

"Maybe another night you can watch *The West Wing* with me."

And there it was. Initiative. An invitation from me was like finding a fucking unicorn.

Wait, did I just invite him to Netflix and chill?

"I'll bring the popcorn," he said before shutting the door.

My pajamas party started two minutes later. Tea was steeping beside my bed; this time I didn't put any liquor in it. I decided to try writing sober to see what my brain could do without any help.

I wanted to write a word, a phrase, a sentence that could affect at least one person. If only one sentence in my whole work sticks with a reader for a lifetime or even an hour I'll have accomplished my mission. If for only fifteen seconds a reader enters a parallel universe where his or her woes are forgotten and displaced by the words on this page, I'll have done what I've set out to do.

When I'm looking for proof that I can make an impact on another person's life I reflect on those who've had an impact on mine. Even just a moment to pretend that something I've written will give others a mere fifteen seconds of pleasure or euphoria is enough to help propel the engine. I sit alone on the bed, trying to make an impression sandwiched between these four walls. Every word, each sentence, they're all in the air like fairy dust. I just need to find the right combination.

I exist in over one million different forms. I am

every writer, every creator; we are no different. We believe in the power of creativity. We internalize our thoughts and enjoy being alone with them. We're comforted by our thoughts, not our actions. We're defined by the stories we tell, and the ones we live. Actions are a means to an end in getting somewhere, but it's our mental awareness that is truly profound.

14 THE CASE OF THE FLEXIBLE SLUT

It was seven-thirty in the morning and could I see the sunlight streaming in through the cracks in my blinds. I stepped outside onto the balcony and stared in the direction of the ocean. It was about a three song walk away from me. By song four, my toes are in the sand. I've spent every day this week at the beach, sipping my martini from a straw and typing until my fingers hurt.

As much as I loved being sexually harassed by the surfer dudes as I sat on my "Give your Friend a Wedgie" towel in my black bikini, I knew I'd rather be chilling indoors at a surf shack watching the ocean from afar.

I wanted a cappuccino and a warm mini-cinnamon bun. I had a three-hour workout session with my personal trainer scheduled for six tonight so I decided I'd be more than able to burn off the sugar and fat I indulged in today. For my birthday this year, my family gave me a year's worth of private training sessions. Twice a week I got my butt kicked into shape, and on the other five days

I kicked it myself.

As I walked along the boardwalk heading to my favorite café, I took note of the wide range of personalities lining the path. There were kids holding hands with their moms, tattooed men lingering and watching the half naked skinny bodies absorbing heat, and there were several sitting on the sidewalk holding a cup filled with coins with their undernourished hands.

By the time I got to the café, I decided that a Moscow mule would be better than a cappuccino. The mini-cinnamon buns looked heavenly, but my initial plan to devour one was slowly fading and instead I order the kale salad.

I sat inside near the window, but close enough to the outdoors that I could breathe in the fresh air.

"Take comfort in knowing you're not the only one that's fucked up," I heard a voice say behind me.

I turned around. A young woman dressed in head to toe black with pink-dyed locks, looked at me as I sat alone sipping my drink. I smiled. Not sure why that made me smile. Perhaps the sheer frankness of her comment, the fact that it was so out of the blue, or the fact that it was so true, resonated for just a second.

I turned to her, smiled and took another sip of my drink. The pink-haired woman left. She seemed to be talking to everyone that she passed on her journey down the boardwalk.

I took her words, attached them to a vagabond, and incorporated them into my manuscript. She was just another unnamed woman in my character's long journey through adulthood.

Two hours later, I was four drinks deep and ten pages closer to finishing my manuscript. I decided to reward myself with a relaxing session lying on the sand.

The sun was beating. I could feel it turning my skin pink. I stared up at the sun, with quilted Chanel protecting my eyes and my toes firmly embedded in an inch of hot sand. I looked away scared of the intensity. I held the cigarette to my mouth, feeling it between my lips, breathing in before letting the air slowly seep out of my mouth. I blew through the cloud of smoke I formed. My fingers relaxed. I put my head back on the towel, inserted my ear-buds and pressed play on *Chasing Pavements*.

I walked home before the sunset. I didn't like being out alone at night, but I didn't want the day to end. The sun had given me a newfound burst of energy and I was going to ride the high for as long as I could.

I accompanied Maksim, Johnny, and a few others to a bar. It was a local bar near us with the best weeknight dance party. A friend was hosting her two year work anniversary party there. I had no idea why someone thought working the same job for two years was something to celebrate, but I didn't care as long as I had a drink in my hand and a stage to dance on.

I hoisted myself up onto the bar, feeling the edges grind into my protruding hipbone. The music got louder in my head. I felt it deep within my body; my bones trembled but my muscles strengthened. I felt my energy ready to explode like the top off a champagne bottle. My arms straightened in a V-shape by my side. I felt the electric current running through my body as I swayed back and forth in an S-pattern. I got my shoulders moving. I stuck out my chest then ran my hands down my body, slightly grazing my breasts.

I moved my gaze to the floor then flipped my head back quickly and forcefully, catching the glance of a dark-haired man in the corner. I held his gaze for half a second. Just long enough to get his attention. Then I turned my head and waited for the next man to visually assault me.

An hour later, Dylan arrived. He's someone I've hung out with several times over the past year. We have a lot of mutual friends. He always treated me with respect when he saw me. I was always happy to see him because I knew I was guaranteed a fun, safe night; a comfortable night.

He walked up to me and pressed his lips firmly against mine as if he owned them. He put his hand on the side of my face as if I were his girlfriend. I took the drink out of his hand and finished it. He bought me another. I finished it. He turned me around so I could grind my body against his. I had one hand holding his and the other holding a rye and ginger.

My mind raced from one thing to the next. I needed to be alone to write down every thought that flew into my brain as I stood there surrounded by hundreds of other emotionally charged bodies. I wanted to keep dancing, but I so desperately needed my laptop to embrace the burst of creativity that six drinks, music, and a crowd full of drunk people could inspire. I needed to record a written version of tonight. I needed to remember how it felt to feel alive in a setting so often disabling to me.

He used more than the warmth of his body to keep me comfortable. I laid under the sheets with an extra fleece blanket that I had all to myself. The heater stood next to my side of the bed.

I broke my golden rule and slept over. I always made myself go home: get that oxytocin then scram. Even when it was three-thirty in the morning by the time we were finished, I'd get up and leave. Some guys would act surprised and ask me to stay. Some guys would say "Are you sure, ok," so fast you could see the relief in their eyes. But last night I made an exception.

When I woke up I was sober: stone cold sober. That juxtaposition between being so high and euphoric from alcohol as I fell asleep versus waking up in such a dramatically different state, nearly debilitated me. When I went to bed the trees were greener, the air was fresher, my prospects seemed within reach. When I woke up in the morning I felt the dead weight of the water I drank to counteract the alcohol and saw the look of fear in my eyes over what was said or done last night.

It was seven–thirty in the morning. I didn't want to overstay my welcome. I couldn't wait to go home and shower and relax on my bed with a giant cup of coffee.

I expected to walk into a quiet apartment. I was surprised to find that the crew was up early making breakfast and sipping on their hair of the dog.

"Hello there, missy," Maksim greeted me the second I walked through the door. "How's your fuck buddy?"

"He's not my fuck buddy. He's my friend who I like hanging out with because he's nice and we have fun."

"Well that sounds boring. When are you Dylan going on a real date?"

"Dylan? Who's Dylan?" Johnny asked with his eyes stationed directly on me.

I ignored his question. "He seems so in to me when we're together, but then I never hear from him. I swear the next time someone tells me that guys are simple, I'm gunna slap them across the face." I grabbed a beer from the fridge. "Guys are anything but simple," I said before taking the first swig.

"That's not true. We are simple. The problem is that women are revisionists," said Maksim.

"Excuse me?"

"We're very clear with our intentions. We can't help the fact that women like to change and interpret the meaning of events after they've happened," explained Maksim.

"If they were so simple and clear we wouldn't have to interpret them," I said.

"What needs interpreting here? Dylan is nice to you so he can fuck you. Then he fucks you. Then he doesn't call you. Clear and simple. He got what he wanted. You hopefully got what you wanted. You trying to make it into something more now is what makes it complicated."

"Huh." I took in everything Maksim said. I let it sit there. I let the silence linger as I pondered my apparently female tendency to over-analyze.

"So what's the plan tonight?" asked Maksim.

"Working at Skinty's," I said.

"Alright, that's your excuse now, but later this week we're going out. I'm feeling tacos and margaritas."

"Mexican it is," I said.

Tonight at the bar it was a particularly slow night. I waited on a guy with his girlfriend celebrating their six month anniversary. Not sure why he'd take her to a dive like this for a celebration but who knows, a shitty relationship like that will probably last a lifetime. I served beers and nachos to two scrawny, pimply guys who clearly got past the bouncer with fake ID's.

In between serving these tables there was a lull. Lulls gave me time to wipe off the tables, clean the ketchup bottles, restock the beer fridge, and ponder the shortcomings of this generation, like the fact that nobody stares at my rack anymore.

There are two very different types of men out there. The ass man and the boob guy. That first kiss I share with any new guy is inevitably followed by an ass grab, but I'd do anything to replace it with a boob graze.

Unfortunately I was born into a generation where ass sex has become mainstream. My theory is that now, since the ass is on the table, literally, guys have become more enthralled with it in general, giving them a new found reason to go after it. Plus porn has made it so widespread, it's almost as if guys have forgotten about our other hole. Before, the ass was just a nice squishy bubble to admire while having sex the conventional way. Now the ass is so much more and it's my boobs that suffer. The next guy that ops for a boob squeeze will be put on a pedestal, but until then I'll do whatever I can to keep my ass out of the line of fire and keep my mind focused.

A friend of mine told me that she meditates in the morning. She said she wakes up fifteen minutes before she has to start her day and sits on her bed legs crossed listening to a calm, de-stressing video. I tried doing this one morning, but it failed to have the same calming effect on me. I sat there on my hardwood floor, cold and bored, focusing attention on aspects of my life that didn't need to be illuminated.

Being alone with my thoughts made me feel even sicker, even more scared, even more in tune with what was wrong in my life. It was then that I realized the people in my life, the movies that I watched, and the music that I listened to, were all helpful distractions that kept my mind functioning. The more I took time to think, the worse it was for me.

Luckily a group of guys walked into the bar just before my mind started running even further off the track. I thought it was for the best, until I had to serve them and found out they were nothing but belligerent fuck boys. Every time I approached their table, they were bragging about their sex lives.

I don't know who Ashley is, but from what I heard, she's one flexible slut. Those aren't my words; I took them directly from the dirty mouths of the immature, unappreciative boys. I always wondered whether any guy ever talked about me that way. I always wondered whether my midnight trysts with the man of the month ever made it past the confines of his bed. Luckily, I'm not very flexible.

15 LATE NIGHT HUNGER

Crash...Bang.

"Shit."

Crash.

"Fuck."

What the fuck is happening?

It was three o'clock in the morning and it sounded like a rabid dog was attacking the stove.

My room was dark. I rubbed the sleep from eyes, slipped on my furry pig slippers and quietly opened my bedroom door just a sliver to peak out.

I saw one of Johnny's shoes sitting by the door. Two seconds later I spotted the other one lying flipped over a couple meters away. I threw on my robe to cover my pajamas and exited my room.

Johnny was in the kitchen with the fridge open, the cupboards open, and food spread across the counter: bread, cheese, pickles, ketchup, raw pasta, something in a blue bottle, an apple, hummus, maple syrup, and barbeque chips.

"You pregnant?" I asked.

"Oh sorrrry, sorrrrry, I didn't mean to waaake you up," Johnny slurred his words.

His eyes went back to the loaf of bread in his hands.

"I'm trying to get this damn bag open. It's like glued fucking shut or some shit. How's someone suppose to make a sandwich with bread that doesn't open? Who wants impenetrable bread?"

"You want to penetrate your bread?"

"Don't be cute with me," Johnny said, with hands planted firmly on the counter. "There's plenty of time for sex jokes but now is not appropriate."

"Okay, okay, move aside," I said wedging in between him and the counter. "I'll help you."

"Thank you, you are so sweet, you know that? Seriously, I just think you're so sexy…"

"Okay, I know," I said, cutting off his drunken ramblings.

He put his hands on my stomach. I put two pieces of bread on a plate.

"What do you want me to do with these?" I asked.

He slowly moved his hands down my stomach. I felt his finger dip down slightly underneath my waistband.

I pushed his hand away, turned around, and leaned back feeling the edge of the counter dig into my back.

"What are you doing?" I ask him staring directly into his drunk eyes.

"What do you think I'm doing?" his eyes diverted down taking in every inch of my nearly naked body.

Two seconds later his lips were on the side of my

neck. I closed my eyes for just a second, feeling his hot breathe on my skin. My stomach clenched into a delicious ball.

I opened my eyes, pushed his body away from mine and put my finger under his chin, lifting his head up. "You're drunk. Go sleep it off on the couch. I'll bring you food in a second."

"Why don't we forget the food and I come join you in your bed?" He smiled while almost falling backward.

A noise startled us. It was Maksim peeping out of his room. "What's going on out here?"

"Nothing," I said. "I'm just going to bed." I took this opportunity to remove myself from Johnny's drunken grip. I left the half-made sandwich on the counter and went to my room.

I laid in bed thinking about Johnny. He was so drunk. I felt bad. I should have finished making him the sandwich. I didn't hear anything happening out there so I assumed he passed out on the couch, but two minutes later my door opened.

"Ray," Johnny whispered in the dark. He normally knocked; tonight he just came in and walked towards the bed.

"It's cold out there and the couch is uncomfortable," he said still whispering.

"You've slept out there a million times," I said.

"Can I sleep here with you tonight?" he asked without actually asking as he plopped himself down on the right side of my bed. He laid there fully clothed and immobile on top of my sheets.

"Thanks," he said slowly and very quietly with his eyes closed as he dozed off before I had time to respond.

"Do you want to get under the sheets?" I asked, not sure if he was still awake.

"Yes."

He lifted half his body as I pulled the sheets down and then up over him.

"Thanks babe. Night," he said, not lifting his head off the pillow.

"Goodnight," I said.

The next morning I woke up with the light streaming in through the blinds. I looked at the clock; it was still early. I wanted a cup of coffee so desperately. Every muscle in my body was screaming for a pick me up. I opened my bedroom door to find Johnny drinking a beer with his cereal. There was coffee already made.

"Hi," Johnny said.

"Hey." I poured the coffee into my cup. "Beer for breakfast? I asked.

"It's the best cure for a hangover," he mumbled.

I walked back towards my room, steam rising from the hot coffee in my cup.

"I'm sorry about last night," he blurted out before I shut my bedroom door.

"Don't worry about it."

16 HE DIDN'T WANT THE GUM

The light streaming through the black curtains blinded me the moment I opened my eyes. The scenery was different. I was looking at two men grabbing a woman's ass while the women kissed. It was one of those erotic posters you can pick up at a sex shop. If I hadn't been so hung over, it may have turned me on, a little bit.

The throbbing pain in my head made the room seem like it was spinning, like I had just entered one of those fun town rides at a carnival.

Somewhere along the way I started wanting to spend more time with Dylan even if we were just sleeping beside each other. I couldn't recognize the feelings. I wasn't sure if they were real or just an extension of extreme loneliness coupled with a misguided attempt to fall in love.

When Dylan woke up I greeted him with a freshly brewed cup of coffee. He looked at me as if I handed him a cup of his own blood.

"How did you make this?" he asked me.

"With your coffee maker," I said.

"Oh."

"Is that okay? I figured you wouldn't mind me using it. After the night we had last night…" I winked at him. "I needed a morning jolt. And I thought you might want one too."

"Okay," he said, not really answering my question of whether or not he minded me using his coffee maker.

From what I'd seen on television, boyfriends usually didn't mind their girlfriends making themselves comfortable in the mornings. I couldn't see why kitchen appliances would be off limits.

His reaction made me question our dynamic. With alcohol still being filtered and the jolt of caffeine making me ride high, I left my inhibitions behind and asked him sweetly, "So, are we like, seeing each other?" He didn't respond right away so I continued. "Like, do you want to actually date?"

"What do you think we're doing now?"

"I don't know. This was just happen stance…you know, taking advantage of circumstances. I saw you at the party last night, so we hung out. It's like when you're at a grocery store in the check out line and you decide to grab a case of gum. If the gum wasn't sitting there you wouldn't have gotten it; you probably wouldn't even think to want it. But once you see it there you think, 'hey, gum would be nice'."

"I'm sorry, who's the gum in this scenario?"

"I'm the gum!"

"So I'm the shopper?"

"You're missing my point."

"No I get it. So you'd like me to plan ahead for the gum."

"Yes, I'd like you to plan ahead about wanting the gum."

"And that's you?"

"Yes, that's me!"

I realized that I had just compared myself to a small piece of artificial sugar meant to provide a few minutes of sweet satisfaction before being chewed to completion then spat out. I probably should have thought of a better analogy, but for now I just went with it. And then I left.

"Wow, you look awful," said Maksim as I walked into our apartment.

I looked at him blankly.

"He didn't want the gum." I said before walking to my room and shutting the door.

The next night Maksim convinced me to go out with him and his friends. He said the best way to get over rejection was to feel wanted by someone else. I told him that a bar full of horny guys asking for my number wouldn't do the trick, but by the time I finished four whiskeys and three tequila shots, I was starting to doubt my previous doubts.

"Rejection feels good." I opened my mouth just enough for the guy standing in front of me to feel my breath in his mouth.

He was wearing some offensive shirt with a half-naked woman on it and a cocky phrase. I couldn't see straight enough to read it, but I'm pretty sure it was something sexist.

"Rejection feels really good," I said smiling just before I pressed my open mouth hard against his.

"Really?" he asked, eyebrows raised in disbelief. "I'll have to see for myself I guess. Why don't you come over to my place tonight then leave without saying goodbye after I'm done banging your brains out? If it feels as good as you say it does, maybe I'll call you for round two."

By this point he was clearly amused with himself. His grin sent a chill down my spine. His buddies eyed me like a perfectly cooked, medium-rare filet mignon. My hands suddenly felt cold against his neck. My eyes regained focus. With my peripheral vision, I saw Johnny waiting at the bar for a drink. He turned around a second later and saw me standing in front of this group of guys.

"Hey," I mouthed to him silently. My eyes must have sent him a help signal because he instantly walked over to me and put his arm around me.

"Everything okay, Ray?" he asked.

The guy with the offensive t-shirt quickly stepped forward and tried to grab my arm pulling me toward him.

"Yeah, we're fine. Actually we were just about to take off," he said so self-assured, confident, and drunk.

"No we're not," I said. I grabbed Johnny's hand and walked with him back to the bar.

"Thanks for the rescue," I said staring at the beer stains on the floor.

"Anytime. You always seem to find the worst dudes, don't you?"

"I don't think good dudes exist," I paused. "I'm

gunna get the fuck outta here."

"Wait, I'll go with you," he said.

"It's okay. You stay and get your drink."

I went home and went straight to bed. In an apparent mission to torture myself, I had agreed to a second date with someone the next night. I was on a role of bad dates, and it was a cycle that became weirdly addictive. I wasn't sure whether I believed there was a light at the end of the tunnel or whether this torture I willingly embraced was actually not as voluntary as I had thought.

Recently, everyone's been telling me that I'm too quick to say no: too quick to pass on a date if I don't think there's chemistry. Following my passions didn't seem to be working for me so well, so I decided not to follow my gut.   There was a friend of a friend of a friend who had been asking me out for months. I was running out of ways to say no so I finally said yes.

Our first date was surprisingly okay. I think it's because I expected it to be so terrible, so when it turned out mediocre, it seemed great. Our second date was a different story though. Somehow we ended up back at his apartment on his couch getting physical. At first, I was turned on, partially because I've been super horny lately and partially because we just watched a very erotic film.

We started making out standing up in front of his couch. I don't know if "making out" is the correct term though. It was more like he was devouring my mouth. My mouth was a sandwich and he was trying to eat it. He sucked on my lower lip like a kid sucking on a popsicle. Then he did this weird thing where he captured my lip with his mouth and sucked in and out, making it almost impossible for me to kiss him back. I stood there waiting for him to be done.

We eventually made it to his couch. He took off my shirt. He took off his own shirt too. I think I would have preferred for him to leave his on. My sex drive was plummeting exponentially with every passing second. He grabbed my ass and started sliding his fingers somewhere foreign.

Is he going where I think he's going?

His fingers inched further and further.

"Ah!"

He tried to part the seas of my anus like Moses. As if his big staff could create a fire in me that I would enjoy. He hadn't even attempted contact with my vagina yet.

What the fuck.

Just when I was getting used to splitting the check on a first date. It'd be like giving a pair of white ripped skinny jeans to a woman in the 1920's.

She'd be all like, 'Excuse me, let me get used to slacks first,' as she goes home to mourn the bustle.

I snapped back into reality and pushed his hand away. This made him kiss me deeper, but it was anything but passionate. I felt like I was being punked, like someone with a camera was going to appear from behind the curtains, laughing and pointing.

Is this guy testing me to see how long I can withstand the world's worst foreplay?

"Ahhh!"

Shit. Fuck. What the fuck?

He just slapped my ass. Hard. My mouth stopped moving. I had to stop my eyes from watering. I just wanted this to be over. Maybe I could try to slow down the kissing.

I pulled away slightly. I tried to close my lips a bit to do that tender lips-closed kissing thing. He grabbed my shoulder and slowed slightly. He pulled away for a second.

Thankfully. I could breathe.

He burped.

Eww.

Then he was back on me, lips on mine prying them apart. He slapped me again. This time he hit my upper thigh. It startled me, like a loud, sudden strike of lighting.

My mind started wandering. All I could think about was my apartment, my bed, my friends. I'd never wanted to escape a date more than I did now. But how do I just get up and leave? He tried to remove my bra. I stopped him. He looked at me like Oliver Twist wanting more.

Up close he was even more terrifying. On our first date, when he wore a suit I kind of thought he was somewhat, maybe, slightly handsome. But now, with his clothes removed, his face inches from mine, and his eyes intent on fucking me, all I could think about was the food in my stomach and the feeling of wanting to throw it up all over his putrid couch.

I started building up my defense mechanisms. Okay, I could pretend I'm an actress. And this was the scene.

If I were an actress, I'd just have to get through it. But time seemed to be moving so slowly. Okay, take two. I hoped it would get better. He grabbed my hand and pulled it towards his package.

Are you kidding me right now? You torture me with the worst fucking foreplay and now you want me to jerk you off?

I pulled my hand away. He grabbed my hand again, this time more forcefully, and pulled it back to his dick.

"No!" I pulled my hand away again. This time I slithered my way out from underneath his runner's body. He stared at me with a confused look on his face.

You've got to be kidding me. You're confused?

I found it hard to believe that he's ever made it past foreplay with a woman. If he has, that woman deserves an award. I truly wondered if he had ever actually fucked anyone before because a woman who could survive that kind of foreplay deserved one hell of an orgasm.

"I should go, it's getting late." I looked at my watch and it was only nine-thirty in the evening. Well, if I were an eighty-year-old yenta it could be considered late. Okay, so it wasn't late, but who cared I just wanted to get the fuck out of there.

"Okay," he said.

I reached for my shirt and threw it on as quickly as possible. I called a ride, slipped on my shoes, and said goodbye. He kissed me again.

Shit.

This time it was that kind of sweet, innocent kiss, but there was no kiss in the world that could ever make me forget the events that just took place five minutes ago. I tried to pull away as quickly as possible, and while doing so I interrupted the kiss quite noticeably. I knew he understood I was dying to get away. I said goodbye, flashed him a fake smile that I manufactured from a hundred percent insincerity, and then shut the door behind me.

I entered the elevators. There were so many freaking ground levels I didn't know which one to press. Is it ground, main, level one, or courtyard that I wanted? I pressed main. Thankfully I chose the right one. When I got downstairs my ride was already waiting for me.

I jumped in and slammed the door. The tears began to form. I did everything I could to stop them from falling down my face. I stared at my reflection in the window surrounded by darkness. We drove by a wooded park area. It seemed foreign enough to feel enticing.

"Actually, can you stop right here?" I felt the fire bursting inside every muscle in my body. I felt claustrophobic in the car.

"Uh, sure ma'am. Are you sure? It's pretty dark and empty here."

Yeah well, so is my soul.

"Yes, right here is perfect," I said.

He stopped the car and I got the hell out. He drove away. I stood still for just a moment, waiting for the car to be out of sight.

And then I ran. I didn't know what else to do. I ignored every signal my body gave me to stop. I ignored the pain shooting through my feet as I ran in my five-inch heels. I ignored the wind pushing my skirt up above my waist, baring my underwear for the wilderness to see.

I just ran. I couldn't stop. I ran past several trees, and buried myself deeper and deeper into the wooded area of the park. I saw a little cliff that appeared to have no end, but once I got to the top I saw that there was an end. I was at the top of a hill, staring down the opposite side, wondering how much it would hurt if I hurled my body off the edge, wondering how long it would take someone to find my body if I didn't survive the jump.

I realized at that moment that my goal was not only to survive but to thrive. I was determined. My heart beat out of my chest. I felt a breeze on my cheeks. I put my head back and fell to my knees. I ran my hand through the rocks on the ground, staring at the imperfections in each little stone. I imagined myself as a lifeless object: just another stone thrown into the mix. I pressed one between my fingers, feeling its hardness, admiring its ability not to crumble under the pressure of my fingers. I squeezed so hard the flesh of my fingers hurt. I felt the pain. I wanted to feel the pain. I wanted to see the blood that kept me alive, sear out of my body and stain the rocks that separated my feet from the earth.

My fingers slipped as a teardrop hit the rock, releasing it from my grip. I couldn't inflict pain on the stone, but it could inflict pain on me. I took off my shoes and stood there, feeling the tiny rocks beneath my feet, some more sharp than others. I don't know how long I stood there, but I eventually made my way home.

As I walked through the apartment door I was greeted by Maksim and his buddies: Johnny, Nick, and

Noland. I wondered what I looked like; I had just ran, cried, and been sexually exploited for the past three hours. I did everything I could to put on a good face. I didn't want to answer questions. I just wanted to go to bed. Take a shower, then sleep for the next twenty-four hours.

"How was your date?" Maksim shoved another handful of popcorn into his mouth, then washed it down with beer.

Johnny stared at me. His eyes were more powerful than rockets launching into the sky.

"Fine. I'm going to bed." I stumbled towards my room, saying nothing more. Not asking them how their night was going. Not letting Johnny eye-fuck me one more time.

I wanted to collapse in bed, but I needed to shower. I needed to wash off the saliva and sweat he'd left on my body. I needed to erase the memory of him sucking my breast even after I told him not to. I needed to punch my pillow just to let out the anger that was building up inside me every time I pictured that smug look in his eyes as he looked up at me with his lips on my breast.

He enjoyed it. He wanted to see the look on my face. He wanted to prove that he could do what he wanted and get away with it. I could have slapped him right then. Right in that moment, but I didn't. That would have given me more pleasure than any guy ever had.

I laid on my bed, trying not to replay every second of tonight, but failing miserably. My mind raced. I heard a knock on my door. I was too exhausted to move a muscle; my body stayed perfectly still. I felt every inch of my body sink into the bed.

"Come in," I moved my lips just enough to speak.

It was Johnny. He smiled. It was not that creepy frat-boy smile; it was kind. It was softer and less assuming. But I was in no mood for pleasantries and I was eager to bite off the head of the next person who wanted to take something from me that I didn't want to give.

"What do you want?" I asked, cold and hostile.

There was nothing but silence. I lifted my head from my pillow just enough to see him standing at my door, eyes looking more sincere than usual. The silence continued. He stared at me and I stared back, but I swore there was communication. I felt his eyes shoot out words that were clear and piercing and whole and silent. He leaned against the door with his strong, muscular arms.

I tried to move my lips, but nothing happened. I tried to speak, but no words came to mind. I let my head hit the pillow again and the tears stroll quietly down the side of my face and onto the pillow.

"Bad date?" he asked finally breaking the silence.

I couldn't answer. My lips were frozen; my mind was exhausted. A simple "yes" couldn't sufficiently answer his question, so I laid there silent.

I heard his body fall back against the wall. I knew he was still standing in my room because I heard the floor creak. I'm not sure why, but for just a second my body relaxed and I felt a subtle feeling of relief.

A few seconds later I heard him open the door to leave.

"Wait." I couldn't believe it. I didn't even lift my head from the pillow. I just opened my mouth and it came crashing out. I wanted to be alone. But I wanted to be alone with someone. I wanted to be alone mentally, but with a physical body beside me for warmth. I assumed he expected me to say something else after I told him to wait, but I couldn't think of what to say.

I looked at him again. He was still standing by the door perfectly still, but I got the sense that he wanted to leap forward onto the bed. Like the force that draws an addict to their vice, I felt myself losing the battle to sobriety.

"If you don't feel like sleeping on the couch, you can sleep here tonight," I said. Maksim's friends crashed at our place all the time because they were always too drunk to drive home. Usually they just sprawled out over the couch or the living room floor. I got used to dodging bodies every Saturday and Sunday morning. Tonight I wanted to feel the heat from another human body.

He moved towards me straight and abnormally steady.

"Why aren't you drunk?" I asked.

"We're out of beer."

"Oh."

He crawled along the foot of the bed to get to the other side. Our eyes stayed locked in each other's gaze the entire time. My heart skipped a beat. He was only inches away from me now.

He laid on his side next to me. We looked at each other one more time without moving an inch. It seemed like we went an eternity without speaking a single word.

I pushed him away for months. He flirted mercilessly with me every time I saw him, which was fairly regularly. He saw me go on dates, I saw him with women, dating, hooking up, or whatever you want to call it. I still enjoyed being around him despite being privy to his whorish tendencies.

Can't say I didn't thoroughly enjoy staring at him with his short dark brown hair, rugged beard, and deep brown eyes, but I just wanted to close my eyes and fall asleep. And so I did.

17 STARCHY DREAMS

There is nothing more cathartic than watching one sweaty man beat up another sweaty man while indulging in carbs and wine in your pajamas. I decided to spend the day watching all the *Rocky* movies, eating euphoria-inducing food, and drinking. I was doing all I needed to forget the disgust I felt every time moments of last night's date crept into my mind. The day was going great.

The front door opened. It was Maksim and Johnny, plus one other couple I recognized from a dinner party I went to just a few weeks ago. I turned around to greet them, not caring that my hair was in a messy bun above my head, my shirt had crumbs on it, and my mouth was probably stained red from the Pinot.

Johnny came and sat beside me while the others lingered around the bar opening up a few beers.

"*Rocky*! I love those movies," said Johnny.

"Me too," I said.

"Adriaaannnne," Johnny said in his best Rocky voice. I smiled at his awful impersonation.

"How's your day going?" he asked.

"Great," I said.

"What are you eating?" he asked as he leaned over to see what was inside the bowl I had resting on a pillow, against my chest.

"Sugary cereal," I said.

"It's six o'clock at night; why are you eating cereal?"

"It's always a good time to eat cereal."

He chuckled. Both of us were looking straight ahead at the television.

"I actually have this recurring dream where I buy fifteen kinds of the unhealthiest cereals, you know, the stuff that's basically candy for kids disguised as breakfast because they throw in a bit of Iron and Calcium? And then I combine all fifteen into a gigantic life-size porcelain bowl and just sit there with my hunk of a husband at our dining room table, eating the cereal as I convince myself that I'm still obeying my diet because I included such variety."

"And then what?"

"What?" I asked.

"And then what happens in the dream?" Johnny asked.

"Then everything goes black, I wake up and realize my cupboards are filled with salted seaweed, not cereal."

"Hmm," he paused. "And how often do you have this kind of dream?" he asked, turning his head and smiling at me.

"At least once a month," I said nonchalantly, still staring at Rocky.

The movie was at the part where Rocky asks Adriane out on a first date.

"Aww." Johnny interjected, turning his attention back to the television.

"I hate dating," I muttered plainly and matter-of-factly changing the subject before I shoved another spoonful of cereal into my mouth.

"Dating can be fun," said Johnny.

"There are two types of people in this world," I said. "People who hate dating…and fucking liars."

"Maybe you've just never been on a great date before," he said.

"Maybe so. But one good date doesn't make up for all the other miserable moments that inevitably ensue."

"That's a pretty bitter way to look at it," he said.

"It's the truth. I've got pictures of the strangulation marks to prove it."

Johnny's face turned to a panic. I awkwardly laughed it off and continued. "You know I always look at happy couples who've been together for a couple years and think, how did they get there? How did they get past that horrible beginning to get to that comfortable in-love phase? It's the fancy dinner with small portions and overpriced wine that marks the beginning of the horrible dating countdown."

"What the hell's the dating countdown?" he asked.

"You know, date one we kiss, date two we kiss again, he tries to have sex with me, I say no cause I don't want to seem easy. Date three, after experiencing the horrible ensuing feeling like at the end of the night we have to have sex, I have to make the decision to either break it off or have sex with him and be left with the wondering questions: are we exclusive? Is he sleeping with other people? What should I do if another guy starts flirting with me?" My words got faster and faster as I continued. "Do I refer to him as my boyfriend when people ask or are we keeping it a secret? Does he want it to happen again or was it just one and done? Then, when it doesn't work out, because it never does, I'm left wondering was it something I did or didn't do? What made him stop liking me? Is he speaking about me behind my back? The list goes on and on." I needed to catch my breath.

I looked at Johnny who had a look on his face I could not recognize.

Shit, what did I just do? Pretty sure I broke all the rules in every single dating article I've ever read about what insecurities you never reveal to a man. Shit. How do I back track? Change the subject!

"You know, I've been pushed out of friend groups before because of random hook-ups I've had that have gone sour."

"Cunts," he said nonchalantly.

"They were mainly guys."

"Bastards."

I shoved a big spoonful of cereal into my mouth.

A second later when I thought Johnny was reaching for the remote he actually put his hand on mine instead and rubbed it slightly before pulling his hand away.

I looked at him wondering what to say. He didn't say anything either. I though it'd be awkward, but it wasn't.

"You've got really soft hands," he said.

Okay, now it's awkward.

"Thanks," I said.

"I'll take you out on a good date," he said.

Wait, what? Did he just ask me out?

"Hey," he continued, "Can I have a bite of your cereal?"

I looked at him. His eyes were focused on the inside of my bowl.

"Sure." I handed him the spoon and let him take what he pleased.

18 THE SIZZLING STEAK

I stood in the kitchen with my bare feet against the cold hardwood floor. I threw a steak in a pan of searing extra light olive oil. I listened to it sizzle as the meat hit the pan, like an external manifestation of how I felt inside. Like that gut-wrenching, rip-your-heart-out kind of sensation that you feel when you hear your ex has a new girlfriend and she's not gross looking. I watched the red meat slowly turn pink. I watched as the juice absorbed into the pan.

Maksim and Johnny were in the adjoining living room having a couple beers on the couch, pre-gaming to go out for the second night in a row. Johnny hadn't mentioned anything about taking me on a date since he nonchalantly dropped the bomb last week.

"Yo, when are the girls getting here?" Maksim asked Johnny.

"They said they're on their way, like ten minutes ago," he responded.

Suddenly Johnny was standing right behind me. He put his hand gently on the small of my back. I felt a lighting bolt race up my spine. I turned around to look at him.

"You want some?" I asked

"Uhh, yes," he said with such conviction. "Wait, are there more steaks in the fridge?"

"Yeah, there's two more."

"Mak, you want a steak?" Johnny yelled.

"Right now? Aren't we going out pretty soon after the girls get here?" Maksim replied.

"Yeah, true, alright never mind," Johnny looked slightly disappointed, like a kid in a toy store being told to choose between two games.

I turned to Johnny, slightly touching his bicep to get his attention.

"You can have some of mine; I won't eat it all."

"Awe, no you eat it, I'm fine," he said. Two minutes later he was back on the couch, beer in one hand, phone in the other.

Five minutes later the steak was cooked to perfection. I turned to the couch, but Johnny wasn't there. I turned around to see the bathroom door was closed with the light on. I cut the steak in half and put each half on a separate plate. I grabbed cutlery for each then put one plate on the living room coffee table. I grabbed my plate and went into my room.

Two seconds into it, all I heard was, "Mmm, steak! Ray, is this for me?" Johnny yelled.

"Yes!" I yelled back.

"Thank you!"

"No worries," I responded.

"Oh my g-d, this steak is amazing," I heard him talking to Maksim in the living room, mouth full.

It was pretty fucking good.

A little bit later the girls arrived. They were all tall, skinny, and over-perfumed. They seemed to know Johnny very well. They greeted him with hugs, kisses, and smiles. I felt like the dirty old housewife or maid, just scrubbing the kitchen counters.

The girls acknowledged me quickly, then asked who I was and whether I lived there. Johnny introduced me as Maksim's friend from college. Then one of the girls with blonde hair and red lipstick asked how I knew Johnny.

Her eyes went up and down my body like an elevator. It was making me a bit uncomfortable.

"Through Maksim," I said, and nothing more.

"Maksim? Who's that?" she asked.

"Maksim, the guy right here," I pointed to him.

"Oh, Mak! Is your real name Maksim?" she asked him.

"Yup," he said.

"Oh! Ha!" She laughed.

"Ray is the only one allowed to call me Maksim though, so don't get any ideas. I'm Mak to everybody else," said Maksim. "You going out with that guy again?" He asked me changing the subject.

"Which guy?" I replied.

"I don't know, one of the ones you've been seeing?"

"Wow, that's specific."

"I can't keep track of your men," said Maksim.

"There's not much to know. So no, not seeing anyone tonight." I caught Johnny looking at me. I returned his glance. Our eyes were more powerful than

109

machine guns, but neither of us pulled the trigger.

"Alright then. We're doing a back to backer tonight. You in?" asked Maksim.

"Nah. But thanks."

"You going to bed early tonight?" Johnny asked me.

"No, I'll actually probably be up pretty late just getting some work done," I said.

Johnny didn't respond, but I could tell the wheels in his head were turning. He had very telling eyes. That's one thing I admired about him. A single glance could tie my stomach up in knots, make my whole body relax, or make me want to just put my hands all over him.

After everyone left, I threw on my bathrobe and sat on my bed with my laptop poised in front of me. I turned the lights off for maximum concentration. I was working on a scene in the novel that was unlike so many others I had written. The character actually got what she wanted. She was pining over a man for months, and finally the two consummated their love. I was very used to writing one-night stands, quickies, and miserable break-ups, but writing a happy ending was something I had to learn how to do.

I watched clips from my favorite romantic comedies. I felt nothing. I thought back to my childhood. I felt lost. I needed to stop overthinking it.

I could have my two characters go out for a nice romantic dinner and then a stroll along the beach at which point he would tell her he loves her and she would tell him she loves him back.

Nah, too typical.

I could have them waking up beside each other in bed with the sun streaming in through their curtains. He could wake her up with breakfast in bed and then she would tell him she loved him, and he would say it back.

Nah, too boring.

Suddenly I realized that I didn't know how to write a happy ending. It had to happen; I wanted it to happen, but I didn't know how to construct it.

Hours later I heard a knock at the door. I looked at my clock; it was one in the morning.

I opened it. It was Johnny. He looked at me, eyes piercing through mine. I opened the door wider, giving him the signal to come in.

I wondered what he was doing here. The bars are open until two and he had some very attractive company with him tonight.

I said nothing. He said nothing. I kept trying to think of what to say, but nothing came to mind. I could tell he was doing the same thing while not being any more successful than me.

We were standing in the doorway, not speaking a word to each other, and yet it didn't feel awkward. Okay, well maybe slightly.

Should I ask him what he's doing here? Should I ask him if he wants to watch a movie? Should I offer him food or a drink? I already made him steak; maybe he wants more? He usually grabs his own food and drinks as he pleases.

He inched closer to me. I finally felt like he was on the edge of making a move.

I tensed up, just slightly.

"I think I forgot my sweater here earlier," he said.

Thank god he made the first lame move.

"Really? Okay come in and check."

He took a quick lame walk around the apartment. No sweater.

What a shocker.

"It's not here."

"Hmm, weird," I said.

He walked towards me with conviction as if I was wearing his nonexistent sweater.

"It was boring not having you at the bar tonight," he said.

"Really? It looked like you guys had plenty of entertainment."

"Nah, still boring." He approached calm, yet determined.

And just like that he embraced my body fully, pushing me up against the wall holding the back of my head with one hand and reaching around my back hugging me with the other. While his embrace was strong and swift, it was also tantalizingly gentle and welcoming.

"Are you drunk?" I asked pulling my lips apart from his for just a second.

"No."

He pressed his lips hard against mine once again. My mouth opened. I put one of my hands on the back of his head and the other on the back of his neck. I pressed my lips firmly onto his, feeling the heat from his breath enter my mouth. It made my whole body tingle.

"Are you sure that…" I began to mumble but he cut me off.

"Yes."

"I just think…"

"Don't think," he cut me off again.

I pushed my hips towards his. I was more riled up than him. He remained calm and determined, kissing my lips firmly yet softly. His calmness started to rub off on me and I felt every muscle in my body relax. We stayed like that for the next five minutes until I wrapped my legs around him.

He walked slowly towards my bedroom without stopping the kiss and without letting me slip even the tiniest bit. It's like I was glued to his body. He turned off my bedroom lights and placed me on the bed gently. Our lips pulled apart for just a second as he laid my head on the pillow.

I looked up at him. He hovered over me, his chest just inches away from mine, his lips just millimeters away from my lips. I turned my gaze away from his eyes and quickly glanced at his lips. I inched forwards just slightly, signaling him to kiss me again. He remained still. I retreated, letting his lips hover over mine, close enough to feel the breath that escaped his mouth, but not quite close enough to touch.

He ran his hand down the side of my torso, starting from my shoulder and moving towards my hip. He put his hand on my cheek. He brushed a few stray pieces of hair back behind my ear then rested his hand on my face again. His thumb inched over the skin of my bottom lip.

My mind was clear.

I couldn't take it anymore. I lifted my head off the pillow and attacked him with my lips. I used so much force to lift my head I ended up sitting up straight. He gave in completely, grabbing my hair, moving his hands around my head from the front to the back, and all throughout my long wavy locks. He gently laid me back down onto the pillow.

We continued like this for the next hour.

All our clothes remained on. My mind was clear.

He finally reached for the button on my jeans, but I stopped him. He didn't seem fazed. He just kept kissing me and moved his hands back up to my head. I paused for a second, wondering why I just stopped him from undoing my jeans. There's nothing I'd want more.

"Wait, stop." I halted our kissing.

He moved his lips away from mine.

He listened. I said no and he stopped. Right away. But the last thing I wanted him to do was stop. I wanted to kiss him all night and into the next morning. I wanted to rip off his clothes, but something inside me stopped my hands from reaching for his buttons.

I focused on my heart beating out of my chest. I ran my hands through his gorgeous dark brown hair sticking up just a couple inches from the top of his head. He let me run my hands along the side of his face as he stared down at me without moving a muscle. My mind was clear.

I was ready to speak. I wanted to speak.

"Stay here with me tonight?" I asked.

"Okay."

19 THE MORNING AFTER

I woke up to the sun beaming in through the blinds, directly into my eyes. I put my arm straight out to feel for Johnny, but I ended up feeling empty sheets and nothing else.

I saw that my bathroom door was open but no one was in there. I heard nothing but silence coming from the living room. I opened my bedroom door and took a peek around the apartment. No one else was home.

He left without saying goodbye. Maybe he was mad. Maybe he regretted wasting his time with me last night; it's not like we had sex.

Oh god, was he mad we didn't have sex?

All I could think about were his arms, his hair, and his lips. I'd never been upset not to see a guy in the morning…until now.

I headed back to my washroom to get ready for the day. There was a note on the counter.

Ray,

I'm sorry I had to leave so early this morning; I had a family brunch. I didn't want to wake you. I'll call you this afternoon.

Johnny

He'll call me this afternoon. I couldn't help the smile that washed over my face. I felt both excited and terrified. My heart felt like it was going to explode. I had that tingly feeling deep down in my stomach. I wasn't hungry. I was too nervous and anxious to be hungry. Not in a bad way, but in a please speed up time kind of way.

I pulled out a journal from a drawer in my bedside table. I wanted to have a few choice words already picked out so that I'd know exactly what to say when he called.

Or, maybe…maybe I should just wing it.

The phone rang. Oh shit, that's him already!

I looked at my phone and it was the guy from the horrendous date I had last week. Shit.

Why the fuck is he calling me?

All of a sudden I went from happy to wanting to puke. It kept ringing. I sat there frozen, less able to move than a popsicle stuck to its other half.

It stopped ringing and I wondered if I should have picked it up.

Doesn't he know it's over?

Maybe I should call him back, just to let him know that it's over. So over. Like nothing could ever make it less over than what it was right now.

I picked the phone up off my bedside table. I sat there letting my fingers hover over his number. Then I did it; I used all my power to dial his number and then I listened to it ring.

He answered. He said hi. I said hi. And then with no further hesitation I said I couldn't see him anymore. He said he didn't want to see me either.

Yeah, no shit Sherlock you mother fucking asshole.

I wasn't going to let one call that had to happen ruin my day. Last night I went to bed as an everyday civilian and today I woke up a soldier. The air around me was clean and fresh, and smelled more invigorating than ever. The simple noise of cars driving past my window inspired me to kick-start my day with a bang and go join the race towards prosperity.

Getting dressed wasn't just about having clothes on today. It was about creating a look that could accurately portray my inner fire that was ignited the moment I opened my eyes this morning. I grabbed a pair of flared jeans: blue with fading in the front and back. They hugged my thighs so perfectly and made my legs look extra long.

I rummaged through my drawers, pushing aside those tops I wore on my bloated days, and going for that emerald green tight-fitted bustier that made my boobs look heavenly. Next I curled my hair with my medium sized curler to create those voluptuous waves that could stop any guy in his tracks. Last but not least, I threaded my favorite large gold hoop earrings through my one and only piercing.

I was feeling too good to spend any longer than five minutes making my face presentable. I looked at myself in the mirror with my bare face. I saw every curvature of my cheekbone, I admired the light freckles dusted sparsely over my nose, I relished in the sexiness of my plump lips. I yearned for a more defined jaw line.

There was nothing in my eyes. Nothing but brown. Nothing special, nothing intriguing. But I had learned to accept my ordinariness and appreciate my uniqueness.

I threw on mascara, evened out my complexion, dusted my eyebrows with brown, and painted my lips with a luscious red. A while ago I discovered that if I applied my red lipstick with my finger instead of with the actual lipstick, it created a more natural look. The red stained my lips so it looked like I just ate a red popsicle. It was exactly what I wanted: not that made up fake red, but the simple and sexy pop of color that made my face look less sickly.

The next day my productivity plummeted. After an hour of siting on my bed in front of my laptop, I realized that I had not touched the keyboard. I spent the entire hour gazing at my bed sheets thinking about my night with Johnny. Eventually I decided to take on the task of compiling my music into playlists that captured a specific mood.

I don't know what we were thinking but whatever we started, really needed to end. I saw Johnny all the time; he was one of Maksim's best friends. Sometimes I even liked to consider him as one of my best friends; that is when he was not being completely annoying. If we got together, we'd surely break-up, and then it would put us in a horrible situation. I'd probably have to move out, I'd get to see Maksim way less, and I'd have to skip most of the parties.

I fell into the same patterns. I rise, I ruin, I repeat. Often I thought it would just be easier to hit rock bottom so that I'd have a clear direction to move forwards. The worst kind of anxiety was the kind that came when I didn't know what was causing it. I self medicated with wine and whisky. I knew those remedies were not clinically proven, but they seemed to keep me sustained for the time being at least. I landed in a sea of fear at random moments throughout the day, but I always seemed to get back ashore as time passed.

Going for a run was one of my favorite ways to de-stress. My shoes were laced up and my exercise bra was holding my boobs down nicely under my ratty old t-shirt. Most days I enjoyed running more than sex. I ran along the beach boardwalk, watching the people and shops fade into the background so quickly while the ocean stayed constant. It didn't matter how fast I ran parallel to it; it was always there. It rushed up close to me then backed away. It was the loudest, calmest noise I knew. The faster the waves moved the faster my legs propelled me.

I remembered my days running track in elementary school. I remembered being focused on the target. Running four hundred meters was all about getting to the finish line as quickly as possible. My legs did the work, but my mind propelled the engine. My eyes saw the finish line, my heart felt the glory of winning, and my body got me there on time. The four hundred meter sprints I ran around the football field in my childhood, weren't anything like the racetrack I was stumbling around now.

As a kid, "winning" was not a foreign concept to me. I was ahead of my peers. I got the highest marks, I won the races, I saw my future and pursued it with passion. Now I'm twenty-eight years old and the only awards I win are free drinks from drinking competitions with Maksim and his buddies.

As children, we're encouraged to look into the future and decide who or what we want to be when we grow up. The skills that were once admirable are now my worst liability. Looking into the future I saw nothing that encouraged me to keep looking.

Somehow I was still running on this path. I was moving forward propelling myself in the forward direction and yet it still felt like I was just wandering aimlessly.

Every time I ran down the street I seemed to discover a new palm tree. It used to make me feel like I was running in a paradise. Sometimes I still got that feeling, but recently it was harder for me to even be able to define what I thought might be paradise. I discovered one of the houses on my street had a rose garden in their front yard; beautiful pink roses were blooming. I wanted to touch one so bad. I wanted to pluck one from the ground and watch it turn black in my hand with no water keeping its color from fading.

I remembered the first time a guy ever bought me

flowers. It was after we spent New Years Eve together. It was such a sweet gesture. It was such a long time ago.

I reached the main doors of my building and looked at my watch. I had just ran for an hour and a half, probably doing about nine or ten miles. My shorts and t-shirt were completely immersed in sweat. My face looked like a tomato and my hair was barely still in its ponytail. I opened my apartment door to find Johnny sitting on the couch watching television with a beer in his hand. He turned around.

"Hey! There you are...you went for a run I see," he said.

"Yeah. What are you doing here?"

"Sorry, I know I said I was going to call yesterday but I got busy so I thought I would just come over today. Mak wasn't here so I let myself in."

I was hoping he would call. Pushing him away would be a lot easier over the phone. The strength and discipline I prided myself in as an adolescent, had been failing me in my adult life. The time I spent organizing my thoughts, making sense of them, and coming to a conclusion could all be railroaded with a button-down shirt, a rugged pair of jeans, a mature belt and a few strategically spoken words.

"You look hot all sweaty like that," Johnny said bearing his pearly white teeth in one of the most illuminating smiles I had ever seen on a man. I could already feel my insides turn to jelly. I smiled.

"I should go take a shower," I said, "Before the sweat congeals."

"Sexy," he said with that look in his eye; I knew he was looking for an invitation. One that I knew he wasn't going to get.

Poor thing.

There are times I couldn't come close to figuring out what ran through the mind of a man, but right now there was something telling me he was imagining me in the shower, perhaps even both of us in the shower together. I hated to admit it but I was thinking about it too.

"I'll be right out," I said.

Standing in the shower naked, I turned the water on cold. I felt my muscles contract and start to shiver. I saw the goose bumps on my skin forming. I let myself feel uncomfortable for just a moment, appreciating the fact that I wasn't back home in Vermont in freezing cold weather.

After my shower I got dressed quickly. I chose to wear casual clothes that were just a notch up from my normal ratty lounge-around-the-apartment clothing.

When I came out into the living room, Johnny was sitting on the couch, a beer in one hand and the television remote in the other.

He turned around to face me when he heard my bedroom door open.

"Ray! What nights do you have off work this week?" he asked.

"Why?"

"I want to take you out."

"Take me out?" I said slowly and hesitant.

"Yeah, I want to take you out on a fifteenth date."

"Fifteenth? Where was I on dates one through fourteen?"

"I figured we'd just skip those. You said you hate the beginning phases of dating right? You know, those awkward and stressful first several dates. I figured if it's a fifteenth date, it should be comfortable and fun by then, no?"

I stared at Johnny like he was a mythical creature. No wait, he was real. I stared at Johnny like he was a candy store and I was a five year old kid walking in with a magical key that granted me all the candy in the world. No, that's not quite right. I stared at Johnny like he was someone I had known for a lifetime.

"Unless, you think it should be our thirtieth date?" he added, anxiously waiting for my response. I was too busy smiling so deep I could feel it in my toes.

"No. Fifteenth is fine," I said calmly and casually while my mind worked overtime trying to counteract this happiness I was feeling.

"Are you sure we should be starting this?"

Wow, I put the brakes on faster than I thought I would, even after all that.

"Yes," he said with great determination and confidence.

I had Johnny's full attention. He turned off the television, put his beer down, and walked over to me.

"We're gunna have fun. I'll take you anywhere you want to go. Even places that require me to dress up or wear a tie."

"This is California; no place requires you to dress up

that much," I joked, lightening the mood a little.

With his body just inches away from me now, I felt that force buried in the pit of my stomach pushing me towards letting my hormones trump my mind.

"I had fun the other night," he whispered to me as he inched closer and grabbed my hand.

Oh no, he's being sweet too.

He put his other hand on the back of my head and slowly leaned in to kiss my lips.

"I have fun every time we hang out, even when we're with the whole group," he said.

"But see, that's the thing," I said.

"What?"

"I don't want to fuck things up between us. I like that we can hang together without me feeling stressed and nauseous."

"I like that too," he said hesitantly.

"If we went out, just you and me, on a date…I'm sure it would be great. But the aftermath could suck. For once, I just want this to stay simple, you know? Like we hang together, have fun, simple."

"Ray, I'm a dude, 'simple' is all I know," he said.

I chuckled then continued, "I wish that were true. What if us dating doesn't work out? As you probably already know, I don't have a very good track record when it comes to dating." As I spoke I realized that my eyes were securely locked on the floor. I couldn't catch his gaze when I was saying things from a place of fear.

He put his finger under my chin and lifted my head to look directly into his eyes.

"First of all, I won't let you screw it up and second of all, I promise you that if for some reason this doesn't work out, we'll go back to being friends and I won't make it weird."

"Easier said than done. I like when you're around. Oddly, I like it when you're sleeping on our couch in the living room...and even sometimes in my bed. I'm okay waking up to find you here in the morning, even though the girls sometimes make me feel a bit weird, but still…" I was distracted for a moment when I looked up and saw a big smile across his face.

Damn, that smile could cause a car accident.

"That won't change, Ray. This is far from a random hook up! My dick ending up in your vagina wouldn't be an accident." His frankness shocked me, but I let him continue. "I've known you a long time. I know your weird habits, and your bad ones, I know most of the dirty secrets in your closet, and now I know that you've clearly never had a good dating experience before so please, pretty fucking please will you let me be your first?"

"You know I'm not a virgin right?" I laughed a nervous laugh.

He chuckled.

"Wait, what secrets do you know?" I asked.

"I know that you only have sex with guys at their apartments, and you never sleepover, and you do it because your fucking lonely but you don't even seem to like any of them."

Holy shit, did he just read my mind?

"Where the hell did you hear that?" I asked. The

conversation was turning hostile and I couldn't help it.

"From the sound of it, it sounds like you only sleep with guys you don't like. How many times have you snuck out of here at midnight to go hook-up with one of your booty-call douchebags?"

"I do not have booty-call douchebags!" I said, indignant.

He ignored that comment and proceeded. "Why do you get so stressed out about sleeping with guys who actually take you out on dates, and yet you have no problem giving it up to an asshole who just keeps it simple. If he's nice enough you'll fuck him, if he actually likes you and wants to date you, you run away."

"You're making this shit up," I said, getting a tad flustered, partly because I had no idea he was that perceptive.

"Am I? What about those nights you say you're going on a date, and you don't arrive home 'til like four-thirty in the fucking morning?"

"Yeah, well how do you know we weren't just at the bars and I'm tired because I've been out so late."

"Bars close at two, Ray."

"We could have gotten food afterwards."

"Every time?"

"Every time? What do you mean every time? I don't do that every time I go out with a guy. Are you trying to say I'm a slut?"

He was about to speak, but I cut him off and continued. "You know what, screw you. You think you know so much about me, but I know your track record too. How many women have you slept with, three hundred? More?" I turned to walk away but Johnny didn't let go of my hand. I just realized that this whole time we had been yelling, he never let go of my hand. I seemed to have a pretty firm grasp of his too.

"No," he said pulling me closer. "I don't think you're a slut and no you overestimate my prowess," he winked at me.

"I don't think you're a slut at all," he repeated. "I think you do things that you don't want to do. I think you're someone that I really like hanging out with and even though you're sometimes difficult and you push people away, and you say things you don't mean, I still like being around you. Maybe I'm a masochist."

I leaned in and kissed him. He kissed me back with such eager force, my knees nearly buckled underneath me. I fell slave to the heat of his body. His lips became magnetized to mine. I just wanted to rip his clothes off so I could feel every part of my skin touching his.

"My bedroom," I said in between kissing him fervently.

"Okay," he said, "But after tonight we're going out on a real date and we'll use our mouths for something other than kissing, like eating or drinking, or use our lips for forming words or making a sentence, or…"

"Shut the hell up," I whispered.

He smiled and wrapped his arms around me, opening his mouth and pressing his lips against mine.

There was a feeling so delicious emanating from my gut. It was like an invisible electric wave that connected his body to mine.

"Thursday night," I whispered between kisses.

"Thursday night it is," he whispered back. "And don't even think about backing out of it."

"Never. But please lets not do something adventurous. I mean, it can be adventurous like woooo let's take our clothes off and go streaking through the quad, but not adventurous like oooh let's climb a mountain, walk up this hill…just for the fun of it…kinda thing, you know?"

"Okayyy," he said looking at me strangely.

"Just nothing that involves work. I just want to chill and have fun," I clarified.

"I can't believe you actually had to preface that. What did you think, I was gunna take you to the gym?"

I laughed.

"You never know. I lived in San Francisco for a summer doing an internship, and those hippy freaks spent every moment they weren't at work, climbing mountains or dancing on bikes."

"Weirdos," said Johnny.

"I know."

"You know people actually belong to groups where they walk up mountains together?"

"You mean hiking groups?" he asked.

"Yeah, weird right? I wonder what they do when they get to the top of the mountain."

"You know what they do at the top of the mountain," Johnny winked at me and smiled.

"No I don't."

"Yes you do, he tapped my arm."

"All those bugs, and dirt, and…"

"Nature?" he summed up my words so perfectly.

"Yeah." I paused. "Eww."

"Okay, let's get back on topic," he said. "I'll take you on a fun date, no exercising required, unless you want to do a workout with me afterward, sans clothes. It is our fourteenth date after all," he said smiling before rolling on top of me and kissing me with more passion than some people express in a lifetime.

20 OCEAN INFERNO

I remember the first night we met. I remember riding in the taxi with the windows down and the wind in my hair to go meet up with Maksim and his nameless buddies at a small sports pub. I remember knowing that I had made the right choice to go out that night. I felt like something good was going to happen. I didn't know what. In fact, I never really understood the meaning of that moment until after that night, until after we met.

Years later the butterflies in my stomach were just as forceful as they were then. Once again I sat here with the same feeling that something brilliant and invigorating was ahead, without knowing what that entailed.

Tonight Johnny and I were having our first official date. He was picking me up and taking me out to dinner at a restaurant near the pier. It's one of those fancy places with decked out silverware, tiny portions, and waiters who treat you like they'd live and die to grant you your every wish and command.

Today was a good day. The energy in my veins was

so vividly present, like at any moment I could explode into ecstasy.

I ran. I ran along the water, deliberately letting my toes feel the warmth of the ocean. I ran. I ran so that I could feel every muscle in my body tighten to propel me forward. I ran. I ran because my mind was secreting those chemicals that gave me euphoria. Those chemicals I dreamed about having every day. Those chemicals I lacked when I was depressed. Those chemicals that could make me feel alive when I felt so lifeless.

Tonight I didn't need help from drugs but I drank anyways. We ordered a bottle of wine at dinner: a red wine from Italy. We ordered three dishes and shared. I could hardly eat with all the butterflies rolling around in my stomach.

Johnny talked about his family. He told me some cute stories from his childhood and even an embarrassing one, after I groveled for it just a little. We laughed a lot. He asked me about my days as a dancer. He asked me why I didn't continue acting. He asked me how I got into writing and why I loved it so much.

Then we got off on a bit of a tangent and began discussing our favorite board games and what kind of games we'd want to invent. I told him about the time I played drunken twister and ending up throwing up all over green, while still holding my position and winning the game. He told me about the time he threw up all over a game of beer pong then woke up in the garden of his neighbor's home, naked.

When our server came by to give us our bill, we

briefly stopped our conversation and noticed that we were the only ones left in the restaurant. We had been there for over three hours. I offered to split the bill; he chuckled and insisted he'd pay.

"I'll drive you home now?" he said with a question at the end of it. I looked at my watch. It was eleven but I didn't want the night to end. I stared out into the distance and saw the lights from the piers casting an illuminating glow over the water. We were close enough to faintly hear the ocean waves crashing against the shore, but I wanted to be closer.

I turned to face Johnny. I flashed a big smile.

"What?" he asked.

"I have an idea," I said.

"Okay," he smiled, clearly intrigued.

"Follow me," I said leading him towards the sand.

"Wait, can we walk around the sand?" he asked, "I got my new dress shoes on."

"You bought new shoes for tonight?"

"Yeah. Ted Baker."

"Fancy. Okay, well never mind then," I said.

"Wait, do we have to walk through the sand to get there?" he asked.

"Yes," I said.

"Fuck it," he said, "Let's go."

"Are you sure?"

"You lead the way," he said taking off his shoes.

I leaned in close to him as if to kiss him, but grabbed his hand instead. I led him straight toward the water. It took him a moment to realize that my idea was the ocean, but it wasn't until I started ripping off my clothes that he realized my idea was skinny-dipping in the ocean.

Johnny followed after me picking up my clothes as I tore them off one by one throwing them on the ground. I stood before him completely naked. He very sweetly stood there staring into my eyes.

"You coming in or am I going in stag?" I asked him. I took a moment to appreciate the pure joy I felt. I relished every moment my lips were curved upwards in the biggest smile I've sported in a while. I walked up to Johnny playfully and put my hands on his waist, with one slightly lifting his shirt to suggest he should take it off. He proceeded to do so. Then I put my hand on the waistband of his jeans with just one finger slipped slightly inside between his jeans and his smooth skin.

The biggest most-telling grin came across his face and before he could even undo his jeans I so fervently laid my lips on his. Seconds later I was off the ground in his arms, straddling his body with mine. I pushed my meager frame hard against his bare chest. He had one of his hands nestled sweetly between the strands of my hair and the other firmly grasping my lower back.

The water was cold against my fiery skin. My heart was beating so fast; the sound of it almost competed with the noise from the waves. I wrapped my arms around his shoulders and hid my face in his neck to hide from a wave coming up beside us.

In the midst of frolicking in the ocean with Johnny, I took a second to imprint a picture of this moment in my mind, from the way my skin felt against his to the way my heart tingled when I focused on his hands touching my back, the way the warmth from the heat of his lips made my whole body feel on fire, and the way his smile made me smile so hard my cheeks hurt.

"Do you still hate dating?" he whispered in my ear.

"I'm coming around to it," I whispered back before planting my lips firmly on his.

"You are so passionate," he said in the brief second our lips weren't touching each other.

I had never had a guy be so openly communicative with me. I always loved my inner fire, but hearing a guy label it as "passionate" made me want to test the limits of what passionate meant.

"I'm glad we skipped dates one through fourteen," I said smiling at him like a child.

He smiled back at me and that was all I needed to feel secure underneath the dark sky. In this moment, it was just the two of us and a body of water with no limits.

I'm not sure how much time passed in the ocean, but by the time we got out, our fingertips were prunes. We had nothing to dry us off on shore except for our sand-ridden clothes. The sand formed to my body like memory foam. I laid on the sand hoping to feel some lingering heat from the day's sun, but it was cold underneath the moonlight. Luckily, Johnny's body on top of mine was all the heat I needed.

21 SURVIVAL OF THE FITTEST

The scariest thing about getting what you want is knowing that if you take it for granted and it turns into nothing, all you'll have left is the bitter taste of knowing it was you that turned it sour. I've learned to admire those that can take something small and turn it into something so special.

People might argue that survival of the fittest is no longer as relevant as it was back in our primal days, but a recent experience at a Chinese restaurant seemed to suggest otherwise. It was a Friday night. I was surrounded by Maksim, three of his buddies, Johnny, and three other women. One of them was a girlfriend, one was a one-night stand tag along, and the other was one of Maksim's good friends. We sat at a large round table with layers of table clothes on top and a large round Lazy Susan in the middle. If you don't know what that is, don't worry I didn't know either. It's a circular table that spins around so that people can easily get access to any of the dishes on it without reaching across the table. At a Chinese restaurant where everyone shares food, it is a vital contraption.

We waited until everyone arrived before we started having the food sent out to us. One of the girls was the last to arrive. She arrived fourteen minutes late and although everyone at the table was relieved when she showed up, they were pissed as hell at her for making them wait fourteen extra minutes.

Finally the food starting circulating one dish at a time. First the spring rolls, then the soup, then the main dishes: chicken, beef, fish, and veggies. Like a lion that had sights on its prey, the people sitting across the table from where the food was originally placed, were eyeing the dish like time was their most precious commodity. With each second that passed, their heart rate rose just a little bit more. But like a kid who just got their first kiss, they tried to play it cool. You could see the flush of their skin and the slight trembling in their hands. The noise level at the table dramatically decreased. All you could hear was the sound of silverware clanging against plates.

Each person was faced with a very specific conflict: stuff the food on their plate into their mouths or try to gather more food before it was gone. Each person seemed to have his or her own strategy. The men at the table seemed more concerned with gathering food. It was all about getting their hands on the serving spoon, taking the largest scoops, and being the first to tear up a dish. The women, me included, were not completely unaware

137

of the race to get the food before any one dish was all gone, but at the same time we knew that a calorie feast like the one we were having, did not happen all the time and therefore shouldn't be rushed without enjoying every innate moment of pleasure that it brought us.

The ones who walked away from the table feeling satiated and happy were the true winners, not the ones that got the most amount of food and were sickly stuffed, nor the ones that failed to gather enough food to satiate their hunger. The ones that were capable of getting exactly what they wanted: the right amount of food, and the right amount of satisfaction from indulging in such salty and sugary fried goodness, were the ones who walked away from the meal victorious. I'm not sure about the others, but I walked away craving more.

22 BREAKING DOWN THE WALLS

I woke up and saw his body lying beside mine. I felt the curvature of my lips deepen as the signals from my heart commanded a smile. I closed my eyes and drifted back to sleep peacefully.

When I woke up the second time, the sun was beaming through the blinds, casting a bright shadow on my walls. Johnny was awake too. I turned around to look at him looking at me. He was shirtless and sexier than ever.

"Hi," I said.

"Hey," he responded before kissing me on the cheek.

"You sleep cute," he said.

"You were watching me sleep?"

"A little."

I took that at face value and didn't dig any deeper into the creepiness of it.

"What do you want to do today?" he asked.

I wrapped my arm around his strong chest and his beautiful muscular arms.

"Anything you want to do," I said. "But…"

"No, no, that's not how it works. I want to know what you want to do today," he said shaking his head then running his hand through my hair. "You always let me choose."

"You didn't let me finish."

"Okay sorry, go ahead."

"There's a caveat," I said.

"Okay…"

"Whatever we do, we have to be able to do it without our clothes on."

"Hmm, interesting." His eyes perked up. "So what you're saying is, whatever I want to do we can do, as long as we're naked?"

"Yes. Precisely."

"Well then, I can only think of one thing." He smiled.

He unexpectedly started grabbing at the pillows on the bed.

"What are you doing?" I asked.

"I'm building a fort."

"That's the one thing you want to do naked?"

He started propping the pillows up on their sides, making what I thought was presumably a wall. He placed the pillows very carefully, with great attention to detail. Then one of the pillows fell down. He turned it back on its side. Two seconds later it fell down again.

"Shit, it's too flimsy. It needs to be harder."

"That's what she said," I joshed.

"Hey, no time for childish antics," he said, serious and determined.

"Yeah, said the grown man making a fort."

He looked at me with those brown eyes I loved. "You'll thank me when I'm done," he said. "You need more pillows on your bed."

"Sorry, I'll get right on that."

"This is seriously what you want to do?"

"Wait, you didn't let me finish. There's a caveat," he said.

"Okay…"

"We must have sex in this fort after it's built."

"Well I hope you know how to make a sturdy one." I winked at him with playful eyes.

"I've had years of practice, trust me. When I was a kid I spent a lot of time playing with myself in the forts I built," he said.

"Playing with yourself, eh?" I winked again with a dirty look.

"Ehh, not like that, although…"

"Okay, too much information. Less chatting, more building, good sir. You want some help? I do have some experience building forts too yah know," I said.

"Yeah, you start with that side, I'll work here and we'll meet in the middle."

"You bet we will." I winked at him.

After building the fort, we enjoyed it. Admittedly, it didn't withstand foreplay, but it was still a valiant effort that gave us a few laughs and some extra calories burned.

For the rest of the day, Johnny sat beside me as I wrote my novel. Every time I looked over he was just sitting there with his headphones on, watching movies on his laptop. I was hesitant to try writing with another soul so close; I was afraid he wouldn't let me get my work done.

"So what do you love so much about writing anyway?" he asked me.

"Close your eyes for a minute," I said.

"Okay."

"Imagine you are standing beside your best pals in a concert hall. You're drunk and holding onto your favorite drink while the band plays your favorite song that you've listened to on repeat for the past ten years. You're not thinking about work on Monday or that horrible date you went on last night where the girl didn't sleep with you."

"Why didn't she sleep with me?"

"Shut it," I said, then continued. "The lights are dark and the audience is loud." I paused. "Remember that feeling."

Johnny kept his eyes closed. I wanted to plant a kiss on every inch of his face, but I stayed composed.

"Now imagine you've just booked the flight to the destination you've been wanting to go your whole life. Remember that feeling. Okay, now imagine you've just bought a new pair of shoes. Actually, scrap that, that won't work for you. Imagine your favorite football team just made it to the Super bowl and your friend called and told you he got him and you tickets for the game as a present for your birthday."

"Is my friend a Rockefeller? Those tickets are thousands of dollars."

"Don't worry about the details," I said.

"Okay, sorry."

"Now, you're there in the stands and your favorite team scores a touchdown. You can hear the cheering, you have to pee like a motherfucker cause of all the beers you had, but that's okay. Your team wins the game and the stadium goes nuts," I paused. "Remember that feeling. Okay, now open your eyes," I said. "If one of my readers can recreate any one of those feelings you just got, I'll have succeeded in my mission behind this book."

INTERMISSION

It's four in the morning and I'm so high off the ground I can't see the ground beneath my feet. I've consumed no drugs, except alcohol. I've been high, I've been low; I've been everywhere but cathartically stable, but tonight it wasn't the alcohol brightening up my spirits. Tonight I had a bottle of wine with Johnny. We laughed, we kissed, we drank the wine until our lips turned red. Like a gentleman he walked me to my door, the one he's entered a thousand times, then kissed me goodnight. Now I lie here more hammered and hopeful than ever. I lie here flying. I lie here waiting to fall.

23 THE INTERVIEW

Johnny rummaged through the fridge looking for some food to soak up all the alcohol he consumed. I used this brief moment to take off all my clothes. I leaned up against the counter, feeling the cold marble resting against my lower back.

He turned around, saw me, and paused.

We just stared. I drank-in his plaid button-down shirt with beer stains, and his dark blue denim jeans held up by his black and silver belt. His eyes moved away from mine to take-in the rest of my body.

I didn't mind.

"Hi," he said.

"Hey."

"Hot?"

"Thanks."

"I mean, hot like is that why you took all your clothes off? I mean you're also hot, clearly," he said fumbling his words like an eighteen year old Jewish boy at a Hillel party.

"Nah, I'm actually cold, now that I've taken my clothes off," I said, very matter-of-factly.

"Hmm."

There was a pause. I briefly and succinctly wondered whether I should have left my clothes on. He looked down at my feet.

"Nice pig slippers."

"My toes were cold."

"Hmm."

Maksim's bedroom door opened.

"Shit!" I whispered and ducked behind the counter scooping up my clothes and putting them on as quickly as I could.

"Yo buddy," Johnny walked to the edge of the counter, preventing Maksim from entering the kitchen.

"Yo, buddy," he said, awkwardly.

"Whatcha doin'?"

"Just grabbing some water," said Maksim.

"Here, I'll get it for you," said Johnny.

"Thanks mom, but I'll get it."

I stood up, clothes on now.

"Hey! I found it. My earring," I said raising the stud I just pulled out of my ear into the air. "Darn things are always falling out," I said.

"Right," says Maksim.

I turned to Johnny. He had a huge smile on his face. He stuck his tongue out at me the second Maksim had his back to us.

Maksim grabbed his water and walked towards his

room. "Resume making out or whatever you were doing," he said nonchalantly.

"Wait, what?" I said, looking to Johnny for answers. I nervously laughed. "We weren't…why would you think…?"

"How stupid do you guys think I am?" he asked.

Johnny was just about to speak, but I put my hand over his mouth.

"I knew you guys were an item like a month ago," said Maksim.

"Wait, we weren't an item a month ago," I said.

"Well I anticipated it then. Just don't break up," he said before shutting his door.

"I guess the secret's out," said Johnny.

"I guess so," I said.

Johnny smiled and wrapped his arms around me.

"Ray," Maksim opened his door for one more second. "I forgot to tell you, I wrangled you an interview at my work."

"What?" I said. He had my full attention.

"A spot opened up. My boss needs an assistant."

"You work at a music production company. Why would they want me? I write books not songs."

"It's an assistant job. All you have to know how to do is answer the phone, look good for clients who come into the studio, and make coffee."

"So what am I now, the charity case?"

"No. You said you wanted to get away from working at Skinty's and you haven't been able to find a writing job yet so I thought in the meantime, this might be a step up."

"I can't believe you didn't tell me about it."

"I'm telling you about it right now," said Maksim.

"When is the interview?" I asked.

"Monday."

"Monday? As in THIS Monday?" I asked.

"Yes."

"I have no time to prepare!"

"You have the rest of the weekend. Now, I'm drunk and going back to bed. Goodnight," he said just before closing his door.

"You suck," I said.

I guess I probably should have said thank you for setting up the interview, but my mind was barreling down a narrow corridor and I just needed to breathe.

"I can help you get ready for the interview," said Johnny.

"I don't even know if I'm going to do it."

"Why wouldn't you?" he asked.

"Because I doubt I'd get it."

"Well that's a pretty negative way of looking at it."

"I have writing to do," I said as I walked to my bedroom.

I sat in my room, nearly naked. The butterflies in my stomach were eating away at the lining. Maksim wrangled me an interview. Already I started picturing how I'd feel when I don't get the job. Already I started thinking about the reasons I'd use to explain my failings. I sat there wishing there was something more I could do. Maybe I could prepare for it? Maybe there was an assistant book I could read to learn everything there was to know about being an assistant.

I felt my nerves quickly consume my soul, and it was like I was sliding down the back of the furriest goat. I reached for the half empty bottle of whiskey on my nightstand. I unscrewed the cap and put the bottle to my lips.

There was a knock at my door.

Shit.

I quickly put the lid on and slid the bottle back in the drawer.

"Come in," I said.

It was Johnny.

Oh shit, I forgot about Johnny.

"Hey, can I get a kiss before you get all wrapped up in your writing?"

"Of course," I said, feeling every nerve in my body relax.

He pressed his lips so sweetly against mine. I hoped that my breath didn't reek of whiskey. I ran my fingers through his messy brown hair. My body and mind needed a relaxer. His lips were my cure.

"You can sit in here if you want, but no distracting me," I said like a puppy trying to mimic a lion.

"How could I possibly distract you?" he asked as he inched towards me, pulling the laptop off the pillow in front of me and laying me down on the bed.

"I'm serious," I said.

He kissed me one more time before pulling his body weight off of mine.

"Alright, alright, get to work," he said.

I set my alarm clock for six in the morning. I liked waking up early because the world was still asleep. I liked feeling like I was profiting from this extra time that most people wasted sleeping. I liked thinking that my productivity would triple if I could spend just one more second awake. And then there were times I'd do anything to knock myself out for just one second longer.

When Monday arrived I found myself sitting in my bed with the sheets draped over my lap, confident that I would conquer the interview today. There was nothing my red patent high heel pumps couldn't accomplish. But when I stepped outside my apartment and headed to the interview, the comfort I found surrounded by the four walls of my bedroom wasn't there anymore. The chilly morning combined with my sudden onset of nerves created a mindset I wasn't prepared to handle.

I arrived at the office, twenty minutes before the interview. I found the nearest bathroom and locked the door behind me. My heart beat fast. I felt like I couldn't breathe. I closed my eyes and pretended I was at home in my pajamas in my bed sitting at my laptop writing. I imagined my blinds were closed and the lights were turned off with only the light from my laptop screen illuminating the room. I was alone. I was safe. I was protected from the world sitting behind a screen and the meaningless unread words that monopolized it.

I opened my eyes and saw that I was looking in the mirror at the reflection of a woman exuding no confidence and sweating profusely in an oversized blazer.

I wished the world would stop for just a second so I could find my breath again and escape this panic.

I spent the morning preparing for the interview. I wasn't doing research, reviewing my skills, or practicing common interview questions. No. I was preparing myself with loud music and reassuring thoughts. I walked myself through the situation: arriving at the office, waiting to be interviewed, and then being confident during the interview. I imagined myself meeting unfriendly middle-aged corporate suits and judgmental potential colleagues. In my mind, under the covers, safe in my apartment I was able to breathe.

Now it felt like breathing was something I needed to relearn. Breathing was supposed to come naturally, right? Walking and talking are all things I took for granted. In this moment of absolute fear, even the thought of standing was taxing my emotional energy. I watched the little hand on my watch tick; only twelve minutes left. I felt a gnawing at the pit of my stomach.

I promised myself I'd appreciate every second alone in my bedroom if I could escape this feeling right now in the pit of my stomach. Like a volcano I could feel the negative energy flush through my body.

It's just an interview.

I thought that again.

It's just an interview.

I could be home under the covers in about two hours. Just two hours.

There was just a few minutes until the interview. I finally built up the courage to leave the bathroom and sit in the lounge area. I pretended today was an audition, a performance. I needed to be someone confident, someone secure, someone competent. I needed to be anyone but me. I had always enjoyed acting; today should be no different.

Two minutes later they called my name. I tried to be ready. I could do this. It would all be over soon.

I thought back to a documentary I watched about guys working on Wall Street. They all had such poise and self-confidence. I mimicked their language. I made my voice sound confident. I didn't let my insecurities taint my overall message. The interviewer seemed to like me. When our interview was over he took me to Maksim's office. Everyone was smiling, laughing, and in good spirits. I had this gig. After all of the initial worrying, I compartmentalized my feelings and held it all together. I was proud of myself. I did it.

Maksim arranged for us to have celebratory drinks later that day. I had to work the night shift at Skinty's so Maksim, Johnny, and the guys were going to come to Skinty's while I worked. Luckily, my alcoholic boss never noticed me taking shots.

Maksim and Johnny arrived at the bar before the other guys. I lined up tequila shots for them.

"Can I talk to you for a sec?" Maksim asked.

"Sure, what's up?" I asked.

Maksim had a grave look on his face. Kind of like the look someone gets before they tell you your dog died.

"You didn't get the job," he said. I loved that he was straight to the point, straight to the sharp, needle-like point like the perfect ballpoint pen.

"Why? Do you know that for sure? The guy loved me!" I said.

"He did! He thought you were great, just not exactly what they needed for this role. They went with someone else. I'm so sorry! But you know what, fuck it, this role would have sucked anyway. You're going to get something so much better," he said as he unsuccessfully searched for something positive to say.

"Yeah, right. I'm going to be slinging cocktails and showing off my ass in these tight dresses for the rest of my life."

"No you're not, Ray. C'mon let's have some drinks and brainstorm your next move," said Maksim.

"Sure," I said. "My next move is pouring us some more shots. Right now that seems to be my only talent."

"Ray."

"This was an assistant job. All I do is assist people. I am overqualified for the job," I said.

"You are! Absolutely! So fuck it," said Maksim.

There was a part of me deep down that was relieved not to get the job. The shame I was feeling was partly from that and partly from being the one stuck on this road I couldn't escape. When I returned to the bar, shots in hand, Johnny gave me a look of sympathy that made me want to puke.

How could I amount to anything more than a bartender when no one would give me a shot? Well, the only shots I was ever given were the ones that give you a headache the next morning, and those shots aren't given to me, I take them myself.

The next morning I went to the ocean. I immersed myself in the cold water. I was wet. So wet. Dripping, cold, and lonely. I stepped out of the ocean waves. I looked around but saw nothing but the clouds in the sky. I ran my fingers along the goose bumps on my arms, cupping my hands around the circumference of my bicep to measure my fat. My hands lost their grip around my arms as the water from the rain enveloped my body.

My ritual swims were planned for every rainstorm. Rain didn't happen too often in California, so when it did I took advantage of it. I tried to capture as many beads of water on my skin as I could. I tried to embed that feeling in my brain, the feeling of being dumped on by gallons of water, that feeling of revival, like the baptism I never wanted. The feeling that there was something moving between me and the sky was what made me feel like there was something moving inside. But this time, I felt nothing.

The noise didn't calm me the way it normally did. I couldn't feel the tingling sensation running through my veins every time the smell of the ocean mixed with the sound of the waves rushing up against the shore. I watched as a six-foot tall wave rushed towards me. I stood there as still as possible waiting to sink down beneath it. I let the force of the wave move my body in the direction of its path. I relaxed every muscle in my body and let the ocean do all the work.

A couple minutes later I found myself washed up along the shore. With blurry eyes, I couldn't see a meter in from of me. The water from the ocean mixed with the rain from the sky and the tears in my eyes to create a cocktail so strong and blinding. The warm water wasn't enough to prevent the coldness of the rain from creating goose bumps on my skin. I could see the physical changes of my body and feel the tears run down my face, but I couldn't feel that spark inside that I had felt every other time I came to the ocean.

I tried so hard to go back and remember how I felt when I was six and went to the ocean for the first time. I tried to recreate that feeling in my heart that inspired my entire life up until this point. I laid on the sand feeling nothing but the gritty dirt staining my pale skin and the wetness from the ocean and the sky making me shiver.

I was reminded of the cold bitter weather of Vermont that I grew to hate so many years ago. But I relished in the memories of a time when I stayed afloat because my dreams were still alive and well. With every breath I took now, each dream dissipated slightly more, slipping like sand through my bony fingers.

I wanted to go back to a place where I still believed in my goals. Even if just for one day, I wanted to feel the way I felt when I thought my actions were taking me somewhere meaningful. Even if just for a second, I wanted to feel the way I felt the first time I stepped into the ocean when I was six.

That night I laid in Johnny's arms as he tried to console me. Despite his kind attempt, the words were meaningless. There was a stillness in my body that not even a fan blowing full speed could disrupt. The warmth of Johnny's body wasn't enough to thaw the hatred I had for myself.

Tomorrow I was leaving. All I had to do now was book the flight.

24 RUNAWAY LOVE

I caught myself today before almost saying I love you. It was about to slip off my tongue so naturally, but I stopped myself and swallowed it down like a horse pill. Johnny insisted on driving me to the airport. We said goodbye and he kissed me ever so softly on the lips. I stumbled forward toward the metal detectors. And then I looked back and he was gone. I tilted my head back just a bit to keep the tears from falling down my cheeks like the water from the Ein Gedi.

His kiss may not have been full of passion, but it was full of something along the lines of sadness. I remembered every touch. His body always felt like the most expensive silk.

I spent the plane ride writing a poem because I couldn't figure out how to channel my emotions into the manuscript. I wasn't usually the poem type; my words never had the right rhythm, the right step, or the right sound. But the more disheveled I felt, the more I yearned for something that I couldn't put my hands on, the more I was able to make my words sing a rhythmic tune.

It went a little something like this:

The lean in, open and touch
The warmth spilling from your lips onto mine
In public, alone, wherever you'll have me
I'll take you

I spent yesterday in love with you
I spend today loving you
I'll spend tomorrow remembering our love

Your kindness doesn't breed often
It doesn't have a word, it doesn't have a phrase
It can't be explained, just felt

The distance can't change my love
I'll love you more with every mile I travel
If you love me half as much as I love you
Tomorrow we'll meet in between

I realized that the poem was horse shit but for some reason I didn't mind the smell.

25 THE GULAG

I stepped into the bedroom I had slept in for seventeen years. I looked in the mirror expecting to see a fifteen year old kid with long blonde hair and a permanent smile, but all I saw were bags under my eyes and knots in my hair.

I opened my closet and rummaged through my old clothes, remembering the nights I spent dancing in the dresses and the days I spent studying in jeans and sweaters. I opened my jewelry box and tried on some of my favorite necklaces as a kid. There was a silver heart with rhinestones and a palm tree with sparkles.

I took my clothes off and changed into sweatpants and a t-shirt. I sat on my bed and starred at the four walls I used to know so well. My bed wasn't as soft as I had remembered it. The sheets weren't as silky as the ones I had in LA. Like so many nights recently, I lulled myself to sleep with the sound of Rufus Wainwright's song, *Across the Universe,* and let my eyes grow tired of the tears staining my pillow.

The next morning I showered, brushed my hair, and bleached my teeth. I stared at the mirror, but no one stared back. I turned around and felt his arms on me, his hand on the back of my head as he planted his lips on mine and pushed me up against the wall. Then I opened my eyes and remembered I was alone in the room.

I thought I had met someone who made my world turn, even if he never knew it. I had uncontrollably grinned every time he liked one of my pictures, every time he sent me a text, and every time he looked into my eyes when I spoke. Our conversations were often interrupted by long, passionate kisses but that's what made them special.

Now with three thousand miles between us, my body was numb. I couldn't feel. The walls around me were visible but not there for me to touch. I spent the day surrounded by the foreign four walls that used to be my bedroom as a child. I sat alone in my room praying for the tides to turn. I tried music, talking with family, sugar, but they all came up empty. It seemed like the only thing I could do was write. I wrote fifteen pages of a novel today and then deleted three of them, which was actually better than my average writing to deleting ratio.

I found comfort in the written word because I had the power to either show or conceal it. My relationship with my writing was mine and mine alone. A sentence I wrote a month ago had the power to make me feel the exact same way I felt when I originally wrote it. It's like I was bottling a million different emotions with each word being more than typography on a page.

I couldn't focus. My light had three settings. The darkest was depression: that lifeless feeling like the world was an even surface and I was just a coasting zombie. And then there was the unexciting normalness phase that left me with a touch of urgency for something more. And soon I hit that sweet spot when the light flicked on like a burning candle with an initial flame that rapidly combusts. This was the dream phase: the phase where everything seemed within reach, like I could reach out and touch the ocean from one side to the other.

Sometimes as my energy started to flourish I realized that grasping for the ocean soon gave me that panicked drowning feeling: that feeling like the world would end if I didn't satisfy my craving, that feeling of longing like shaking a bottle of champagne and leaving it in the freezer for days.

I couldn't hear my own thoughts. There was no music loud enough to drown out the look in his eyes when he said goodbye to me at the airport. He didn't want me to leave. I wasn't used to being wanted. He let me leave. I told him I had to leave. He told me to stay and I stared back into the warmest and softest eyes I had ever seen and said I couldn't. That was it. Two words that I couldn't explain. I just needed to get away, run away back to a place I hated more than I hated myself.

I'd been trying as hard as I could to see past this one moment: to feel the way I felt last week, last month, last year. The past always looked better than the present. The noise in my head was turning into screaming. The rose petals I tracked into my room were black and crunchy and starting to smell.

Every decision I made was worse than the one before it. I started to question my every move, my every play, so much so that I found myself amounting to nothing and aspiring towards no goal in my hometown of Rutland where dreams go to die.

Tonight I went to my favorite dive bar and sat at the same booth I sat at when I was seventeen pretending to be Lyla Collette, a 21-year old from Springfield, Massachusetts. Her cheekbones weren't quite as defined as mine, but bouncers didn't seem to notice. With my boobs practically hanging out of my shirt, I didn't think they really spent much time looking at my ID back then.

Who knew that now at the age of twenty-eight with real ID to prove it, I'd be pretending to be someone else even more than I did back then. I was on my fourth whiskey neat when my high school crush walked into the bar.

He was tall, dark, but not quite as handsome as I remembered. His hair wasn't as messy as Johnny's, his jeans weren't as baggy, and his smile wasn't as powerful. I felt an aching deep inside and it wasn't from the shot of whiskey pouring through my body right now or the drinks before it. I don't know why I came back here. I needed to go home. But first, I needed fresh air.

I left Vermont without leaving a mark. There was no goodbye party, no breakup, no I'll miss you, just the very poignant feeling in the pit of my stomach that if I didn't leave that place and discover a new way of living I wouldn't be living at all. I wanted to feel like something was pulling me back to California. I wanted to know that upon my return there would be more than the ocean and a bar filled with booze I'd need to pour. I had fallen so out of love with myself and had grown into someone in so much need of love from any source willing to provide it.

I wanted Johnny so bad. Every time we kissed, it felt like the first time. Every time he touched me, the warmest ball of energy ran through every vein in my body so strong that if it didn't kill me a lightning bolt never could.

I couldn't breathe. The pavement beneath my feet wasn't strong enough to keep me sturdy and the chill in the air wasn't helping. I couldn't breathe but I hadn't fallen yet. I'd fallen for the perils in life. I'd fallen for the sexiness and allure of hedonism. I'd been sucked up and spat out by the big bad leather-wearing boy, known as life. I looked down and saw a bird eating a dead rodent on the street. I looked up and saw the same sky I saw in California. I looked back at the lights from the bar behind me; it looked just like the one I worked at in California.

I looked down at myself and saw the same short dress I was paid to wear at Skinty's. I saw the same skinny legs I used to run away. I saw a bruise I gave myself when I fell into the kitchen cabinet when I was drunk. I saw the scar on my wrist looking more and more like the fate I was going to experience once again if I didn't get myself back on that plane and back to the place where I had nothing figured out, but everything I wanted available. My mind started racing faster than I thought possible.

I felt the mixture of whiskey and energy drinks in my system. I felt the coffee from this morning. I felt the valium from an hour ago and I felt the cigarette in my hand lead my body down to the concrete that I was so unlucky to be dwelling on alone right now.

There was no pillow for my head, just a jagged curb with ants and cigarette butts, one of which was probably mine. My eyes closed ever so slowly as I drifted away to the beach just blocks away from where I wanted to be right now. I squished my toes hoping to feel sand, like on my first date with Johnny, but all I felt was the strap of my high heel digging deeper into my skin.

I don't remember what happened next. Time became irrelevant. I needed to pass out before I could come to and change everything I hated about my life.

The next morning I threw up whatever I could from the dinner that I didn't eat last night. I took a bath in the tub I had used since the time I was a baby. I remember spending hours pretending to be a swim instructor as I watched my hands turn into prunes. After the bath I got out and had the house to myself. I stepped outside onto the porch with a big cup of coffee and started reading a book I found on my mom's nightstand: a book about how meditation can lead to better sex. Twenty pages in, I got bored.

An hour later I went for a run outside despite it being freezing. The colder I felt the faster I ran until I was sweating through my workout gear. I ran past the candy store I used to love as a kid, I ran across the train tracks I feared as a kid, I ran alongside the riverside and nothing stopped me until my phone rang. I looked at the screen and saw Johnny's name.

My fingers hovered over it. I wanted to hear his voice but I was afraid of his words and even more afraid of how I'd explain my actions. I hated the person I was becoming; the person who ran away from everything, but I didn't know how to stop it. I ignored his call.

Two weeks went by, but everyday was the same. I woke up, tried to busy myself with some writing, went for a run, spent time with the family, went to the bars, and then passed out. On good nights, I passed out in my bed, on the bad ones I passed out in the streets.

By the end of the fourth week I was so lost in a sea of misery, I could hardly force myself to get out of bed. I missed the cologne and whiskey smell of my apartment with Maksim. I missed the four walls of my bedroom in LA with all of their tape marks and scratches. I missed coming home to an apartment filled with people. And…Johnny. I missed Johnny.

I went for a walk today and discovered that my childhood neighborhood had no distinct scent. The ground bred new life in the form of small wimpy weeds and no flowers. I came across a disheveled bush and nearly tripped on one of its broken branches. And while I had socks and sneakers on my feet to protect me, I would have rather been barefoot in sandals.

I walked all the way to the river about two miles

north. I wanted to hear the rushing of water and feel the waves against my skin, but when I got there the water was brown, the smell of algae was already so pungent from thirty feet away, and the movement of the water was slow and timid. I kept my distance and waited to see if anyone else would come to visit the river. Nothing but crickets. I was alone amongst tall, dirty trees with broken branches, a muddy terrain, and a lifeless river.

The walk back to the house was cold and quiet. I hated the silence. I couldn't wait for the concert tonight. I was going to see one of my favorite bands, Jack's Mannequin. I remembered spending hours listening to their albums from start to finish when I was in school. I remember daydreaming about the perfect man; the one I'd fall madly in love with and marry. I remember feeling so young, like my whole future was ahead of me.

Tonight I hoped those feelings would be reignited during the concert. I had already gone back in time to Rutland. I was hoping the endless flood of flashbacks would turn into something positive tonight. I always turned to music for answers. I was hoping I'd get some reassurance tonight. I needed to figure out my next play.

INTERMISSION

I fell so far down; I looked up and saw nothing. My mind escaped to my favorite place. I stood in the concert hall drunk again, feeling hopeful for the first time in as long as I could remember, praying that maybe moments like this could happen more often.

I dreamed of a love so strong that even though we were thousands of miles apart I could still feel the touch of his skin on mine. If I could close my eyes and wake up in LA I would do it now. When I opened my eyes I was still in the concert hall. I was feeling good but in the wrong city. I was flying in my mind. The clouds were soft and silky, and I loved the way they felt. I found comfort in the loudness; it drowned out everything else.

Do I stay or do I leave?

That's when the band started playing their song, "Miss California" and I knew.

I'm going home.

26 THE NEW GIRL

It was nine o'clock in the evening when I stepped off the plane at LAX. I was happy to have shed the sweaters for a pair of jean overalls. My hair was in a messy ponytail and my face was makeup free. When the warm air touched my bare skin and the smell of exhaust fumes and palm trees reached my senses, I knew I was home.

I left LA with nothing but question marks and a bitter taste, and I knew that upon my return I'd have to explain, defend, and work to get myself back on the track I fell off of a long time ago. My first stop was my apartment. I wanted to shower and clean myself up before I headed to Johnny's. I had no idea what I was going to say, but I couldn't wait to give him a hug and feel his body on mine.

As I walked through the hallway to my apartment I heard voices coming from inside.

I didn't tell Maksim I was flying back today. I

wanted it to be a surprise. I opened the door and saw him in the kitchen with a beer in one hand and a grilling fork in the other. There was a strong smell of caramelized onions and steak.

Maksim looked at me, jaw dropped just a bit before a big smile crossed his face.

"Ray! You're home!" he said.

He put the fork down and walked towards me to give me a big hug.

"I was just about to send in the wolves," he said.

"I missed you too, yah goof!" I responded.

The rest of the room was silent. I turned to my right to see Johnny sitting on the couch, beer in one hand and television remote in the other. He looked at me, his eyes sending lightning bolts of something unrecognizable towards me. He kept a straight face.

"Hi," I said to Johnny, smiling and hoping that my smile would induce him to do the same.

"Hey," he responded very machine-like.

There were a couple other guys and girls on the couches, a couple of whom I had met briefly at other parties.

"Sweetie come over here, check this out," a female voice yelled from the other room. She stepped out of the bathroom and saw me.

I guess Maksim's got himself a new girl.

"Hi, I don't believe we've met. I'm Ray. I live here with Maksim," I said.

"Oh hi, I'm Gigi. I'm with Johnny," she said with a smile.

169

That's when it happened. That feeling I wasn't sure whether I wanted to throw-up, faint, cry, scream, or close my eyes and not wake up until the feeling passed. I closed my eyes and opened them. Johnny stood there next to Gigi, holding her hand. I looked at Johnny. He looked at me with a stone cold expression that could have made snow fall in the desert.

There was a sharp feeling in the pit of my stomach like the forming and falling of icicles from the roof of a house. Every time I took a breath the pain got worse.

I stared at his hand holding hers and all I could think about was our first date when he held my hand. I wanted to fall asleep with my lips still touching his. I wanted to stay intertwined with his body every second of the night. I wanted to curl my icy toes around his feet. I wanted each one of my fingers touching every inch of his body. I wanted to see what his body looked like next to mine, on mine, in mine... I couldn't feel it, but my mind could imagine the feeling of it.

I fell so far I could feel my stomach hit the floor. I screwed up. I screwed up so bad I wondered if I would ever take another breathe without feeling like I was punched in the stomach.

"Ray, do you want to come out with us tonight?" Maksim interjected, most likely to fill up the awkward silence that I was initiating.

"No." It was all I could say.

More silence ensued.

"What are you going to do tonight then?" he asked.

Rip my heart out and watch as little tiny schoolgirls step on it?

Practice putting needles in my eyes? Walk on nails. Drink all the whiskey I can handle before I pass the fuck out.

"Sleep," I said.

More silence. I walked to my room and shut the door.

"She's just tired," I heard Maksim say to explain the awkwardness.

Johnny has a girlfriend. Johnny is putting his dick in someone else's vagina.

I kept repeating that in my mind and somehow every time I said it I still had to force myself to believe it. I was supposed to be his girlfriend. How could so much change in a month?

I returned to my room and fired up my laptop. I opened my manuscript and started reading. My character was the same as I had remembered her from the last time I sat on this bed deciding her fate. I looked around at the four walls surrounding me, and they were the same too. The nightstand was filled with whiskey and wine; that hadn't changed. I sat there still for a second and practiced opening and closing my eyes. It wasn't a dream. It wasn't a nightmare. It was real life and I couldn't stand the feeling of it.

I've always known that writing was my only form of control. I couldn't control what happened in real life, but I could determine the life of my characters I created on the blank page in front of me. I bottled up all of my bad date experiences and incorporated them, pushing them off onto fictional characters, giving my main character more sex and distress than any one person could handle.

Sometimes I found it very hard to write about something that I couldn't understand.

Tonight the world slipped slightly further out of reach. My character didn't do what I told her. Her race to the finish never ended. She just kept running and before I knew it I couldn't control her. Her legs protruded off the page. Her voice was louder than mine. Her words spoke clearer, but like a woman in the height of a manic attack, her words didn't make sense to me. She spoke in hyperboles, she spoke in code, she spoke and ran and leapt and tore across the page, and I was left sitting and staring and wondering how a fictional character could out smart me.

And then I looked at the night table beside me and saw the open bottles: the empty bottle of beer, the pain pills, and the empty message in a bottle that symbolized my fate. Suddenly I realized my character was me. My character had somehow morphed into the god-awful human being that I had become, and had overruled any sense of normalcy that I had hoped to portray in the writing of a woman who's fate was supposed to be better than mine.

Sometimes I wondered how loneliness could take on such a severe form, one that could make me feel so close to the words I had written to describe a fictional character. The tears came crashing down on my keyboard so fast. My eyes were so blurry I could hardly see my laptop screen, but that didn't stop me from typing. I typed so vigorously to create a character that could keep me company and comfort me when I mourned the death of my real life relationship with someone I wanted to spend everyday loving.

It was time to call it a night. My character was going nowhere good and I was just seven whiskeys away from entering an even darker zone than hers. I couldn't remember the last time I had seen a full moon in the sky, but tonight I looked out and saw the full circle lit up so close I felt like if I didn't reach out and push it away, it would obliterate me. The weight on my shoulders trickled down through my body and I knew all I had was an empty bed to support my sinking soul.

27 CONDESCENDING CUBES OF TUNA

I woke up to find the walls moving towards me. It felt like I couldn't breathe unless I consciously told my body to do so. Sun streamed in through my blinds but it couldn't illuminate anything except the darkness that was emanating from a place even I couldn't reach. I wanted to feel numb. I needed to escape into a new world like the one I had known for so many years before this one.

I took a deep breath. It didn't help. I tried again. The panic was still there. I took another shot of whiskey, but nothing worked fast enough.

I needed to escape. I needed a rose garden filled with flowers and the hot sun beating down on me. I needed to feel loved but have no one around me. I was fading so fast I could hardly feel my legs. My heart was beating so fast but not fast enough to make me feel alive. I needed to escape this feeling of no feeling but panic.

I went from a single shot to guzzling. I felt the liquid burn all the way down my throat and into my stomach. I needed it to work quicker. I needed to cry, but I couldn't remember how to manufacture the tears. I hoped that the written word could get me out of this horrible feeling of nothingness, but I couldn't open my eyes.

The lifeless statue sitting on our marble floor walkway had more spirit in it that I did. I kept trying to make the world I remembered reappear, but nothing would change until my mind did. Resting my head on the pillow, I felt nothing beneath the skin. My eyes squinted so hard, the stress reverberated through every muscle in my body.

Tonight was Maksim's twenty-eighth birthday party. The timing couldn't be worse. This year I told him I'd arrange his celebration so he could focus on his work. He was super stressed lately and I just wished there was more I could do to help.

I wanted this night to be super special and memorable for him. He said he wanted it to be dinner and then a bar afterwards; he said I could pick the places. I chose sushi for dinner then a rooftop bar with one of the best views in the city.

I created the event page and invited all of his friends. My heart skipped a beat when I clicked on Johnny's name. He was skillfully ignoring me lately. Every Friday or Saturday night when I got home from bartending at Skinty's I opened the apartment door and held my breath in anticipation to see Johnny laying on our living room couch. Every time he was not there I felt that heavy,

175

brutally painful feeling in the pit of my stomach; that visceral feeling that made me want to throw up or knock myself into a long, drugged up stupor.

All day I was restless. At two o'clock I sat down to write. At three I realized that I had just spaced out for an hour, listening to music without typing a single word.

I didn't know how tonight would play out. I kept imagining different scenarios, but in each one I ended up in Johnny's arms. They started off realistic, with Johnny ignoring me and me trying to talk to him, but they always ended in the same fairy tale way.

My eyes glazed over as I continued staring at my blank laptop screen. An email message notification popped up and stole my attention away from Johnny for a split second. It was from Edgar Publishing. I opened it. It took only the first two sentences to make my heart sink.

Dear Miss Raya Rivers,

After reviewing your submission we regret to inform you that we will not be going forward with publishing your manuscript. We commend you on the effort and time you put into your work, but at this time we will be moving ahead with other candidates.

Months ago I sent in my first novel manuscript. Since then I had completely put it out of my mind and had moved on to writing manuscript number two. I had already gotten past the pain of rejection when I didn't hear back from any of the publishers. This letter just made the rejection more salient and more real.

My work lied dormant in its file, mocking me. Maybe my ex co-worker was right. Maybe the guy who tried shoving his tongue down my throat and his hand up my dress was saying something I should have heard. The main character in that novel was dark, morbid, and a loner. Maybe the creative mind that I relied on to write it was not capable of producing something people actually wanted to read.

All this self-reflection made everything worse. It was only four in the afternoon and already I just wanted a glass of something alcoholic in my hand. No actually, make that two, two glasses of something alcoholic, one in each hand.

Johnny didn't show at the pre-party, which gave me all the time I needed to dissolve my fears in drinks before we headed to dinner. By the time we got to the restaurant I was starving. I ordered scallops for the appetizer, a tuna tower, and a fancy house special roll for the meal. A few people were late, including Johnny, but we started ordering anyway. Apparently manners disappear when an excess of wine and beer have been consumed.

When my scallops came I indulged in every bit of their buttery goodness. Sweet, soft, and gooey just like I had hoped.

"Happy Birthday dude," I heard a man's voice say to Maksim. I looked up to see who it was, even though I already knew. Johnny's voice was husky like a wolf, while still soft and endearing. My body was a sound system in sync with his voice. When he spoke I could feel the reverberation through every nerve. When he spoke, my cold hands stopped shivering and my heart started pumping faster and faster like the beating of drums in a crescendo.

When I looked up I saw Johnny standing next to Gigi. Gigi smiled at me, but Johnny avoided my glance. He sat down on the other side of the table. I watched as he pulled out Gigi's chair and touched her shoulder as she sat.

My tuna tower arrived and I stared at it, waiting to see the walls fall down from the pressure of my gaze. Nothing happened.

"Ray."

Tonight was Maksim's night. I wanted him to have the best birthday.

"Ray!"

I tuned out the conversation for a moment. When I tuned back in Maksim was trying to get my attention. Gigi and Johnny were waiting for my response, so were a couple others.

"Sorry, what was that?"

"I was telling Gigi what you do," said Maksim.

"And what did you say?" I said, not really knowing the answer myself.

"You're a writer."

"Right, yes, I write."

"Cool, what kind of writing do you do?" asked Gigi.

"I write novels."

"Oh that's great! Which ones have you written, I'd

love to read one!"

"Well, I haven't published any yet," I said looking at my tuna tower hoping I could hide my shame in it.

Damn chef didn't make it big enough.

"Oh," said Gigi, clearly not sure of what consoling thing to say.

But that's okay because Maksim chimed in with an even bigger buzz kill: "She's sent some work to publishers, she's just waiting to hear back."

"Actually," I said knowing that it couldn't get any worse, "I heard back from one today. They weren't interested."

"You didn't tell me that," said Maksim.

"Well I'm telling you now," I said. Unfortunately, I let my eyes slip away from Maksim to Johnny. I saw him looking at me, or at least in my general direction, with a look of compassion. That pity made me want to throw up. My tuna tower seemed less appetizing as food and more appetizing as a potential landmine to smash onto the floor into a million tiny pieces of ripe avocado and perfectly condescending cubes of tuna.

Who the fuck cuts tuna so precisely?

Every cube was an exact replica of the one beside it.

"Who wants a sake bomb?" I asked, changing the subject as best I could. I may not be able to eat, but I could certainly still drink.

I set the sake on top of the chopsticks that I placed across the top of my beer. I watched as the weight of the sake was supported by two thin chopsticks that were just millimeters away from letting the sake and beer explosion commence.

After dinner we headed to the rooftop bar. It was overflowing with guys in dark jeans and button-up shirts, and women in skin-tight cocktail dresses and high heels. Rooftop bars always seemed to attract the prettiest people, at least on the outside.

I walked toward the barriers that prevented patrons from falling off the edge. All I could hear was the loud clink of the metal from my broken high heels hitting the pavement. No spa had ever given me the same serenity that I felt when enveloped by the warmth of Los Angeles' warm wind in my hair. When the heat in the air mixed with the darkness of the night I started to think that consuming the drink in my hand wasn't the only way to feel something.

I pressed my hands firmly around the metal bar lining the edge of the rooftop. The city was lit up with lights coming from every street and building in the distance. I looked up in search of a star but found none. In the corner of my eye I saw a young and physically fit, brown-haired man approaching. I turned my back to him, trying to find the group.

That's when I saw Johnny kissing Gigi and I started to wish that the metal bar under my fingertips was the only thing that I could feel. So I flung myself overboard, waiting for that rush of adrenaline. I was ready to fly.

…I'm just fucking with you. My heels remained firmly planted on the ground, but my senses did go into overdrive. I felt every muscle surrounding the pit of my stomach contract. I felt every thin fiber of hair rise on my skin. I could almost touch this visceral pain with my hand, but it was buried too deep inside. Every breath I took hurt more than the one before it. I clutched my martini glass with fervor. That longing I'd felt just a month ago had now turned into this never-ending yearning for something that I had destroyed. I just wanted it to end; I needed it to end. I needed to breathe deeper. I needed to feel something; anything but this never-ending sickness stemming from every organ receiving blood from my broken heart.

A hand touched my shoulder. I turned around, ready to kick this horny bastard in the groin, but to my surprise it was Maksim.

"I was about to kick you in the groin," I said.

"Well hello to you too," he said. "Is that your version of birthday treatment because if it is that could explain why you're single?"

I ignored his stupid sarcastic question. We both knew that there were a million reasons why I didn't have a man.

"What are you staring at?" he asked.

"Nothing," I said. "I'm going to get another drink. Can I get you another?"

"Your martini is still more than half full," he said.

I drank the rest in one big gulp.

"Now it's empty," I said.

Maksim's eyes wandered, most likely searching for long legs and long hair potential in the bar. My stomach turned the moment I saw Maksim spot Johnny still making out with Gigi. He turned to me with a look of pity that just made the situation worse.

"I'm going to get another drink," I said.

On my way to the bar I turned around to see Maksim heading towards Johnny.

Shit.

My penchant for self-destruction had me ditching the bar to listen in on their conversation. My self-esteem and pride were non-existent by this point, so lying low behind a bush to listen to Maksim and Johnny talk was not at all demeaning for me.

"Dude, do me a favor for my birthday," Maksim said to Johnny.

"Anything, what?"

"Don't be a dick," said Johnny.

"How am I being a dick?"

"You're making out with Gigi right in front of Ray. Stop trying to rub it in."

"Ray and I aren't dating. I can make out with whomever I want, wherever I want, whenever I want."

"Yeah well, that also makes you a dick, but whatever. It's better you're not with Ray anyways."

"What's that supposed to mean?" asked Johnny.

"Nothing." Maksim walked away and headed towards the bar, eyes open and wandering.

Shit, he's looking for me.

I snuck out from behind the bush and circled back to the bar.

"Hey." Maksim spotted me. "Where's your drink?"

"Still waiting," I said.

We approached the bar and got our drinks within

minutes.

"Want to go dance?" he asked.

"Seriously? But you hate dancing."

"Not when I'm drunk, I don't," he said.

"Okay, fuck it, let's dance!" I said, holding my gin & soda and my whiskey neat. Buying two drinks at once was more efficient. Less time was spent waiting at the bar without a drink. In college, I mastered the art of holding two drinks on the dance floor while not spilling and still being able to dance to my fullest capability. Although, at this time of night my dancing skills consisted of trying not to fall over drunk.

It was one-thirty in the morning, only thirty minutes before everyone would be clearing out of the bar. I couldn't wait to leave. I put my arm around Maksim and said happy birthday one more time before telling him I was heading out.

"What? We're probably going to go for late night pizza down the street."

"I'm not hungry," I said. "Just tired."

"Alright. You're the best," Maksim gave me a big squeeze. "Thank you for planning tonight. It was incredible," he said with overzealous drunken enthusiasm.

"I'm glad you had a good night," I said almost knocking over the drink next to me with my unsteady drunken hand.

I turned away from the table and was met with Johnny standing just a meter in front of me with a freshly filled drink in his hand and no Gigi attached to his face.

"You leaving?" he asked.

"Yeah."

I saw him open his mouth slightly, but nothing came out.

I wasn't sure whether I should try to hug him goodbye or respect his space.

"Night," he said one second before walking past me to sit down on the other side of the table.

"Night," I responded.

I needed to hit the restroom before leaving. Of course the ladies' waiting line had about ten women standing in it, while the men's restroom had only one. Twenty minutes later I was ready to leave. I headed around the corner to the stairwell. I opened the big black door and drunkenly walked down the steps in my five-inch heels.

"Hey."

It was Johnny. We were both in the stair well. He was heading up and I was heading down. He acknowledged I was there by giving a slight head nod, then preceded to walk past me.

I turned around. "Wait. I wanted to tell you something tonight," I said.

All of a sudden the thoughts in my head were completely gone. The chalkboard was erased clean. My mind just went blank.

Johnny stood there looking at me with his short brown hair spiked up and his arms resting awkwardly against the stair banister. I clenched the banister like I was holding on for dear life.

I tried to open my mouth again, hoping that if I

opened my mouth the words would automatically flow. Unfortunately again, nothing came out.

Johnny stood there patiently. I wanted to run up to him and wrap my slender arms around his strong, muscular body. I wanted to put one hand on the back of his neck and the other on the side of his soft cheeks while I attacked his lips so passionately with mine, but instead I just stood there one second longer before saying, "Actually, never mind. Another time."

I quickly turned around and started walking down the steps completely mortified.

"Wait," he said. "I'm sorry your book didn't get published. You should keep trying."

"Yeah." That was all I could say. I didn't want his pity or his advice. I wanted all of him or none of him.

"What did you want to say?" he asked.

I wanted to be standing there with the old Johnny: the Johnny who made a bed fort with me on a Saturday morning to remind me of those wonderful childhood years and to put a smile on my face.

"I wanted to say that I'm sorry," I paused for a second. "I wanted to say that I'm sorry I didn't answer your calls or call you back when I was in Vermont. I wanted to, I really did! I just, I don't know. I just needed to get away from everything for a minute. When I arrived back home, I hated myself for taking the easy route and just taking off. But at the same time, I wanted to make sure that when I came back to LA, I would come back a different person. Someone who wouldn't run away after a failure. But I never expected you to…" I paused.

"To what? Move on?" asked Johnny. "So you think I was just supposed to wait in silence?"

"If we were meant to be then…yes," I said, somehow not believing my own words. "I mean, I didn't think that you thought that I didn't care. I thought I had made it clear that I cared and that I wanted to give us a try."

"Why the fuck should I have assumed that, Ray? You just shut me out! You didn't respond to my texts, my calls…"

"I know! I was figuring things out."

"And you couldn't text me back or make a two second phone call in between figuring shit out?"

"I thought about you…all the time."

"Huh, well that's great. I'll think about you tonight when I'm fucking Gigi. You can let me know how that feels."

That stung. Much worse than the bee sting I got on my ass cheeks when I was four years old, having a picnic with my porcelain dolls. I immediately imagined the worst porn video I had ever scene and mentally imposed Johnny's face on the tattooed meathead and Gigi's on the over-enthusiastic screaming girl. I wasn't sure how to respond, so I didn't. But he did.

"Since when is just thinking about someone a good form of communication?" he asked.

"I suck at communication and you know that already," I said trying to defend myself knowing that it wasn't going well for me.

"You suck at everything, Ray. And I'm tired of you

just stating it as if it's okay because you copped to it. Just because you know you suck, doesn't mean it's okay. And if you did give a shit about me, even slightly, you wouldn't have ghosted me. You would have responded to at least one of my fucking calls or texts."

"I didn't know what to say," I said quietly, trying to bring down the heat a bit.

"Well now you don't have to say anything. I have a new girl who actually answers my fucking calls. And get this, sometimes, wait for it, she'll even call me first. How about fucking that! We're not back in the fifties where men took all the initiative and women were the doe-eyed little deer waiting for their precious phone calls from their heroic gentlemen. We're in the twenty-first century Ray, and while I tried to accommodate your weird quirks and unfounded fears, maybe I just got tired of being the one to initiate everything."

I hated that every word he said was right. I hated when I came to the realization that he deserved someone better than me.

"You're right," I said, staring at the floor and wondering how silly I must have looked wearing a pair of five inch high heels with glitter all over them. My voice was so quiet I wondered if he heard me. "I'm sorry if I hurt you," I said forcing myself to look him in the eyes before I turned around and walked away.

My eyes were dry, but I knew that in about an hour when I'd be between those four walls in bed under the covers, the tsunami would flow, and I'd be the only one in bed to catch my tears. But then I thought of the kids with no beds and remembered that my sorrow wasn't real, it was manufactured by the combination of hope and disappointment that I had no right to feel, and that thought just made everything worse.

28 NO SYNONYM FOR SAUDADE

After last week's rather hostile run-in with Johnny, the main character in my novel took a rather dark turn. Her positivity diminished. I somehow found it impossible to write a protagonist who was thriving in life.

I walked into the kitchen. Maksim made food in his boxers.

"Hey, what are you up to today?" he asked.

"Skinty's," I said.

"When are going to look for something better?" said Maksim.

"I don't know. The best thing about wearing a short revealing dress is that I make a lot of tips," I said. "Are you going out with the guys tonight?"

"Not tonight. I'm just gunna chill, have some dinner, then go to bed early. You eaten yet?"

"No."

"You hungry?" he asked.

"Yes," I said.

"Cheer up soldier. How's your writing going?"

"Fine."

"What's up, Ray?"

"Has Johnny talked about me to you at all recently? Like since your birthday a month ago?"

"Ray."

"What?"

"Stop thinking about Johnny."

"Do you think I'm crazy to think that we're meant to be together? I mean, you know me. I hardly ever fall for someone for longer than it takes to put my clothes back on."

Maksim laughed.

"And," I said with extra emphasis, "It took me a long time to come around to Johnny. For the longest time, I thought he was just a player. But in his weird way, he made me feel like a princess. I think I miss that feeling." My mind wandered off, back to the ocean where we skinny-dipped on our first date.

"Why don't you invite girl friends over and have girl talk?"

"I don't have any girl friends, well, except you."

"Very funny. Do you want a beer?" Maksim asked.

"Yes, please," I said with no enthusiasm.

"Look Ray, if you and Johnny are meant to be, you'll get back together," he said.

"But in the meantime, how do I be around him without feeling like a... I dunno, like a shitfuck?"

"A what?"

"A shitfuck…Someone who feels really shitty," I explained. "Every time he talks I want to like run over to him and rip his clothes off. Every time he laughs I want to like face plant my face onto his and just kiss him until we both run out of breath."

"That's…a little weird," Maksim responded with hesitation as he tried to comprehend my feelings. "You ever think that maybe you only like him because you know you can't have him?"

"No. Not even slightly," I said, indignant. "When I went home to Vermont I still thought about him every second of every day. I just needed to get away, but I never, seriously NEVER, wanted it to be the end of us."

"Well maybe this Friday is the perfect time for you two to work things out at the party," said Maksim.

"What party? I asked nonchalantly.

"Johnny's birthday."

"What?" My body tensed up into a little ball like a bully's fist. I unwound my lips and vocal cords just enough to say, "But Johnny's birthday isn't until next week."

"Yeah, but his party is this Friday."

"I guess that means I'm not invited," I said.

"I'm sure he just made a mistake and forgot. He's probably not done inviting everyone yet. I'm sure he's inviting you," he said.

Maksim was never a very good liar. That was always a quality in him that I admired, until now.

Maksim put his arm around me. "But hey, I'm inviting you," he said. "The party invite said we can bring friends."

I laughed a very unenthusiastic laugh. "You know there's no way I'm going to that party unless Johnny invites me himself, right?"

"Yeah I know," he said.

My mind was tired. I wanted to change the subject.

"I need to get out of my mind for a night," I said. "I need to breathe and not feel like the weight of a three-hundred pound man is resting on my chest. I would like to take one hour, one minute, or even just one second to breathe in without feeling a lingering of hatred for myself and all the decisions I've made. I keep telling myself that I'm not with Johnny because of what I did; I left abruptly and didn't stay in communication. But I fear I'm just saying that because it's better than the alternative."

"What's the alternative?" Maksim asked.

"That he actually just doesn't like me that much. He likes Gigi more. Me going away was just the perfect opportunity for him to discover someone else he enjoyed being with more than me," I said.

"So what."

"What?"

"So what. Do you really want to be with someone who doesn't want to be with you?"

'No' seemed like the right answer but I couldn't say it.

"You'll meet someone else, Ray. You'll meet someone better."

"And if there is no one better?"

"There are billions of people in this world, I'm sure

you can find one."

"Everyone's turning on me," I said laughing uncontrollably like a teenager trying weed for the first time.

"No they're not," said Maksim.

"I'm serious. There was this nice old lady that used to make deliveries to the bar; I swear she used to love me, she even brought me homemade brownies once. But the other day I swear she gave me the fuck face."

"She wanted to fuck you?"

"Nooo, she wanted me to fuck off. You know the face, it's the 'go fuck yourself face.' I don't even know what I did."

"See, that's your problem."

"What?"

"Actually you have two major problems."

"Just two?"

"Yes. You give too many fucks about shit. And two, you always assume you did something wrong. Maybe that old lady was just having a bad day. Maybe her cat died or her husband stopped going down on her."

"I think I know the difference between a 'sexually unsatisfied' face and a 'go fuck yourself' face. The 'go fuck yourself' face is way more hostile."

"Is it?" asked Maksim giving me a wink. "You need to drink."

"You know for once, I wish there was something besides alcohol that could solve my problem," I said.

"Get laid?"

"I have no one to lay me right now," I said

unenthusiastically.

"Uh, what? That's one of the best things about being a woman. You always have someone who will 'lay' you."

"Fine, but there's only one person I…" I paused. "But he's probably laying the shit out of someone else right now," I said.

"Johnny and Gigi won't last," said Maksim.

"Why do you think that?" I asked, suddenly feeling slightly lighter on my feet.

"Because she's not you," he said eyeing me directly.

"Yeah, right. That's what makes her so perfect."

"Don't do that," said Maksim.

"What?"

"Don't sit here being all self-deprecating and self-pitying. If you want him back, tell him. If you want to be a better person, be a fucking better person."

"Okay this conversation was okay until you came in with that tough love to make me feel like a real piece of shit. Lets just grab a drink," I said.

"I thought you just said you didn't want to drink."

"No, I just said I wish there was something else I knew we could do that would make me feel as good as I feel when I drink, but there isn't…so lets drink."

29 DINNER AND A MOVIE

I was in my room preparing for a long night of writing. I brewed a giant cup of coffee and an even bigger bowl of cereal, grabbed a water bottle and prepared myself to be in my room all night. Maksim told me Johnny might be coming over. I wasn't exactly avoiding him, I just didn't want anything or anyone interrupting my flow.

When I looked up or tried to look forward, I saw nothing but a far away terrain with an outline so fuzzy no lines could be drawn. The music I listened to was quieter, the scent of food cooking in our kitchen was less appealing, the view of the ocean was less thrilling, kicking the soccer ball into the net was less of an accomplishment.

There was only one feeling I could find and it was a feeling that comes after your soul endures a sadness you don't want to comprehend. It was a feeling somewhere between a lifeless body and a living, breathing person with no soul. I remembered that time I fractured my anklebone sliding to kick the soccer ball in the net, while simultaneously bumping feet with the opposing team. I remembered lying there thinking the pain was so deep and so real that it couldn't be ignored despite my teammates trying to comfort me. My ankle swelled up to double the size. Now I've learned that pain doesn't need scars. It doesn't need a physical representation. It lies within: deep within, like algae at the bottom of the sea.

I remember those cold nights in New York City, the ones I spent outside waiting in line to get into a bar or walking back from class. But what sticks in my mind most vividly were those nights I stayed indoors lying on the bed next to the window, staring out into the bright lights of the buildings and street lamps as I waited patiently for the unknown. I remember those days I wasn't afraid. Those days when I tried to stay out as late as possible, those days when sadness was short-lived and fleeting, not constant and enduring.

If I could write something that would make someone feel something, I'll have won; it would all be worth it. I'd still be the one feeling nothing. Like a still leaf on a tree on a day with no wind, no breeze, no movement of life in its vicinity, I sat there trying to remember how it felt to feel. It sounds weird. How could I remind myself how to feel? How could I relearn what I never had to learn in the first place?

I was searching for happiness in a world that should make me happy, but didn't. I tried to drink it, shoot it, smoke it; nothing seemed to work. There was something about the pursuit of love that kept me hoping there'd be something worth feeling one day, something stronger than a shot of whiskey.

For now there was nothing but hollowness. I sat there like a human shaped cookie cutter, waiting for my insides to be filled with dough, waiting for something sweet, something soft, or something full of energy to turn my hollow shape into one of substance.

I went into the kitchen to fix myself a coffee cocktail. A stimulant with a depressant; hopefully if one didn't work, the other one would.

"What are you up to tonight?" asked Maksim as he sat on the couch watching a football game alone.

"Well, I was writing my novel, but I had to take a break," I said.

"Why?"

"I had my character go on a date: dinner and a movie," I said.

"So?"

"Dinner and a movie? What person wants to indulge in a book where the lead character has a more boring dating life than they do! The whole point of indulging in anything whether it's a book or a movie or television show is that for a moment you get to dive into something that is either more exciting than your own life or way worse so that you can feel better about yourself."

Maksim looked at me trying to understand. "So then why did you have your character go to dinner and a movie? Why didn't you write her doing something more exciting?" he asked. "Like attend a Buddhists-only orgy night?"

"That's good!" I said with fake enthusiasm.

"Really?" Maksim perked up.

"No," I said. I paused a moment before admitting to the shame, "I couldn't think of anything more exciting. I have no real life inspiration to draw from and my creativity has reached an all-time low this week."

"Does that have anything to do with Johnny dating Gigi?" he asked.

"No," I said quickly. "Yes."

"You need to go on a date," he said very matter-of-factly.

"I know."

"A good one," he said.

"Yeah, like I can just pull that out of my hat quickly. Why don't I also whip together some world peace and solve the homeless problem in America while I'm at it. Heck, lets think big and feed all the children in Uganda too."

"Okay okay."

There was a knock at the door.

"That's probably Johnny," said Maksim, warning me so I could either run and hide or suck it up and stay in the room like a normal human being. Of course I hid…in my bedroom…like a spineless sad little girl too afraid to face her fears.

Five minutes later there was a knock at my door. I assumed it was Maksim trying to convince me to come in the other room and say hi.

"Come in," I said.

It was Johnny.

JOHNNY.

"Hi," I said.

"Hey, what are you up to?"

I put my hands on my laptop keyboard and pretended to be writing.

"Writing."

I didn't mean to speak in one-word answers, but my mind was incapable of elaborating. Johnny looked as handsome as ever in a pair of dark-wash jeans, a silver belt, and a blue-striped button down.

Johnny's eyes wandered around my room, never really sticking with me for longer than a second.

"Well, I'll let you get back to it, I just wanted to let you know I'm doing birthday drinks this Friday, if you want to come," he said with no expression in his voice like a court reporter reading back a transcript.

"Thanks," I said.

"Alright, see yah," he said before leaving my room.

I sat there frozen. He invited me, but why? It didn't seem like he actually cared if I went to the party.

Oh my god. What if Maksim forced him to invite me? Shit, I hope Johnny doesn't think I'm not interested.

Something other than my brain propelled my body to get off the bed and walk into the other room. I saw the bathroom door was closed, and only Johnny was sitting on the couch with a beer in hand and the football game on the television.

He turned around and saw me.

"Where are you having the party?" I asked.

"That bar downtown, the one we went to a couple

weeks ago, with the rooftop."

"Oh cool, yeah that bar was cool. Okay cool, I'll see you there."

Why did I keep repeating the word 'cool'? I sound like a fucking moron.

"Cool," he said.

I awkwardly walked back to my room. It's not like I was expecting to see a smile on his face after I told him I was coming to his party, but I still felt like the kid in class who got invited to a fellow classmate's party just because everyone else in the class did. I'd felt that feeling many times; I was able to recognize the feeling again.

30 VAGINA LOVE

Tonight when I took the trash out at Skinty's there was a young girl with long, thick and wavy sandy-black hair sitting on the ground against the building wearing headphones and smoking a cigarette.

"Aren't you a little young to be smoking?" I asked her.

She looked at me with an expression I understood. She was sitting there alone in ripped skinny jeans, a pair of kick-ass black sneakers, and a t-shirt that said "fight for waffles" on it.

"Are you okay, hun?" I asked.

"I'm fine," she said, "Just enjoying the nice view."

"There's a nice view from here?" I asked jokingly, staring at a few palm trees partially hidden by a dumpster, and some houses in the back.

"The sun should be setting soon, but I think the view would be much better if you walk a mile to the beach," I said.

"You work here?" she asked me.

"Yeah, I'm the worst bartender they've got."

"Would you be a peach and make me your worst drink and bring it out here?"

"Huh! So I can get fired for serving someone underage and bringing alcohol off the premises? I don't think so," I said.

"Fine." She took another puff of her cigarette.

"Is someone coming to pick you up?"

"No."

"You okay?"

She looked at me. I think she was wondering why I was being nice. I was a stranger. Why the fuck should I care?

I sat down beside her. "What's your name?" I asked.

"Mila."

"I'm Ray. So what brings you to the back of this trashy establishment?"

"I stole money from my mom's wallet so that I could buy a dress for junior prom," she said. "Cooper Preston, a high school senior, who every girl loves, asked me to go. He asked me a month ago, way before anyone else even got asked. Today he told me he couldn't take me anymore. He has a girlfriend, Zara. He's taking her." She paused for a moment then continued, "The prom is this weekend. Everyone who is capable of getting a date already has one. Now I'm stuck with this dress just sitting in my closet, staring at me, mocking me. My mom will probably beat the hell out of me if she finds out I stole money from her."

I paused for a second, drinking it all in. "First of all, what's with all these modern names, like Cooper? And Zara? Seriously? Where are all the Johns, Jakes, Ryans, and Joshes that I dated? They all got their Brittanys, Katies, and Rachels I guess. Now we're stuck with the loser Coopers of the world."

"That's all you picked up from that? Seriously? The names?"

"No," I said. "Second of all, don't smoke," I grabbed the cigarette from her mouth and whipped it on the ground. "That shit will kill you. Why don't you go to prom anyway? Alone. I went to my prom alone. Keep the tag on the dress and return it after, then put the money back in your mom's wallet."

"I'm a sophomore. I can't go to the prom unless I'm invited by a senior."

"Oh."

"Plus that's not even what I'm upset about. I couldn't care less about prom. It's just embarrassing. I liked this guy and he acted like he was crazy about me and then all of a sudden he's got a girlfriend, and I'm the one left being a loser having to tell all my friends that the guy I was crazy about likes someone else more. All my friends know how much I liked him. Why wouldn't he want me?"

"Well, I'm probably not the one you want advice from because my life is running off the rails faster than yours I'm sure, especially in the dating department, but there is one thing I will say…"

"Then why'd you ask me if I wanted to talk?"

"Let me finish," I paused. "Feeling wanted is one of the best feelings in the world. When it leaves, when someone who used to want you, now wants someone else, it should make you realize that there's someone better for you out there. You're a beautiful girl and trust me many guys will want you. So what, this loser doesn't. Fuck him! You should have a party that night. How old are you anyway?" I asked her.

"Fifteen."

"You shouldn't be worried about anything at your age. You still have your entire dating life ahead of you. Not that it's something you should look forward to, if I'm being completely honest." I chuckled.

"Thanks for the optimism."

"Sorry kid."

"Does anybody love you?" She looked at me with her big brown eyes waiting to hear my answer. "I'm sorry, that came out weird. I mean do you feel loved by anybody? A romantic love? Not like your mom or something, who has to love you because you came out of her vagina."

"I don't think so," I said, letting my back sink into the brick wall behind us. "Plus, my mom doesn't 'vagina love' me anyway."

"What?"

"She had a C-section," I said.

"Huh?"

"Never mind."

"Have you ever had a guy say they love you before?"

"No. Wow, I just realized, I am twenty-eight years old and I've never had a guy tell me he loves me. I had a guy text it to me once, but that doesn't count. Jeeze. Thanks for that, yah loser," I stated bluntly, wishing I had kept her cigarette for myself.

"Hey, what did I do?"

"You pointed out how pathetic I am," I said.

"I just asked you a question. You came to that realization on your own."

"Fine," I said.

"I have friends who have boyfriends, and they get to hear 'I love you' all the time: before every class, after every class, before they go to bed, when they wake up in the morning. Every time they see each other or say goodbye they say, 'I love you'. I'd do anything to hear it just once," she said.

I let out a deep breath.

"I love you," I said, serious look on my face.

"What the fuck?"

We both busted out laughing.

"That's creepy," she said.

"Sorry," I said.

"Hey, are you sure you can't bring me a drink out here?"

"You're fifteen years old," I said to her, "No!"

"Yeah as if you didn't drink at fifteen."

"I didn't," I said.

She looked at me with a face of disbelief.

"I didn't! But I've made up for it since then," I said, as I looked at her and smiled. "What night's your prom this weekend?" I asked.

"Saturday."

"You wanna have a real party instead?"

"What do you mean?"

"I live near here. I live with my best friend, Maksim. We've hosted more cool parties than you'll ever have in your entire lifetime. Why don't you come over Saturday night?"

"Seriously?"

"Yeah," I said.

"You just met me. How do you know I'm not some crazy freak?"

I loved her naivety. "When it comes to making a quick judgment about a person's crazy freak factor, I compare it to my own. My gut tells me I've got a lot to teach you…that is if you desire to become a crazy bitch in the first place," I said.

"Will there be alcohol there?"

"In the apartment, yes. Will you be drinking it? No."

"What if I drink my own alcohol beforehand and bring the rest in a flask?"

"Wow, you really are like me, aren't you?"

"You said you didn't drink at my age," she said.

"I didn't. But I was a quick learner. You just got a bit of a head start."

"Seriously, you have plenty of years where alcohol will be your only method of enjoyment. Enjoy the years you're young when you can still have fun without it."

"For a woman who claims not to be loved, you seem mighty wise," she said.

"I'm a bartender. It's my job to pretend to love and listen to others."

"So you're just doing your job now?"

"No, you're not a customer. You're just a young woman that could use a good time. Am I wrong?"

She looked up at me. After a second of silence she said, "Okay."

"Alrighty, then." I got her number then headed back inside.

Over the next few hours of my shift, I wondered whether it was the right decision to take this girl under my wing. I was born with wings that couldn't fly and now I've let another one grab onto them. Suddenly I felt pressure to learn how to fake it.

31 SAY THOSE 4 WORDS NO GIRL WANTS TO HEAR

On Friday mornings I liked to go to my neighborhood coffee shop and get there early before all the tables were occupied. So when my alarm clock went off this morning I sprung my body from my silky purple Egyptian cotton sheets and slid my feet into my pink piggy slippers. I wore a black lacy nightgown to bed. I wanted something that would make me feel sexy. I've tried sleeping naked, but I always woke up cold in the middle of the night. Waking up naked sometimes gave me anxiety in the morning. It normally took me a minute to realize that no one else was in my bed before I could finally relax. This time, waking up without anyone there made me sad, but I didn't want to waste a moment thinking about it.

When I got to the coffee shop there were a few other early birds there. I sat at a table for two next to a young woman at a table with ten books piled high. She was obviously a college student. I glanced over and saw an "Intro to Psychology" book on top of the pile.

In college I took one class in psychology. The professor was involved in a lot of clinical studies outside of class. She was searching for students who wanted to participate in a paid study analyzing the behavior of men and women at the beginning of new social relationships. I was intrigued by the concept of the experiment, but even more so by the money.

I had to find 30 students that I had never previously met and ask them to grab coffee with me. The only catch was that I couldn't ask them in person. I must have technology between us, meaning I could send a text, email, or online message. The experiment had two parts to it. First, it hoped to analyze how hard it would be for strangers to agree to meet someone who they've never met and to do so for no specific reason except to talk and get a free coffee. Once I was talking to the individuals over coffee, I was supposed to get their opinions and feelings about making new friends and starting new social relationships.

I soon learned that women would not return my messages. Even when I dropped a mutual friend's name, no message back.

My friend gave me the name of one of her guy friends who she said might be interested in helping me. I reached out to him via an online message and got a response within the hour.

From that point on I decided to search for and reach out to only men. It took me a week to find all thirty students, and two weeks to meet with each of them for coffee.

I analyzed the results of our conversations and submitted the results to my professor. Each guy had interesting things to say about how they formed new friendships, which was the mission behind the study, but I learned a whole lot more.

I learned that it's important to know your audience. Men are my audience. When I started the study I went into it with the false hope that thirty strangers, both men and women, would be willing to take time out of their busy days to meet up with me, a stranger, for coffee for no reason other than to have a friendly chat about their social behaviors. I also learned that when you ask a guy about their social behaviors they almost always try to bring up their dating life in some way.

Even though all participants knew this was a study, twenty-eight of the thirty guys asked for my number at the end of our chat and twenty-eight times I had to say no. The two that didn't ask, sent me an email later that day thanking me for meeting with them as if I did them a favor.

This was my favorite class. I learned a life lesson that would stick with me forever and unlike my other classes, this one taught me a lesson applicable to real life. I learned a valuable lesson about being successful. At the time, I didn't take into consideration that those twenty-eight guys didn't know me, which is probably why I seemed so alluring and confident. All I wanted was that power back or even a taste of that feeling. Although, I wasn't expecting to get it at Johnny's birthday tonight. I tried not to spend the day worrying about it but this was a war that I was losing.

When I got to the bar that evening he ignored me just like I expected he would. I stood there next to Maksim with a drink in my hand and a slow emerging sense of calm. There was a darkness in my soul that the moon couldn't illuminate. I stood there near the edge of the building watching the lights of the city stay still and the noise get louder in the background. I felt the effect of my sixth drink.

A group of us were congregating in a disorganized circle near the bar. Silence settled in when Johnny walked over with Gigi on his arm.

Maksim awkwardly tried to make conversation by asking me how my writing was going.

"I just finished writing the stripper scene today," I said.

"There's a stripper scene?" asked Maksim.

"There is," I said.

Suddenly the guys were listening. I caught the drunken attention of Johnny's best pals, Nick and Noland. For one second they stopped circling the bar in a desperate search for nearly nude fresh tender white meat. There were never any chicken fingers on their menu.

"What happens?" asked Noland.

"Well, my main character's friend is a stripper. So in this scene she's grinding against the pole in a very drunken state and a male patron has his head in her crotch going down on her."

"While she's dancing around the pole?" asked Noland.

"Yeah, well she's just kinda leaning against it all sexy, yah know?"

"But I thought the stripper is the one that's suppose to be giving the show, not reaping the rewards," said the beautifully misogynistic Nick.

"First of all, that's sexist, second of all, it's my world, bitches," I said with false confidence dripping from every single word. I was drunk. "I could have her eating cupcakes while three cowboys lick the crumbs off her va-jay-jay if I wanted."

"That's pretty graphic," said Maksim.

"The mind is our most dangerous playground," I said.

"How many stripper scenes are there?" asked Noland.

"Just one. But it's not nearly as graphic as the vacuuming scene."

"What?" Noland spit out his beer.

"There's a slutty vacuuming scene?"

"Well, I wouldn't necessarily label it 'slutty,' but more…" I paused as I searched for the right word, "…informative," I said, flashing him a knowing wink.

"Informative?" asked Nick with intrigue in his voice.

"Yeah."

I looked at Johnny. He hadn't piped into the conversation. He stood there still and quiet but clearly listening and absorbing. I kept looking at him trying to get his attention but his eyes never met mine, not even once. So I just kept talking about the disasters in my manuscript, the scenes that could disturb a civil society and disrupt a normal life, but when read in the context of my characters would hopefully seem perfectly normal.

"Are all your thoughts this fucked up?" asked Nick.

"No, not all of them," I said very plainly and matter-of-factly. "Tonight all I'm thinking about is having a guy come up to me and say, "Oh your hair is so soft; how did you get it like that? Kiss me!" I said with a sad impersonation of a guy with a deep manly voice.

"What?"

"So you're looking to find a gay dude?" asked Maksim.

"At this point I think I'd settle for any guy with a soft pair of lips and a full head of hair."

"That's funny cause right now I'd settle for a woman with two sets of lips and a full set of tits," said Noland.

"As opposed to a half set?" I joked.

"Yeah, as opposed to small tits. I want full voluptuous tits," he clarified.

"Well keep taking that Estrogen, hopefully one day you'll get them." I laughed.

Noland gave me an evil stare.

Johnny laughed. It was small and short, but it was there.

Oh my god, I made Johnny laugh.

He was listening. I may not be able to get him to talk to me, but I could talk to him.

My platform to speak was soon diminished when

Nick and Noland spotted a group of women congregating near us. Maksim went to get himself another drink. That's when unfortunately I found myself standing there with just Johnny and Gigi.

The cloud of weed was nearly suffocating me, and my proximity to Johnny and Gigi wasn't helping.

"Are you warm enough?" Johnny asked Gigi so sweetly as she stood there in her spaghetti strap mini dress.

"Yes, thanks hun," she said.

I stood there in a cloud of smoke, listening to words I didn't want to hear, seeing the budding of a new relationship that I didn't want to see, but I couldn't escape. No smoke was thick enough to cover it all up. I screamed so loud but only I could hear it. The music was a construction of notes crashing into one another like a drunk person stumbling down the stairs.

Time was passing by so slow. I was waiting for it to be midnight so I could go home. Leaving earlier would have been perceived as a slight. Midnight was lame but acceptable. I was okay with that. As each second passed, I felt further and further away from the setting I could see in front of me. I felt the warm breeze, I saw people I knew, but I stood there alone letting my words fail me and my soul dive deeper into it's coffin.

In the midst of a social life crisis all I could think about was going home to hide behind the protective glare of my screen. I'd labor over a manuscript that was built out of fear and loneliness, praying that just a few words could jump off the page and protect me from the loneliness I felt.

I learned to feel something when my own hand grasped the other one. I'd gotten better at pretending there was another soul lying beside me when I woke up in the morning alone.

Maksim popped up behind me, grabbing my shoulder and surprising me back into reality.

"Hey you! You having fun?"

"Does it look like I'm having fun?"

"Nope."

"Everyone sucks here," I said.

Maksim looked at me as I looked at Johnny and Gigi. "Cheer up soldier," he said.

"I'm sorry, I'm really not that spiteful, I'm just lonely as fuck."

"You're a lonely ass fuck?!"

"Nooo, I'm lonely. As. Fuck," I clarified.

Maksim was still looking at me like he didn't understand what I was saying.

"I'm fucking lonely!" I blurted out, way louder than I had intended. I turned around to see if anyone overheard. There was a group of three guys, all miraculously wearing plaid shirts. They were looking at me like predators surrounding a newly sighted prey. Feeling lonely wasn't the worse part of being lonely. The worse part was the consequences that occurred with that feeling. It was knowing I'd do anything to make that feeling stop, to get just one moment that I could pretend to be loved.

"Dude, don't be lonely, you got me!" said Maksim

with that sweet, naïve tone that I adored.

"I know and I love that," I said.

Maksim put his arm around me and I reveled in the feeling of having a best friend that was so sweet and caring. But I had been watching the time very closely and it had just struck twelve, so I was able to leave.

Since it was Johnny's birthday party, I figured I should say goodbye. I walked around the bar looking for him, hoping that Gigi wouldn't be draped on his arm. After a couple minutes I spotted him. He was talking to a group of five people: three guys, two girls. Gigi wasn't one of them. I walked up to them and waited for a second until an appropriate moment to say goodbye.

Johnny turned around and saw me there.

"I just wanted to say happy birthday and goodbye. I'm heading out now," I said.

"Thanks, Ray." He said with less than zero enthusiasm in his voice. The nun at my church spoke with more vigor for life.

"Are you having fun tonight?" I asked.

"Yeah." Again, no enthusiasm.

"Good," I said. "Alright, bye."

"Wait," he said, "Come here," he said before wrapping his perfect arms around me.

I played with his words like a young boy learns to play with himself. Feeling out every inch of solitude to get to that jaw-dropping moment of pleasure stemming from a newfound knowledge deep within: maybe he craved exactly what I did.

Although stunned, I wrapped my arms around his

body so tight, with one hand grabbing his back and the other grabbing his shoulder tightly. I kept the hug going for as long as I could. I wanted to stay like that forever. All the thoughts came rushing back into my head, and then I remembered what I wanted to say.

"With both arms still wrapped around him, I whispered into his ear, "I'm sorry."

He kept his grip around me tight.

"I'm so sorry I left," I said again, with one single tear escaping my eye and trickling down my cheek. I know my apologies were old news, but I just needed him to know. I was so relieved to have my chin resting on his shoulder and my body resting against his. I wanted to memorize the rhythm of his heartbeats.

He rubbed his hand up and down my lower back in that calming way a mother soothes her ailing child. A second later he let me go.

"I should get back to the party," he said. "I'll see you soon."

I'll see you soon.

I guess that's progress. Just hearing him admit that we'd inevitably see each other again sent a warm shiver down my spine. Our story wasn't over here. I knew it, but I still wasn't sure if he did.

When I got home I had my own after party. I settled onto the couch with a whiskey in one hand, a bag of popcorn in the other, and *Mad Men* playing on the screen in front me. I sat there admiring Peggy for her ability to get what she wanted. She wasn't a screw up like everyone initially expected. She could roll with the men like a lady, like a confident lady.

I turned the show into a drinking game. Every time someone on the show drank, I drank. Before I knew it my glass was empty. Then it was empty again, and again, and again until my body was lying horizontally on the couch sinking into every crevice that supported my hollow heart.

I put my head back and drifted away into pure satisfying bliss. My body felt heavy and my heart felt numb. In that moment I couldn't shove aside the fear that a phone call would bring because when the world was sleeping, that's when I stayed awake. I breathed easy knowing that no one would try to reach me in this world where none of us were unreachable.

Time passed at a rate I couldn't comprehend. Suddenly I was startled by a noise behind me. The front door opened. Maksim, Johnny, and a slew of other unfamiliar male and female faces entered. I looked for Gigi, but she wasn't there, at least not according to my blurred double vision. Johnny appeared surprisingly lucid, considering it was his birthday. If anyone should be drunk it should be him.

"Party on the roooooof," one of the girls yelled.

We don't have a roof.

"We don't have a roof," said Maksim repeating exactly what I was thinking. "I mean we have a roof of course, but we don't have a roof we can go on," he clarified.

"Well then lets go to a building that does," she said slurring each word more than the previous.

"You want to trespass into some building drunkenly searching for a rooftop? Yeah, that sounds like a good idea," he said sarcastically.

"Whatever," she said just like they did in *Clueless*. "Then what are we gunna do here?"

"Drink. Watch TV. Grill some burgers," said Maksim nonchalantly. This was a game plan he was very familiar with because it is one that he had done over and over again.

"Mak, I'll fire up the stove and get the burgers going if you wanna get the drinks and figure out what we're watching. And get the ladies settled on the couch," said Johnny.

At that moment I used every drunken muscle in my body to collaboratively hoist my head, which was attached to a hundred and fifteen pounds of dead weight, over the top of the couch.

Johnny happened to glance over in my direction and saw me.

"Hi," he said.

"Hey."

"Sorry, I thought you'd be in your room sleeping. You left early tonight," he said.

"I stayed till twelve," I said, very machine-like. "Then I had my own after party."

"I can see that," he said staring at the half empty bottle of whiskey beside the couch.

"Do you want a burger?" he asked.

"No thanks. I'm going to bed."

I wanted to be tucked in my bed so bad right now,

but as I sat there drunk, looking at the hallway leading to my bedroom I knew that a smooth journey to my room was overly optimistic. I tried lifting my arm, but it sunk back down into the cushions. The room was spinning faster than the ceiling fan. I let my body collapse into the cushions again.

"Ray."

I opened my eyes. Johnny was kneeling down beside me with a look on his face that wasn't necessarily inviting, but also not angry.

"Let me carry you to bed," he said placing one arm under my legs and the other under my shoulders.

"How are you not drunk right now?" I asked.

"Because I didn't throw myself a sad and lonely pathetic after party," he said.

There it was. The disdain.

"Come on," he said as he hoisted my body off the couch.

I let my head relax on his shoulder. I wrapped my arms around his muscular arms and nuzzled my nose in his neck to take in the fresh scent of his cologne.

When we got to my room he placed me down gently on the bed, but I kept my arms firmly around his neck. He grabbed one of my arms, softly trying to remove my grip from around him. I flexed my muscles and stayed strong, fighting for just one more second to be this close. I lifted my head up to look him in the eyes, but he tore his gaze away from mine.

"Johnny…I miss you," I said, hoping he'd let me stay like this for just a second longer.

I tried to put my lips on his but he turned his head so I settled for placing my soft lips on his cheek.

"Ray."

I continued to kiss his cheek as if I were kissing his lips.

"Ray, stop," he said firmly, but without anger.

I closed my eyes, stopped kissing him, and instead just wrapped my arms tighter around him.

"Ray."

I normally loved the way he said my name. It used to give me shivers running down my spine, but this time I felt the distance between us more and more every time he said my name without holding me the way I was holding onto him. Johnny was moving further out of my reach. The tighter I held him, the further away I felt and the more I felt like I was holding onto something so wildly unattainable.

"Tell me you don't love me," I said.

"What?"

I took a deep breath before I explained: "I need to know that you don't love me because it's the only way I can move on. If I thought that you loved me and that the only reason we're not together is because I deserted you for a month, I wouldn't be able to live with that."

Johnny looked at me with a blank stare that I couldn't read, so I just continued speaking: "I came back here thinking that you and I would continue from where we left off, falling in love," I said.

Oh my god, did I just admit I'm in love with him?

I scrunched my eyes, trying to ignore the urge to

throw up. "When I found out you were mad at me and had moved on I told myself that if we were meant to be, and if you truly loved me, we'd get back together. It's been some time now, and that hasn't happened, so I need to hear you say that you don't love me." I paused again and took a moment to focus on not puking.

The nausea was coming in waves. I just needed it to hold on for a few more moments.

"Then I will move on and we can remain friends," I said.

I looked up at Johnny who remained speechless. When I looked up, there appeared to be three Johnny's. I kept my eyes gazed on the one in the middle. I just needed to hear those four little words no girl ever wanted to hear: 'I don't love you.' I waited for him to speak but he still said nothing.

"Say it," I said, closing my eyes and resting my head on the pillow.

There was silence.

"Get some sleep," he said before turning off the light.

I closed my eyes but that just made the room start spinning even faster. I fell asleep without the answer I asked for, but with an even better answer than I was expecting.

INTERMISSION

I stared at the white porcelain like it was my grandma's fine china. Whiskey going down is always better than whiskey coming back up. There was warmth from our heater that was heating my already flush cheeks so well. I guess it's not always true what they say: heat doesn't always rise. Unless I'm actually floating above the clouds like I am in my mind, and my head is not resting on our dusty bathroom tiles right now. But the mold beneath my fingertips convinces me otherwise.

32 FEAR AND CHOCOLATE

I woke up the next day with my head pounding and a sick feeling in my gut. I only remembered bits and pieces of my conversation with Johnny last night, but I did vaguely remember begging him to declare that he didn't love me.

But did he declare it?

Mila was coming over later today. I needed to pull myself together and sober up as quickly as possible. I guzzled coffee by the gallon. I drank water and had my favorite kale and cucumber green juice for breakfast.

I wanted to think that I invited Mila over out of pure caring for someone else. Maybe I did, but inside I also realized that part of me wanted a night to indulge in the past and relive my simple teenage years, even if they didn't appear simple at the time.

I told Mila she could bring a few friends. I wanted tonight to feel like a party even if it was my first one in ten years that wouldn't have alcohol. I made popcorn and chocolate chip cookies. I figured we could order Chinese food for dinner, something greasy something unhealthy.

Mila arrived with three girlfriends, all of whom were gorgeous and vibrant in their own way. They all had that relaxed California style that East Coasters could only dream to embody.

"Hi Ray!" Mila seemed to be in much better spirits than the day I met her. "This is my friend Emma," she said pointing to a tall and skinny red head with freckled cheeks and gorgeous green eyes. "This is Sophia."

Sophia was very petite, with long dark brown hair and a sweet smile.

"And this is Isabella, we all just call her Izzy," said Mila.

Izzy wore dark black eye liner that reminded me of my own high school days before I learned how to apply it without looking like I had been punched in the face…twice.

"This is my friend, Ray," Mila introduced me.

"Hey girls! It's so nice to meet all of you. We're gunna have a blast tonight," I said with a kind of enthusiasm I hadn't felt in a long time.

"What's the plan?" asked Mila.

"Well, here are our options: we've got karaoke, a million board games, chick flicks, enough junk food to keep us in a sugar coma for the next year, and best of all, we've got a super sick sound system so if a dance party doesn't erupt at some point, I'm gunna have to kick you all out."

There are moments in life you enjoy as they're happening and then forget about them the second they're over. There are moments you enjoy, but not enough and then you pray you'll get the chance to relive a similar moment soon. Then there are moments you let yourself feel the nostalgia for the past, while you enjoy the moment in the present, and feel excited about a future filled with more moments like that.

When I looked at Mila I saw myself and someone different. I saw a better version of myself. I saw someone open to new adventures. I had never seen so much energy in people that weren't wound up by alcohol or caffeine. They were just high on life. They were listening to the music and singing loud, they were dancing with no boys around to watch, they were using their hands as microphones, and they were having fun. Or at least I hoped they were having fun. I had to admit it was a little nerve racking planning a party that didn't have booze as the main special guest.

Testosterone was the other obvious missing element. I knew Maksim would be out for most of the night, but I just hoped he wouldn't come back with his friends until late. All five of us women were sitting on the floor gossiping about everything stereotypical you'd expect from a teenage slumber party: boys, sex, parties, celebrities, nothing was off limits. About an hour into the conversation, we dug a little deeper than condoms and risky locations to give a hand job.

It all started when Sophia started talking about her fear of spiders. Before we knew it, everyone was admitting their fears. It was like everyone was waiting for a moment to share in this safe space we created surrounded by nothing but four walls, a whole lot of popcorn and chocolate, and way too much soda.

"What about you?" Mila asked me after everyone else had spoken. What is your fear?"

"I have to pick just one?" I laughed.

"No, what are your fears, with an 's'?" Mila asked.

"Well, I told you guys earlier that I'm a writer, on the good days at least. But I keep thinking that there's something beautiful I'm missing. I've been so caught up in my own misery with Johnny lately…"

"The tall dark and handsome man you ran away from?" Mila asked for clarification.

"That's the one," I said. "I've been so caught up in my own shit that I can't even see the path my characters need to take. I don't want to screw up this manuscript. I feel like there's something beautiful that I'm missing, and I just can't get it onto the page. Do I wait? Do I wait until I'm in a better place to keep writing? What if I keep pushing through it and end up moving my characters into a direction I don't want them to go. I feel like I have no control over my life right now. How could I possibly have control over the lives I've created?"

"Well, I'm not a writer," said Mila, "Math and science are my jam, but I think that even if your life seems like it's out of control, you should just use it!"

"What?" I asked.

"Use that force to create a new one in your manuscript. Write something that stems from chaos if you have to, but keep writing because your words will mean something and one day someone will be reading those words, and they'll mean something to that person."

"What's your goal for your book? Money? Inner satisfaction?" asked Emma.

"All I need for my work to be successful, at least in my own eyes, is for someone to read it and feel something when he or she does," I said.

"That's beautiful," said Sophia.

"Izzy bursted out laughing. "Okay, this moment is getting a little too emo for me, it's making me uncomfortable. Does anyone even still read anymore?" she asked.

"Don't be a bitch," said Emma. "That's clearly why you're failing English class."

"Cause I'm a bitch?"

"No, because you don't read!" said Emma.

"Now now, settle down. I think sometimes I do put too much emphasis on the effect of my writing. Sometimes I just need to remind myself to let go. I want to write because I love it and not because I'm expecting anything from it," I said. "At least now it's on my terms. I'm not at the mercy of anyone."

"Have you ever tried getting a publisher for your book?" asked Mila.

"I did for the first one I wrote. I actually used to intern at a publishing house, but there was so much politics. That gig was brutal."

"Why? What happened?"

"My bosses were jerks."

"What did they do?"

"They once told me they wouldn't let me in the room for a meeting unless I told them how I masturbated," I explained.

"Let me guess, you didn't end up going in that room," said Emma.

"Are you kidding? In this industry I knew I had to do whatever it took to get one step further."

"So you told them how you masturbate?"

"Yup. I said I secure a rope to the top of my building, shimmy out the window, tie my feet up and hang upside down while I flick the bean in front of oncoming traffic."

Everyone in the room was silent for a second. Then Izzy piped in, "And they believed you?"

"Doubtful. But I answered their question. Telling the truth wasn't necessary. Those in power just want to feel powerful. As long as they thought they were exploiting me, they'd remain confident that they're position wasn't being threatened," I said.

Our front door opened and it startled me for a second. Maksim walked through first. I prayed to God that he was alone. Then Johnny walked through and caught my gaze for just a second before turning to my guests. Nick and Noland entered as well.

The girls all stared at the guys with smiles on their faces.

"Hi," said Emma.

"Hey," Maksim responded. "You must be Ray's new friends."

"We are," Izzy said as she got up from the floor and walked over to Maksim to shake his hand in an ultra-flirty way.

"I'm Maksim, her roommate," he said.

"You live with him?" Mila whispered to me.

"Yes. He's been my best friend since freshman year of college."

"Which one is Johnny?" she said very quietly.

"The one wearing the blue plaid button down," I said.

"Jesus Christ on toast," said Emma.

"What?"

"He's fucking hot," Mila chimed in stealing Emma's words straight from her head.

"I know," I said. "Why don't you girls set up our next board game and I'll make us some more popcorn?"

"Sure," said Sophia obviously a bit more anxious after the guys entered.

I walked into the kitchen waiting to explain myself to the guys.

"How does it feel corrupting the youth?" Maksim asked, half-joking.

"I'm corrupting the youth? It's more like they're making me less cynical and I love it." I was smiling and it felt great.

Well, it felt great until Johnny piped in: "What, you haven't ruined your own life enough yet? You got to destroy innocent adolescent lives too?"

Recently there was a dark cloud following me everywhere I went, showering down on me when I least wanted rain. That cloud was Johnny, and I was just starting to realize it.

I couldn't stop my mind from racing. I was running so fast I could feel every inch of my body fuelling with fire. I felt my chest rise and fall; I felt the coldness of the kitchen floor on my feet and I felt my heart beating faster just like I expected it too. And then I let it go when the microwave beeped and the popcorn was done.

"I'm using the living room now. You guys can stay in the kitchen," I said with authority as I completely disregarded Johnny's comment.

I walked back to the girls with a smile on my face. Tonight was going to be fun because I wanted it that way. The world was there; I'd never be able to erase it from my surroundings, but I could stop it from burdening me with fear, anxiety, and sadness. Tonight I practiced living in the moment and blocking out all the negativity.

33 INTO THE OBLIVION

While a pre-party erupted in the living room, I joined Maksim in the kitchen.

"You're finally out of your room," said Maksim.

"Yup. I'm pretty sure I was just fuckin' up the novel today anyway. So, it's better that I stay far, far away from it," I said.

"I'm sure that's not true," he said. "At least you've been writing lots recently, right?" he said.

"I always write more when I'm lonely. The characters become my only friends," I said.

"That's because you can control them," said Maksim.

"That's not true," I exclaimed indignantly. "The other day I was writing when all of a sudden my character told me to go fuck myself. That's when the delete button really came in handy. I just erased that motherfucker." It took me a second to realize it, but I was smiling.

Then Johnny walked into the kitchen looking for

another beer.

"Whatcha guys talking about in here?" he asked.

"Ray's fictional characters from her novel are turning against her," said Maksim.

I wished he had just kept his mouth shut.

"Smart characters," he muttered under his breath, saying it loud enough that he knew I could hear.

Maksim looked at me with endearment. I took in a deep breath and let out a big sigh. I was used to Johnny's little jabs, but I was waiting for them to stop hurting.

"I'm heading out now," I said trying to deflect from the awkwardness, "You guys have fun tonight."

"Where you going?" asked Maksim.

"I have a date," I said knowing Johnny was still in the room. He always felt so comfortable parading Gigi around in my face so I figured I should be open about my dating life too. Actually, this was the first time I was hanging out with a guy since Johnny and I ended.

"Nice," Johnny interrupted. "Who's the unlucky guy? Just kidding," he laughed an awkward laugh.

I knew he wasn't kidding. "Dylan," I said.

"Dylan?" He choked a little on his beer. "The guy who didn't want the gum? How did you get him to actually ask you out?"

"I didn't. I asked him out."

"Huh, so you are capable of taking the initiative. Guess you only do it for guys that don't give a shit about you," he said.

Every time Johnny and I talked post-breakup, even when it started out as simple pleasantries, it always ended hostile. I hated the feeling of knowing he hated me. I wanted this conversation to end, so I didn't respond. He obviously wasn't ready to let it go though.

"Why did you change your mind?" he asked.

"What do you mean?"

"I mean you stopped hanging out with Dylan before because he never took the initiative to ask you out, right? Weren't you guys just fuck buddies? I mean, it's pretty clear he didn't want the gum."

"First of all, can you stop referring to me as a piece of gum?"

"You were the one who drew the analogy in the first place," he said.

"I'm bored. And I'm lonely," I said matter-of-factly, staring him directly in the eyes, wishing that it was his arms I'd be in tonight. I never realized how good it felt to be blunt. Judging from his silence, I don't think he expected me to be blunt either. "And plus, why the fuck do you care?"

"I don't," he said.

"Great. And for your information we weren't just fuck buddies, we were friends."

"Who fucked," he said.

"If you're lonely you could walk into any bar and 'not be lonely' within five minutes I guarantee you. So why Dylan?"

Why does he keep pushing this?

"Because I don't feel like a piece of shit after I hang out with him," I said. "Again, why do you care?"

"I don't," he repeated himself.

"Great, then go be with your girlfriend," I said, instantly regretting the hostility.

"Alright you two, play nice," said Maksim finally stepping in as the referee.

I grabbed my purse by the door and slipped on my heels.

"See yah," I said before shutting the door behind me.

I fell into nothingness the next day. I lifted my arm just enough to rest it on my laptop keyboard, but then it fell from sheer boredom and didn't rise again until an hour later, maybe two, maybe three; I lost count of time when my eyes stationed themselves on the four walls that blocked my mental capacity.

I heard the sound of my ex-hales. I heard the sound of cars passing by my window. I tried to get up an hour ago, but failed. I tried to feel something other than the deadweight of my body protruding into the mattress.

I couldn't fathom how rough these soft sheets felt against my skin, how they felt like something so deadly. I wanted to be as far away as possible, but still I sunk deeper.

I tried to go for a run. I put on my gym clothes like every other day, I tied up my hair, I laced up my shoes, but when I got outside, my muscles didn't follow. I kept trying to move one foot in front of the other, but my body was being controlled by two minds, and the foreign one was the one that was winning. I sat down on the closest bench. I turned my music up louder. I hoped that one note from the song could turn nothingness into feeling, turn boredom into inspiration, and turn exhaustion into energy. Still no luck.

The misery lasted for weeks.

I went to a strip fit class hoping that getting naked and sweating in public would help invigorate some deep sense of feeling. I slid up and down the pole like it was an extended arm of the devil. I breathed in so deep; I felt my ribcage expand and collapse like my dreams.

I walked into the apartment after the strip-fit class.

I stood in the doorway with my perfectly toned abs showing and beads of sweat lingering on my body. I thanked god that I wore my slim fit black and pink leggings and not the holy pieces of shit I used to wear.

Johnny sat there, beer in hand, hair gelled, teeth whiter than ever. It was my place. I decided to own it like it was mine because I was still riding high on the exercise euphoria.

"Hey," I said to both Maksim and Johnny, and the other two dudes smoking on the couch.

Johnny did his best not to stare at my bare skin. I did my best to make sure I had maximum cleavage showing. I washed my hands in the sink then shook my hands in the air deliberately dripping water on my skin for that extra touch of sex appeal. Then I waited for Maksim to ask me what I was up to for the night.

"I'm going to take a shower," I said, hoping that Johnny wouldn't be able to help but picture me naked.

"You gunna drink with us after?" asked Maksim.

"Sure. Be right out," I said.

When I got out of the shower I put on my favorite pair of flare jeans and a plain white tee overtop of a black lacy bra. I towel-dried my hair to get sexy beachy waves. I grabbed a beer from the fridge and joined the guys on the couch. Gigi wasn't there. I wanted to stir the pot.

"Where's Gigi?" I asked.

"Work," said Johnny.

"On a Tuesday night? She a bartender too?"

"Lawyer," said Johnny. He looked at me, knowing that would hurt to hear.

Silence washed over the room like a racist grandmother finishing a toast.

"Work must keep her busy. It's surprising she even has time for a boyfriend," I said.

"Yeah well she often works late weekday nights cause I monopolize all her time on the weekends," he said, digging the knife in deeper.

"I bet."

I took another sip of beer, then another until I finished it. It took me about fifteen seconds. Johnny eyed me intently for every one of those seconds. I repeated it eight times before switching to Merlot.

Three hours later I laid down on the couch while the guys continued to argue about sports, calling each other "lil' bitches" for cheering on certain teams or thinking highly of a specific player. I focused on Johnny who kept looking at his phone when it buzzed then kept putting it back in his pocket, ignoring it.

I walked away into my room, not saying a word. I looked at myself in the mirror. I stared at the bags under my eyes. I stuck my tongue out to see its wine-colored tinge. I noticed the walls in the background moving slightly in a circular motion. My door opened. I turned around and saw Johnny standing there. He walked in and closed the door, leaning his back against it.

"Hey," he said.

He was surprisingly still sober. He wasn't slurring his words.

"You hiding from me in here now?" he asked.

"No. I was just out there for like three hours. I didn't think you needed a babysitter." That came out a little more hostile than I had planned.

"Alright, never mind, I'll see you out there." Johnny opened the door to leave.

"Wait," I said.

He closed the door again.

"What'd you come in here to say?" I asked.

He took a moment to think.

"I don't remember," he said.

"You think you'll ever forgive me?" I asked.

"For what, tonight?" he asked.

"What did I do tonight?"

"All your little jabs?"

"No not tonight. I mean for everything else. For leaving and shutting you out. And taking you for granted. I mean, I just figured you'd always be there, but…"

"You're seriously trying to make me the bad guy?"

"What? No. What are you talking about?"

"You're trying to say that I should have been there for you. You assumed I would be, so why wasn't I, right?"

"No! That's not what I was saying. It's my fault

because I took you for granted and didn't appreciate what I had. You had every right to move on, I just…"

"What?"

"I mean I just assumed you wouldn't, but that was the wrong assumption, I guess," I said.

"So you're saying I should have waited out the radio silence from you and hope you come running back into my arms?" He got very flustered.

"No." This was going terribly.

"You're the only pussy in this relationship, Ray. I can't read your mind. How did I even know you were coming back, you never answered any of my calls?" The anger in his voice was almost palpable.

"I know. It was my fault."

"Well there's one thing we agree on, but whatever, it was a while ago. It's over now, " he said abruptly without even pausing a second before trying to leave my room again.

"Wait!" I said as I grabbed his arm holding him from leaving. "Talk to me." I hated how much it sounded like begging. "Why'd you come in here?" I asked.

"I don't know. I have nothing left to say."

"I do," I said.

"I don't really want to hear it, to be honest, but say what you must," he said so coldly.

The intensity of Johnny's full attention scared me. His impatience was probably warranted, but talking on any given day was not my forte and his attitude was making it even harder. I couldn't find the flowery words to dress up my thoughts, so I just said them the way they came into my head and hoped something would make sense.

"I think somehow I convinced myself that if we got together at some point I'd screw it up, and losing you down the road would be harder than losing you now," I said. All of a sudden the words seemed so stupid to me. I didn't want to lose him. Every time I saw him I got that feeling that made me want to envelop myself around his body and never let go.

Now I stood there looking at him, looking at me. His eyes so soft, his breath so slow, his hair so perfect like always. I wanted to hug him. I wanted to grab his hand and tell him a million times that I was sorry, and I'll never shut him out again.

I wanted him, and only him, but I said this: "I'm moving to another apartment by myself. It's a little studio in Studio City. So I won't be seeing you as much anymore," I said.

His eyes perked up, he stared so intently back at me. I could almost feel the heat radiating from his body; his eyes were the lasers. He went from staring, to letting out a big breath, to shaking his head, to pursing his lips, to shutting his eyes for just a second. And then he emerged with a mix of emotions propelling hurtful words.

"Fuck you, Ray," he said calmly before the crescendo of hatred. "Fuck you and your low self-esteem. Fuck you and your tendency to push people away. Fuck you and your inability to say what you're fucking thinking! And fuck you for always thinking the absolute opposite of what I'm actually thinking!" he yelled before finally taking a breath.

"And super fuck you for permanently stationing yourself in my mind," he said losing his momentum slightly, but just for a second. "I'm tired of you running away like a fucking child. Then you come back and when I'm mad you're all sorry until two seconds later when you're rubbing Dylan or whoever else you're fucking, in my face."

"I'm rubbing it in your face?" I asked indignant.

"You're the one that flaunts Gigi around me. I said I was sorry and you didn't accept it, so I've been trying to move on."

"Yeah well, you keep it moving alright. I'll let you know if I ever want back on that bandwagon," he said.

"You fucking asshole. Who says I'd ever have sex with you ever again, you arrogant, selfish son-of-a-bitch?" I said, angry as hell.

I stood there drinking in his hostility with one big gulp. I felt my eyelashes becoming wet; I saw my vision becoming blurred. I've made so many bad decisions, I couldn't even tell which moves were right and which ones were wrong.

He looked at me so fiercely I could feel his eyes on my skin like lasers. I was so mad at him, almost as mad as he was at me. He moved a few steps closer to me until he was standing so close I could feel his breath. He put both his hands on the sides of my head, with one firmly grabbing my hair between his fingers and the other clutching my cheek. But still, he continued.

"Fuck you Ray. I fucking just wanna…" His lips

hovered close to mine.

He used his thumb to wipe away the stray tear that got away from me. I wrapped my arms around his upper body. I wanted to rip off his clothes, but instead I slid my right arm under his shirt to feel his skin against mine.

"I don't want to fight with you." I looked up at him. I couldn't get a read on his expression. His eyes were cold. I waited for him to say something, but he remained silent.

"I know I screwed up and now I have to live with seeing you with someone else," I said before pausing. "But I just really want to know what you want from me," I said.

I waited for him to say something comforting, but instead he just said this: "I want to fuck you."

A second later my nightgown was up around my waist. I heard the jingling from his belt as he undid it and slid his jeans off.

I stepped backwards towards the bed. I put my hand behind me, feeling for the bed, but as I did that, Johnny pulled me down onto the floor.

He hadn't kissed my lips yet. His lips were on my stomach, my chest, my neck, my arm, but not my lips. I let him do what he pleased. I rested my hands and arms on the floor, out of his way, and let him explore my body as he wished with my only wish being that his lips would end up touching mine.

I felt him pushing into me, strong and firm. His head was resting beside mine. I felt his cheek rub against my cheek. I could hear him breathing, but it wasn't enough. I wanted to feel his breath on my lips. I put my hand on the side of his face and gently pulled his head towards mine. I picked my head off the floor to put my lips on his but he pulled back before I got the chance.

He grabbed my wrist and held it down on the floor above my head. Without my lips touching his, all I could focus on was his body on mine. I'm not sure how much time passed until he stopped. Before I knew it his clothes were on and he was saying goodbye.

"You want to stay for another beer? Watch some TV, or a movie, or something?" I asked, as I laid there still naked on the floor wondering why he was leaving in such a hurry.

"I can't. I have plans tonight. Besides, if you're moving out soon, I need to start getting used to not seeing you as much, right?"

"Yeah, but it's not like I'm never going to see you. We do still have mutual friends," I laughed a kind of nervous laugh that shouldn't really be classified as a laugh at all.

"Sorry, got to run," he said like a freshly oiled machine.

I washed all the grease off in the shower. I watched as the moisture fogged up the mirror slowly erasing this portrait of nothing, helping me slide deeper into the oblivion.

34 KARL

The next day I woke up feeling strange, like I was living in two worlds, neither of which coincided with the other. I went for a run to clear my head. It was three o' clock when the nausea hit me like a truck crashing into a brick wall. My muscles felt heavy; I couldn't lift my arms long enough to wash my hands. My whole body felt weak. My head felt like it was consumed by San Francisco's Karl the fog. Keeping my head up straight was a difficult task that consumed what little energy I had left.

There was a knock at the door. Trying to coax my body off the bed into an upright position was difficult. Maksim was at work so I was the only one home. I opened the door. Mila stood there in ripped jeans, an oversized tee, and a blue raincoat.

"What are you doing here?" I asked. "Shouldn't you be at school?"

"I usually skip Monday mornings. I like my long weekends," she said very nonchalantly.

"Okay."

"You look like hell."

"Great, I'm glad I look better than I feel." I took in a deep breath. "You know I'm not really up for company right now."

"Right, I'm sorry, I just really need to talk," she said.

I paused to look at the younger version of myself asking for a little help. "Okay, what's up? Here, sit," I said pointing to the couch. I walked over to the fridge and opened it up.

"Do you want…?" I looked inside the fridge, which was filled with beer, wine, and hotdogs. "Water?"

"No I'm okay," said Mila.

I grabbed a beer.

"Do you think beer is really the best thing for you to be having if you're sick?"

"It's ginger beer. It'll settle my stomach."

"Whatever works," said Mila giving me a strange look.

"So what's up?"

"Okay so, I texted Cooper last night because I was missing him, and I know I shouldn't of but I just…I don't know. Maybe it was that natural female tendency towards masochism that you were talking about earlier that made me do it, but the point is, I did it."

"Okay, did he respond?"

"Yes."

"What did he say?"

"Well I said, 'Hey, how are you doing?' Then he said, 'Hey. Period. Good. Period.'"

"Period? Why would he say period?"

"No he typed a period after the word 'Hey' and 'Good.'"

"Okay, then what?"

"What do you mean then what?"

"So he responded saying he was good, and you hate him why?"

"One word with a period after it means, 'FUCK YOU' in textual language."

"Fuck you means fuck you. Any miscellaneous word with a period after it does not."

"Yes, it does."

"Unless you text me like, 'Fuck you,' I'm going to assume we're cool."

"Well you shouldn't," said Mila.

"I think you're reading too much into this," I said.

"No I'm not. Things are really bad. If he cared about me even slightly, he would of at least followed up 'Hey. Good.' with 'How about you?'"

"Yeah, maybe," I paused to think, "Alright well I thought we decided you should be over him anyway?"

"We did, but it doesn't work like that. I can't just be over someone because I say so," she said.

"Trust me I understand that."

"So what should I do? Should I text him again?"

"No, I think you should leave him alone," I said.

"I was afraid you'd say that." Mila pulled a cigarette out of her pocket. "Can I smoke in here?"

"No."

Mila grunted then put her cigarette away. "Do you

think he'll ever message me and say sorry for being an asshole?" she asked.

"No."

"Thanks," she said.

"I'm just being honest. A male apology is an oxy-moron," I said.

"An oxy-what?"

"Oxy-moron. You know like," I paused to think of an example, "Like having a one-night stand with an accountant."

"I don't know what that means. I've never done that," she said.

"Exactly."

"Okaaaay then."

Mila's phone buzzed. She looked at the screen.

"Shit, I got to go," she said. "My friend needs help defining the parameters of her consensual sexting arrangement with her new boy toy."

"Consensual sexting? Is that a thing?" I asked.

"Yes. Yes it is," she said as if I should know.

"I'll save that lesson for another time," she said as she slipped on her shoes.

When she left I called Skinty's to tell my boss I wouldn't be in today. Then I started making chicken soup from scratch. My mother taught me the secret to a truly flavorful chicken soup: parsnip. I let my mind be free as I focused solely on the preparation. I peeled my carrots and the parsnip, threw in some onions, celery, and chicken, and let it come to a boil. I reveled in that salty savory scent that used to comfort me as a child.

After a day and a half of eating nothing but chicken soup and drinking lots of tea, I slowly started to regain my strength. I was dreading a call from Johnny, but at the same time I hated that I hadn't heard from him since the other night. I was confused and somewhat hopeful, all while being terrified. I didn't know what he was thinking, but I had a feeling that was a good thing.

I had been waiting for some event to thaw the ice between us. Although our intimacy normally would have reassured me, there was something that told me that the physical form of expression that happened the other night came from a place of anger not love.

I didn't want Johnny to know that I had been sick. I didn't want to show any signs of weakness. I wanted to be who he needed, do what he needed, and communicate whatever he needed to hear. I stuck to myself for the next few days and stayed out of trouble. I wrote; I used the confusion in my mind to write something so beautifully disastrous. I went to Skinty's and delivered the best customer service; I kept a smile on my face. I waited for his call.

I looked at the couples in the bar, waiting for that to be me and Johnny. I know it was a lot to assume from one night: one night that didn't even end well, but it was the only fuel I had to keep me running. Days went by and I still didn't hear from Johnny. Maksim was away for the week on a business trip, so the apartment was particularly lonely. It would have been the perfect week to have Johnny over for one on one time.

I was just a few days away from signing the lease for

my new apartment in Studio City. In a rash decision to escape seeing Johnny with Gigi, I told Maksim that I was going to move. Within a week I found the perfect place: a tiny little box of an apartment with a balcony overlooking the garden. When I pictured myself living without Maksim it made me sad, but the alternative was unpleasant too.

After Johnny and I hooked up last week I instantly regretted telling him that I was moving. Maksim didn't want me to leave but he said he'd respect my decision because he knew it was hard for me to see Johnny all the time. But now I actually wanted to see Johnny all the time. There was that glimmer of hope telling me that I might be able to fix the damage that I caused in our relationship and find a way for us to work past it.

I ran along the Santa Monica boardwalk when my phone buzzed. It was a text from Johnny.

Come over?

Silence for days, and then he sends me just two words and a question mark. I wanted to see him. I hoped that one by one we could take steps towards the way we were, even if I didn't really like the way he treated me now. So I went. With a dull light flickering just a few miles away, I followed it in my car hoping to drive myself out of the oblivion.

When we were done my body settled so nicely into the mattress.

I laid there hoping we would talk. Johnny started

putting on his clothes. When he put on his pants I started doubting that he had any plans to come lay with me in bed. He glanced in my direction quickly then started spewing out random words I didn't understand.

"Man, this is great isn't it?" he asked.

I wasn't sure exactly what he was referring to.

"I mean there we were this whole time trying to make an impossible relationship work when all we really needed to be happy was sex," said Johnny.

In that moment I felt sicker than ever.

"Who knew the solution was sex," he said so plainly again.

Sex.

Somehow that word was invoking a visceral feeling in my gut, like when finger nails scrape along a chalkboard.

"So everything's solved between us?" I asked already knowing the answer myself but wondering if he believed in another one.

"Sure," he said, "Seems much better than before, right?"

"Right."

How had I let him slip so far away? How did I let my interests dissipate into something so opposite from what I wanted? I thought I was taking steps towards making smart decisions to pursue what I wanted.

Suddenly knowing what I didn't want, was making what I did want seem so much clearer, but still so far away.

"What about Gigi?" I asked.

"What about her?"

"Well, are you gunna tell her, or end it with her?"

"Gigi and I aren't exclusive," he said so plainly.

"What? Does she know that?"

"She was the one that suggested we see each other and other people."

"So does she know you're sleeping with me?"

"Well of course you don't tell the people you're dating who it is that you're sleeping with you just make sure they know they're not the only one."

"Right."

In just one sentence he so perfectly summarized everything that's wrong with the dating world. When I left Johnny's place that night the air seemed colder than when I had arrived. There was a full moon in the sky. I looked at it, so far away from me, so out of reach. I opened the car windows to let the wind tear through my knotted hair.

Another week went by with every day feeling more and more like a routine. I wrote, I went to work, and a couple nights a week I saw Johnny. Tonight when I got home Maksim sat on the couch with a beer. There was an unusually good aroma in our place.

"What's that kickass smell?" I asked Maksim.

"I made dinner for us. I texted you earlier to see when you'd be home, but you never answered. So I put the leftovers in the fridge," he said.

"Sorry, I had plans after work tonight."

"Plans, eh? You've had a lot of late-night 'plans' recently," he said with an accusatory tone in his voice.

"What are you trying to say?" I asked, hoping that he wouldn't question me. I figured he knew about Johnny and I, but it was one of those things like taking a shit that I just wanted left unsaid.

"Are you judging me?" I asked.

"Nope, just want you to be happy, that's all," he said so sweetly.

I didn't say anything.

"Are you happy?" he asked me.

"Is anybody?"

"Yes. Are you?"

"Well I got something that I thought I wanted. Or, something close to what I thought I wanted, so I should be happy," I said.

"Can we speak in less obscure terms?"

"No. I'm hungry." Just like that I changed the subject.

"Okay."

"What did you make?" I asked.

"Zucchini noodles with a Bolognese sauce, a side of vegetable spring rolls, and garlic bread."

"Huh, three of my favorite things. Am I dying?"

"Nope. Just wanted some quality friend time with you," he said.

"I'm sorry, I would have made sure to be home if I knew you were making dinner," I said. "Can we do this again, but next time I'll make dinner for you?"

"Sure," he said. "But only if you make my favorites."

"Of course. Foie gras, right?"

"I don't condone torture," he said.

"Neither do I. Tofu and mashed potatoes it is!"

"Eww."

I filled my belly with lots of good food, drank a couple beers with Maksim, and watched the weekly sports highlights. I found myself delighting in the simple things: a good cold beer, delicious food that I didn't have to cook, and a pal who cared about my happiness.

Another week went by and I kept up the same routine. Maksim was out tonight, so Johnny came over to my place.

"So when are you moving into your new digs?" Johnny asked.

"I'm actually not going to move yet. The new place was slightly more expensive than I thought. I didn't want to spend that much." That was a lie but I said it because I didn't want him to think I wasn't moving because of him.

I had decided on my own that I wanted to stay with Maksim. I realized that he didn't want me to leave and I didn't want to leave. I wanted to stay somewhere that I felt wanted; I didn't want to run away in fear.

INTERMISSION

I stood frozen in an over heated bar. I was sandwiched in between a fear of saying no and a fear of complying. I agreed to come out tonight. I said yes to all five shots of whiskey; I kept saying yes to every beer, every dance on the stage for the whole crowd to see. I was slipping through every step I took, my skirt rose higher and higher, I felt the ground beneath me moving closer and closer but I kept going like a wound up music box. I kept spinning, I kept thinking about him, I kept hating, kept wanting, kept wishing, kept hoping for something I knew I'd never get. And there I stood, barely standing, hardly walking, barely hearing the sounds around me but still standing nowhere near upright.

35 CLOUDS

The clouds came rolling in quickly tonight. The day started out sunny like every other day in the city of Los Angeles. While I never really spent much time in the daylight, I still always liked knowing it was there if I needed it. I liked knowing that if I stepped outside I'd be greeted by rays of sunshine so strong my skin would turn red.

I left Skinty's a couple hours early tonight because it was slow. I walked down the street to another bar with strong whiskey drinks, live indie music, and a rooftop. Everyone was inside in the main bar because it was starting to get chilly outside. I walked straight to the roof and stationed myself at the bar facing the city's skyline.

"Aren't you cold up here without a jacket?" the bartender asked me.

I was sitting at the bar with just one other middle-aged guy sitting a few seats down.

"I like the chill in the air. But if you want to be a peach, you'll pour me a whiskey neat to help warm me up," I said, giving the young tattooed bartender a wink.

"Sure thing, young lady."

I drank my whiskey with cumulonimbus hovering above me. My phone buzzed. It was Johnny wanting me to come over. Every time his name popped up on my phone I felt like I couldn't breathe, like a kid took a mallet to my stomach. I sat there trying to revive myself. I sat there drunk, hoping I wouldn't make the inevitable decision. My body craved his heat. It craved another human being touching me, holding me, giving me a false sense of security and comforting me at least enough to reassure myself that I was not alone.

I texted Johnny asking him if he could pick me up from the bar, but he said he'd been drinking so I just ordered a ride. I slid off the bar stool and walked downstairs to the street to wait.

My driver was a balding middle-aged man with a beer gut. He talked about how he was always pulling twelve-hour shifts for his family. He was nice. He probably had a few kids. He talked about his love for fishing. He probably hadn't fucked his wife in months. He asked me a little bit about myself, trying to create small talk. I had no interest. I just wanted to relax and enjoy the radio. I wanted to get lost in the songs, so lost that I could pretend I was in another reality heading home to a man that loved me, a man that cared about my happiness, a man that showed affection, not anger, compassion not indifference.

Coasting became easy. Each day collided into the next. Every time I saw Johnny I hoped something more would come out of it, but every time it was just the same physical acts with no caring, no conversations, and no love.

When the car stopped I opened my eyes and found myself just steps away from Johnny's apartment. I reminded myself to take one step at a time, to feel every moment the way it should be felt without reading too much into it. When I saw Johnny I asked him about his day. He grunted an answer.

"You want a drink?" he asked.

"No I'm okay thanks, I'm already a little drunk," I said.

"Alright."

Johnny grabbed the whiskey off the counter and took a shot. Then he washed it down with a soda. He stood in the kitchen looking at me. I stood there awkwardly at the door.

"Come in," he said. "You wanna go chill in my room?"

"Sure." I followed him into the other room.

The second we got in there he started ripping off my clothes then I ripped off his. He laid there looking up at me like I was a body without a soul. I switched off the lights so I didn't have to see. I waited for the warmth of his body to reverse the enduring chill in mine, but it never did.

When we were done I closed my eyes and let my body melt into the sheets. I closed my eyes and enjoyed the oxytocin boost. I let the day wash over me while I passed into a calm and relaxed state.

"Ray." Johnny put his hand on my side gently shaking me. "You're falling asleep," he said.

I opened my eyes and rolled over to look at him sitting there without his shirt on showing off his six-pack, laced with beautiful beads of sweat.

"You want me to order you a ride?" he asked.

"What?"

"The rules," he said. "No emotions. No cuddling. No sleeping over, right?"

"I don't remember agreeing to those rules."

"Well I thought they were just assumed when we decided to keep things simple."

I tried to hold back the tears. I tried to swallow and breathe. I tried not to feel angry for being dragged out of the most peaceful state. My heartbeat hadn't even returned to normal before he was trying to kick me out of his bed.

I didn't say anything. I just got up from the bed and searched for my clothes hoping they'd be laying right there waiting for me. I put them on one by one: my underwear, my bra, my shirt. He watched and waited as I said nothing and just did as I was told. There was a silence so loud it was hurting my ears.

"I mean, you can stay if you want to I just thought we were keeping this low key and unemotional," he said.

I just nodded my head as I put on my pants, soaking up his words like a sponge.

Unemotional? I never agreed to that.

"Say something," he said.

"I don't know what to say." I kept my words monotone. They weren't weak, they weren't strong; I just said them.

I grabbed my purse then left his room without saying goodbye. I didn't know who the fuck I just slept with but he had no resemblance to Johnny. At least, not the Johnny I'd been pining over for the last few months.

He followed me to the door. I looked out the window. It was pouring rain. I didn't have a rain jacket with me.

"Stay tonight," said Johnny. "It's pouring rain. Please stay, I'm sorry. I didn't realize it was so shitty out there. You can stay."

I couldn't bring myself to look at him. I had become the person I hated. Johnny had become every other guy that I'd dated…and hated. I opened his front door and slammed it shut behind me. When I got to the elevator, I could hardly see my phone through the tears. I ordered a ride. I sat inside the main entrance watching the rain come crashing down. The car was a minute away. I wiped the tears from my eyes and off my cheeks. I needed to learn how to stop hurting myself. I needed to compose myself for ten minutes until I made it home to my room between those four walls that protected me from myself.

When I got home, the real tsunami began. Tears flew so rapidly down my face it was like champagne exploding from a bottle that had been violently shook. I felt weak in the most pleasurable way, like naked pictures of me were released on the Internet for the whole world to see. Like a live feed of my naked body was streaming on prime time television. The power was in my hand to make it stop, but I didn't. I just stood there letting the tears surround me with a clear layer of shame.

INTERMISSION

I couldn't feel anything. My knees dropped to the floor. I scrunched my eyes to try to force tears but nothing happened; my eyes were dry. I squeezed my hand so tight trying to draw blood with my nails. I tried to feel the pain; I tried to feel the fear. I couldn't feel anything. I put my head back and let my body collapse to the floor. I reached up to grab the coffee off the counter and then I poured it on my stomach. I still couldn't feel anything. I looked down and saw my skin turn red. Why didn't it feel hot? Finally, I lifted my dead weight off the floor, opened the freezer, and stuck my hand in the ice tray and left it there waiting for my body to turn cold.

36 PIMPING OUT A LAB RAT

"Why'd you decide to do it this way then?" asked Mila.

"I don't know, it was kind of a shit or get off the pot type of moment, you know?" I said.

"Not really." Mila helped me carry groceries through my building's hallway.

"Have you ever bought a dessert before and then in the middle of it just thought, damn I should have bought the chocolate chip one or the lemon one or the extra fudgy one, but you finish it because you know it's pure sugar and carb goodness and you feel bad because you asked for it and you should be enjoying it right? And then the next time you see it you buy it again because you just think of it in terms of it's sugary goodness and high carbs and rich velvety texture, and then you're left with another disappointing experience, but this time not only are you disappointed during the act of eating the cupcake or cookie or whatever it is, you have an extra inch of fat around your waist to remind you of it. So you're sitting there touching yourself, hating that extra layer of fat you could have avoided but weren't strong enough to, and suddenly you just start freaking out because you realize that if you don't get some self-restraint, you'll look like someone else by Christmas." I finally took a breath.

Mila stayed silent.

"Well?" I asked.

"I'm Jewish," she said.

"Good for you," I said. "And?"

"And I could really go for some hamantaschen right now," she said. "Sorry, was that not the desired effect?"

"You have no self-control," I said.

"Well I already knew that, but what fifteen year old does?"

"That's the thing, I'm not fifteen I'm a twenty-eight year old woman who keeps making these stupid mistakes with Johnny…and every other person with a dick that comes within a five mile radius of me."

Mila leaned in towards me and put her arm around my shoulders.

"Don't worry," she said, "There are always treadmills." She smiled.

I laughed even though it was so not funny.

Mila and I walked into my apartment carrying a couple bags of groceries and sipping our hot tea. I turned towards the living room and spit my tea halfway across the room when I saw four guys feeling each other's ass while the basketball game was on in the background.

"This isn't what this looks like," Maksim spoke up

instantly.

"I hope not," I said. I covered Mila's eyes, but she pushed my hands away and laughed.

Johnny was there too. I was hoping to avoid seeing him as much as I could, but somehow watching Maksim grab his ass was mildly cathartic. I didn't think he was THAT lonely.

"We were just checking to see who had the tightest ass because it's clearly me," said Nick.

"Not having an ass doesn't count as a tight ass," said Noland.

"I do fifty squats every day to get this shape," said Nick. "You're just jealous."

Johnny sat down on the couch the second he saw me.

"You hungry?" I asked Mila.

"Starving."

"Great, I'll start cooking."

"What can I help with?" she asked.

"You know how to make fresh garlic bread?"

"Can't say I ever have, but I can wing it," she said.

"Great."

Mila still stared at the guys in the living room.

"Focus on the bread," I said as I pulled the long French baguette out of the bag in front of her face. "I'll worry about the meat."

"I bet you will," she said as she winked at me.

"Ugh."

The manhandling stopped. Johnny was sitting silently on the couch.

"Did you happen to buy enough for all of us?" Maksim asked as he turned his attention away from the TV for a second.

"Yeah, there's lots," I said.

Johnny ended up leaving before dinner was ready. He didn't even say goodbye to me. He left while I was wrist deep in the meat forming the most savory meatballs.

After dinner Mila went home to do homework. Nick and Noland drank a few more beers then met up with a few people at a nearby bar. Maksim stayed home with me to help me clean up the kitchen, then the living room. The whole apartment was really in desperate need of a clean. He turned on some music then we plowed through it all: the laundry, the scrubbing, the tidying, the sweeping, and the dusting.

It wasn't exactly the most riveting night, but it gave Maksim and I time to catch up and air out our problems. He told me about his attractive female boss that hated him. I told him she was probably just trying to assert her authority. I told him to respect her.

When I was done telling him what he didn't want to hear he let me vent. At first I refused. I was done talking about Johnny and how he made me feel. But while I dodged the subject for a few minutes and focused on the world instead, I eventually found myself using the world to explain my plight with Johnny.

"I thought we were on the right track," I said. "But it seems now that while I thought we were on a tram exploring Italy, we were actually veering off the tracks somewhere near the Rideau Canal," I said.

"Huh?"

"I thought we were in Italy, but we were actually in Canada," I said, "Freezing our butts off in Ottawa. Running around like naked chickens getting frostbite until one of us, i.e. me, got frost bite and had to chop off a limb."

"I'm confused," said Maksim.

"We were on two different playing fields," I said. "I was playing hockey while he was playing soccer. Or the other way around."

"Still not making any sense, can we drop the metaphors please?"

"We wanted two different things I guess. I thought he just needed time to forgive me. I thought doing anything to stay in contact with him would help us mend fences, but I was sorely wrong. I don't even want to mend fences anymore."

"Then don't."

"I won't," I said. "I'm going to focus on myself. I'm going to better myself and grow as an individual not reliant on anyone else for my own happiness."

"That sounds like a great plan," said Maksim, "I fully endorse it. How can I help?"

"That's the thing," I said, "You can't. I have to do it on my own because I am strong, confident, and fearless."

"Fearless women can still ask for help you know."

"I know. I just want to do this on my own."

"Alright then."

We sat there in silence for a moment. My mind was running a marathon, but my body was immobile.

"I don't know how I could have possibly let Johnny think that he could use me like his little voodoo doll. I am no one's voodoo doll," I said.

"I think you mean ragdoll," said Maksim.

"Not the point."

"Okay."

"I'm sorry. I know he's your good friend," I said. "And I know this has got to be weird for you sometimes."

"It's fine," he said.

"Does he ever vent to you about me?" I asked.

"I don't tell him what you say, the same way I wouldn't betray his trust and tell you what he says."

"So he does talk about me!" I said.

"That's not what I said," he said.

"Yes it is." I let out a sigh and looked around the apartment. It was super clean. "I don't care anyway. I'm ready to move on," I said.

"Clearly." He looked at me as I eyed him intently, waiting for him to spill some beans…or at least add heat to the pot.

"I think Johnny feels bad for being a dick," he said. "Honestly I think you're both a dick sometimes."

"Hey!" I said, alarmed.

"You wanted to hear my opinion," he said.

I stayed silent and pondered his accusation while he continued: "Johnny's a dick because he's mad at you for being a dick and you were a dick because you have the self-esteem of a lab rat," said Maksim so matter-of-factly.

"Is that a good thing or a bad thing?"

"Ugh," Maksim ignored me and started walking into his room.

"Hey no wait, come back. How much self-esteem does a lab rat have?" I asked as I followed him towards his room like a chicken waiting for the slaughter.

He shut the door on me.

So I yelled through it. "Are you trying to tell me I'm not in control of the situation?"

There was silence.

"I'll take that as a yes," I said before walking away feeling defeated.

The next day I went into work early for a meeting. My boss at Skinty's demanded that each and every employee be available for this pivotal meeting. I was dreading it once he told us it was good news. Good news for a bar owner is most likely to be nightmare news for the staff who work for him.

"We're acquiring the bar above us," he said. We're putting in a shallow pool for décor to give our bar a classier rooftop pool bar vibe."

As if LA doesn't have enough of those.

The machines around me smiled. I remained hollow. I waited to hear what that would mean for me.

"Because of this, our culture amongst the staff will need to change. First and foremost, there will be a uniform change. Instead of black dresses, women will be wearing white and gold bikinis, and the men will be wearing black and gold swim shorts."

How classy.

It was happening. Slowly my clothes were starting to dwindle. My job was becoming less about the brain in my head and more about the shape of the flesh that lies between my skin and bones. My smile wouldn't be enough.

"Sarcasm and negativity won't be tolerated," he said, practically calling me out by name. "Guests will need to be treated with the utmost respect. We are here to provide a great, pleasurable and luxurious time for each and every one of our guests."

I could no longer be a servant, a machine; I had to be my own pimp. I had to be the sexualized version of perfection. I had to be the object of attention for those who wouldn't even know my name.

"The renovations are expected to be done by midsummer," he said.

I had four months. Four months to leave before I'd never be able to recover from the hurt.

When I got home I curled up like a baby underneath my silky sheets. It was a long day that ended with a bottle of wine. I drifted off into a relaxed sleep with the breeze from my open window aerating the room with just the right amount of freshness.

I heard the front door open. There were footsteps: a few of them. I assumed Maksim brought friends home again. I looked at my phone; it was one in the morning.

The banging got louder. I heard what sounded like shoes being thrown against the wall.

I heard talking but I couldn't make out what they were saying.

A second later my door opened. I assumed it was Maksim. I figured he'd leave when he saw my eyes were closed.

"Ray." It wasn't Maksim's voice. It was Johnny's.

"Ray," he whispered again as he touched my arm, trying to wake me up.

I kept my eyes shut, pretending to be asleep.

"Ray."

He shook my arm harder and put his other hand on my hair.

I tried to keep my eyes from watering.

"Ray, wake up."

He climbed on top of me. I opened my eyes.

"I want you," he leaned down and whispered in my ear. His breath was tantalizingly warm.

I felt his hand sliding underneath my nightgown.

"No, stop," I said. "Get the fuck out."

I pressed my hands firmly against his chest, pushing him back.

I saw him staring at me in his drunken state. Finally looking into my eyes for the first time since I left for Vermont. His eyes were so glazed. I looked into them and saw nothing but the effect of severe inebriation. He sat there, totally still, for another moment.

"Get out," I repeated, this time slightly less hostile, but still abnormally stern for my temperament.

"I'm not your fucking voodoo doll or…ragdoll for whenever the urge arises."

Johnny didn't say a word. I could tell he was trying to think of what he should say. He probably didn't expect me to turn him down. Honestly, I didn't expect it either.

"Whatever this thing is that we've been doing, it's done," I said.

"I thought you were okay with casual," he said.

"You've never been just a hook-up to me and you should know that."

"You left!" He stammered his words.

"You can't keep using that as an excuse. I'm came back."

He didn't say anything so I continued.

"I know I shouldn't have left you so abruptly with no explanation but at some point you needed to decide whether you liked me enough to get over it and be in a relationship with me, or move on," I said quickly. "I don't need another dick in my life."

He put his head down, staring at the sheets. I wasn't sure what he was thinking, but he wasn't moving.

"Get out!" I said again.

"Can I sleep on the couch?" he asked.

"Sleep on the couch, sleep on the floor, I don't give a shit, just leave my room."

I don't know what happened but a second later a tear fell from my eye. I don't know how it happened. It came on suddenly. I hoped he'd be too drunk to remember that, but not drunk enough to forget that I was done with him.

"I'm sorry Ray," he said quietly before opening my door to leave.

I heard the door shut behind me. When I woke up

in the morning, I found Johnny asleep on the couch.

"I'm sorry about last night," he said, sounding sincerely apologetic.

I was still in no mood. I was done with Johnny. I was tired of feeling at the mercy of someone who clearly didn't love me. I was tired of feeling like I should always be the one pleasing others.

"You know you do have your own place, right?" I said to Johnny with a cold ambivalent tone in my voice.

"Are you saying you don't want me staying here anymore?" he asked.

I ignored his question and continued, "We do have taxis you know. In fact, we have those ones that you call from your phone just by putting in your location and clicking request. It's not that high tech, even you could figure it out," I said, coming off a little too bitchy for my old self, but perhaps just bitchy enough for the new confident woman I was trying to become.

"I'm sorry. I'll leave," he said as he gathered his sweatshirt off the couch and reached for his wallet on the coffee table.

I had to do everything in my power to let him walk out the door on those terms. I had to physically hold myself back from apologizing and telling him he could stay as long as he wanted. Not offering him coffee or making sure he had hangover food, made me want to puke. Sometimes I wondered if the pain I felt being cold to someone was worse than letting them be mean to me, and then I reminded myself that this world doesn't reward pushovers.

I let the sex go on longer than it should of, thinking that if we kept our bodies close, soon his heart would follow. I didn't always expect to learn a life lesson everyday, I didn't always expect to know more than what I did the day before, but today I could honestly say that the ocean in my mind was clearer and more pure.

I was so busy fighting for the Johnny I thought I knew, that I didn't realize I was fighting for a completely different person. I dreamed of that morning we turned our pillows and sheets into a fort and laughed as we indulged in the memories of our childhoods. I dreamed of the Johnny who took me out on a date to cheer me up and show me a good time. I dreamed of the warmth I felt when we would finish a bottle of wine and lay on the bed passionately showing the love we had for each other.

INTERMISSION

I sit alone on my bed, hair pulled back into a bun, face bare, hands freed from their cage. I sit here almost sober, but more clear than ever. I remember the blue skies and oranges. I remember the safety of having my parents on the sidelines cheering for me. I remember the simple tasks seeming less cumbersome: putting on socks, waiting for the game to start, waiting for it to end. Time rolled by naturally. I knew what I was doing in this world. I kicked the ball and it went in the net. Now I sit here alone, thousands of miles away from those that I love, separated by so many years from the self that I used to know and admire, with nothing but a vast body of water as my reason for moving away. It's hard being on the opposite side, trying to explore what I've trained myself to want. I've reached a precipice, but I don't know how to get to the other side. The bottle hangs off the edge, but my feet are still planted on the ground.

37 TWO NUNS WALK INTO A SYNAGOGUE

Some days I waited before jumping into the circle of hell. On others I dove right in, head first, waiting for the flames to consume me before the tides had a chance to swell up on shore. There was no air between these four walls, but that didn't stop me from breathing.

Maksim was my emotional dartboard once again. We sat on his bed, as I aired out my grievances. "Everyone around me is doing something," I said, "And here I am wasting away spending my days writing bullshit that no one will ever read, and all those nights I spend slinging cocktails for wannabe actors and movie producers…" I paused for a second to catch my breath. "What skills do I have huh? What do I have to contribute?" I asked.

"You done yet?" Maksim looked bored. "That brain in your head isn't as fucked up as you may think it is, and until you realize that, you're just going to continue going down this shitty road you've built for yourself."

I didn't know how to respond. I'm not in the dark. I'm aware. I know that the decisions I make are what get me into trouble. I see myself heading down the wrong path and I know why, but I don't know how to stop it.

"I can't stop," I said. "It's like I'm running towards the edge of a cliff. I see that it's a dead end. There are other ways to go, but I just can't stop running in that same direction because along the way there are donuts and sex stops and adult beverages and tank tops that push my boobs up, and they just keep me coming."

"I bet they do," said Maksim, winking at me, trying to make a cheap sexual innuendo that didn't quite work.

I ignored it and continued. "So I'm running further and faster, and I see this cliff. It's right there in front of me. I see that in about two minutes I'll be over the edge, but I just can't stop running because dangling off the edge is a shiny new diamond necklace with the rocks cut directly by the hand of the devil's most beloved intern."

"The devil has interns?" asked Maksim completely missing the main point of the story.

I paused, breathing heavily. "Yes. Now how do I stop running off the cliff? I want to stop running. But I don't know how to stop."

The door to Maksim's bedroom opened.

"Maksim, where are the... oh, sorry." Johnny looked at me. I wiped the wetness off my face and kept my head down. Maksim kept his arm still around me. I could feel the intensity of Johnny glaring at me, but like a coward I kept my head down. "I'll just be in the kitchen. Take your time," he said.

"No, what's up?" asked Maksim.

"I was just wondering where the bottle opener is? It wasn't in the usual drawer."

"It's on the desk in my room," I said.

"Kay, thanks." Johnny closed the door behind him.

"Shit," I said. "That's all I fucking needed. Johnny seeing me emotional one more time."

"It's okay," Maksim said. "I think you worry too much about what other people think and I think you don't give yourself enough credit."

"I don't deserve credit. No one's read a single word I've written, nor would anyone ever want to. I'm a slutty bartender with a bad attitude and masochistic tendencies."

"Yeah? Well, it's your own fault," he said, coldly delivering the truth.

"I know," I said.

"You can change it if you want to, Ray. If you want to write, then write. But your writing doesn't mean shit if you don't get it out there. You're not a slave to publishers anymore. You're living in the age of technology and entrepreneurialism. If you want others to read your words, get them out there yourself," his voice continued powerful and confident.

I always admired Maksim's confidence.

"What if I get my work out there and no one reads it?" I asked.

"Then you and the other millions of people who go unnoticed will continue to work. And when ninety

277

percent of those people give up, you'll keep going."

"So I can encounter more humiliation?"

"Failure isn't humiliating. Not trying because you think you suck, is," he said.

The TV was on in the background. A catchy food advertisement played. A family of five danced in their kitchen because they were so excited after eating a meal. They danced like a sexually confused monk, but the expenditure of energy seemed oddly enticing.

"You know I used to be a great dancer," I said.

"I know," he said.

"I used to love it. I still do, but dancing in a crowded bar with a hundred sweaty guys grinding around me isn't exactly the same. I miss performing," I told him. "I miss that feeling in the pit of my stomach when I knew every inch of my body was being consumed by hundreds of eyes on me."

"Then you should dance again," said Maksim. "Sign up for a class."

"I will. I'll look into it tonight!"

"I like the spirit," said Maksim. "I'm happy to have glimmers of my best friend back."

"Back? Where did I go?" I asked.

"Into the fiery darkness of hell. But I knew it was just a phase. After all, destructive breakdowns aren't for the weak."

"Aren't they?"

"You know what they say right?"

"No what?"

"Only white privileged females are allowed to

breakdown."

"That's so racist!"

"Just saying…"

"I think hitting rock bottom helps me thrive," I said.

"I know it does," he said.

Maksim stood up.

"Can you tell Johnny I just had something in my eye, and you were helping me get it out? Like a stick or a crab leg or something?"

"You want me to tell him I was helping you pull out a long, narrow…"

"Stop," I said. "Allergies then?"

He shook his head.

"Plead the fifth?" I asked.

"Sounds good to me," he said.

I snuck into my room. I was afraid to walk in the living room because I knew Johnny was there. I pulled out my laptop and began working on my novel. My fingers hovered above the keyboard, but no words formed. My hands were still. There was nothing there; nothing in the mind that was working overtime to block out everything that was happening outside of these four walls that defined my failure in life.

I always wanted to be more powerful and more in control of my relationships, my friendships, and my jobs. I was stuck in an endless circle that wouldn't end if I didn't step outside the lines. With that in mind I stepped out of my bedroom wearing no makeup, having no lines rehearsed just the simple conclusion that I needed to change this back and forth between someone I claimed to love.

Johnny turned around when he heard footsteps.

"Johnny, can I talk to you for a sec?"

"Sure," he said so softly.

Johnny followed me into my room. Maksim winked at me and made a crude gesture supposedly suggesting that I shouldn't have sex with Johnny. I discreetly flashed him the middle finger.

"I know what you're thinking. 'Why the fuck is this chick always crying?'"

Johnny couldn't deny it.

"Well, I just want to say that I'm sorry and I want you to know I would really like to go back to being friends like we were before all of this. I'm at peace with the idea that we're not a good fit." I took a moment to stare at the floor as I continued in fear of being too open and honest. "You were honestly the sweetest guy that I had ever dated. You made me feel like a princess whenever we hung out. You were patient with me. I just think timing was bad and I wasn't ready for a relationship. And then, well I can't really blame you for what came after." I spoke like a machine but there was a whole complex mechanism working behind it.

I spoke from the deepest place in my heart, but it came out like a rehearsed speech. I lost my ability to feel. I numbed my senses to protect myself from all the pain and now I just spoke to protect myself from any further damage.

"Ray, you have nothing to be sorry about. I was the asshole this whole time."

"I made you that way."

"No one's capable of making me an asshole but me. That's all on me," he said.

"Well, I just want to put it behind us now. I wish you the best with everything in life and…"

"You make it sound like you're never going to see me again," he said.

"No, I just want you to know that I care about your happiness, and I hope you find it with someone."

"I'm not seeing Gigi anymore," he said, nearly taking my breath away.

"Oh," I said. "I'm sorry."

"Are you?"

"I just want you to be happy," I said.

Johnny didn't respond, he just looked at me with those eyes that could pierce a whole through the clearest diamond.

"I'm gunna go make something to eat," I said, breaking up the unbearable silence. "Glad we could clear the air."

"Right," he said.

He wasn't really adding a lot to the conversation. He stood there looking at me. I stood there afraid to make things worse.

I walked into the other room and he followed.

"Well, kids," said Maksim making it a lot more awkward.

"Well," I said. "You guys want some popcorn?"

"That's it?" asked Maksim.

"No, I can make something else too if you want," I

said.

"That's not what I mean," he said.

"I didn't think it was."

Maksim looked at Johnny. Johnny sat on the couch and took a swig of his beer.

It's hard to describe the scene accurately. Imagine a group of nuns sitting in an orthodox synagogue, listening to Hebrew waiting patiently for the part when they get down on their knees and cross themselves. I stood in the kitchen waiting for the popcorn to pop, hoping that the sound of popping kernels would block out the silence that was making me want to scream.

The next few weeks progressed slower than ever. Each day ran into the next. I went into work at Skinty's. I came home and sat alone in my room working on my novel. The storyline was coming together fine, but there was nothing new. I stayed away from the clubs. When I felt like I couldn't breathe, I opened my lungs with coffee followed by red wine. I joined Maksim for the occasional beer at our local dive around the corner. I wore very modest clothing. Life wasn't dramatic. It was fine. It was happening. Time was passing by, and that's about all I could say.

It didn't take me long to realize that I needed more. That boring, plain daily life was everything that I didn't realize I had been fighting against. I was drowning in a sea of boredom. My legs at times would collapse beneath me or my arms would fall to my side because I had no motivation to turn anything into action. I wasn't stupid enough to call on Johnny again, but I needed something to keep my soul alive. I realized that feeling pain, feeling hurt, or feeling scared was still "feeling," which right now seemed a lot better than feeling nothing at all.

For weeks I was afraid to let myself go so high when I knew that it would undoubtedly be followed by the lowest low: one that would be even harder to handle after experiencing such brilliance. But then I realized I needed those highs. I needed all of them. I was a body and a soul festering like phytoplankton at the bottom of the sea, but it was that feeling that I needed in order to prosper.

That's why I decided to start hooking up with a guy named Chad. He fit every criterion I had on my dwindling list. He was attractive, narcissistic, unavailable, and an undeniable douche. I was on my way to hitting another rock bottom that would soon let me be free to soar.

When he touched me I cringed on the inside and waited for him to leave so I could write. My manuscript flourished. I wrote from a place I never wanted to be again, and I relished in my ability to create work that I would be proud to show people one day.

I hated myself and loved my work. I was mentally free. I ran from work to Chad's place to my bedroom between those four walls that seemed like less of a barrier now that I was learning to embrace my enemies.

Johnny was being pleasant when I saw him. He seemed to be hanging out with Maksim and the other guys fairly often like usual. Maksim kept asking me to have a drink with Johnny. I kept putting it off saying that I was on a roll writing and although I was anything but happy, I was inspired. Maksim didn't really understand but he didn't push it.

Johnny texted me one day asking me to meet him for a drink. I told him I was busy, but promised we'd do a drink soon. When I saw him the next day at our apartment watching a game with the guys, I assured him that I wasn't mad I just had to get work done.

I smiled and gave him a hug. He was confused, but he said he was glad to see me happy. It made me feel good to think Johnny thought that I was happy. I was glad that he didn't know how unhappy I really was inside these fleshy walls that hosted a soul that had no meaning. I was just grateful Johnny wasn't the one leading me to that dark place I let every other man take me to.

By this point, I was so delirious from all the uppers and downers I was taking. I really couldn't tell what it was that I was feeling or whether I was feeling anything in the body that I had crafted to perfection. When I laughed I had to remind my body how to recover, when I smiled I had to remember not to cry, when I watched Johnny look at me with confusion I had to force myself from sprinting into his arms and tackling him with all the love I was waiting so patiently to give.

One day I decided to bring Chad back to my place. When we walked in, Maksim was on the couch talking to his mom on the phone. It was the perfect time to sneak into the kitchen, grab a drink, and then run off to my room.

"I got to call you back mom," said Maksim.

When he hung up the phone, Chad and I were

already headed back to my room.

"Ray, wait up. Who's this?" he asked looking at Chad.

"This is Chad. Chad, this is my roomie, Maksim."

"Sup," said Chad like a true bro.

"Alright then. We'll be in my room," I said.

"Ray, can I talk to you for a sec?" asked Maksim.

"Sure."

Chad waited in my room.

"What?" I asked Maksim.

"Who the fuck is that?"

"What do you mean, I just told you. That's Chad."

"Okay, yeah mhm, I know his name is Chad, but why the fuck are you hanging out with him?"

"Because I'm in desperate need of an oxytocin boost."

"Okay. Ever tried banana pancakes?"

"What?"

"Banana pancakes? Something about the bananas and sugar and carbs. They'll give you an oxytocin boost too."

"Right…" I said. "Nah, I'm good."

"Why don't you call Johnny?" he asked.

"Why would I call Johnny?"

"Because you like him and because he likes you and because he's been patiently waiting for you to reach out to him and make things better."

"What are you talking about, I already made things better. Johnny and I are good," I said.

"No you're not."

"You know something I don't?"

"Well I know a lot you don't, but yes I know that Johnny's been asking about you constantly and I know that you don't want to be fucking Chad right now?"

"You got a direct line to my vagina?"

"God I hope not."

"Thanks for the concern my friend. Love you for it. But I'm good," I said as I walked into my room awaiting hell.

Chad laid half naked on my bed.

Well that was fast.

Two minutes later there was a knock at the door.

"Ray," yelled Maksim from the hallway. "Where is the toilet paper you just bought?"

"The bathroom," I yelled.

I was on top of Chad. He held my hips and kissed me.

"Okay thanks, did you happen to buy more air freshener too?" he yelled.

I stopped kissing Chad again. "No!" I said frustrated.

"I've got a date tonight," he said, "Do you have any extra condoms lying around?"

I buried my head into the pillow.

"Cause I'm all out," said Maksim from behind the door.

"Go away!" I yelled.

"I can't. You want me to get a disease? I've only known this chick for a week."

"For the love of god, go buy a box of condoms," I

said, filled with frustration.

"Okay," he said timidly.

I looked at Chad beneath me.

"I got a couple," he said to me in that husky voice of his. "I can give him one if he wants. Unless, we're planning on going a couple rounds tonight?"

I rolled off of him in defeat.

"He doesn't need a condom," I said. "He's just being an ass."

The mood was dead. Maksim was quiet for a minute.

"Ray?" Maksim was still at it.

"What?"

"I have this weird rash on my back. You think you could come look at it? I don't want to like give her scabies or anything."

"Is he into you?" Chad asked me.

"Eww, no he's like a brother. He's just helping out a buddy," I said.

"What?" He was clearly confused.

"Never mind. Let me just shut him up," I said. I put my shirt back on and left the room. When I shut the door behind me, I shot Maksim the most evil death-stare drudged up from the underworld of my ignored coochie.

"That's not a cute look," he said.

"What the fuck?"

"Johnny's on his way over," he said.

"Why the fuck would you call him?" I asked.

"I didn't. I texted him. He said he was on his way over to stop the slaughter."

"What slaughter?"

"I dunno those were his words, not mine."

"The only ones who are going to be slaughtered are you and him if you both don't let me destroy my own happiness in peace," I said.

"We're willing to take the risk."

"I'm not joking," I said. "I'm ignoring you both."

I went back into my room. Ten minutes later I heard the front door open.

Shit.

"You might hear some weird things coming from the other room," I said to Chad. "Just don't let it distract you," I said, kissing him.

There was a knock at the door.

"Ignore it," I whispered.

Another knock.

Fuck.

The knocking continued.

"Ray," said Johnny. "Ray, can I talk to you for a sec?"

"No, I'm busy right now."

"Uhhh, uhhh aagh yeah, right there," Maksim was yelling from the other room.

"What the fuck man?" I heard Johnny say quietly.

"Pretend to fuck me," Maksim whispered to Johnny.

"Dude, I am so uncomfortable with everything you just said," said Johnny.

"Ray won't be able to fuck him if she hears her best friend fucking her past and future boyfriend. I mean, talk about a lady boner killer right?"

"You have a disturbing point," said Johnny. "I guess we got to do what we got to do, right?"

"Ahhh, yeah, oh yeah, mmmm," I heard Johnny yelling completely unrealistically from behind the door.

"Harder," yelled Maksim.

"Mmm, I like it, I like it," Johnny shrieked.

By this point, I was lying beside Chad staring up at the ceiling, still fully clothed. Then I heard Maksim laugh.

"Wait, here, use this," I heard Johnny say.

"Okay, now this is really making me nauseous," I said. I got off the bed and opened the door. Maksim and Johnny were standing there fully clothed.

"Huh, I didn't know that devils don't sweat when they have sex."

"Hey," said Johnny, trying to sound out of breath. He ignored my little jab and quickly pushed past me into my room. "Hey, can you leave?" he asked Chad.

"Uh, no man we're actually kinda busy right now, why don't you go back to fucking your boyfriend?"

"What are you doing?" I asked Johnny.

Johnny ignored me once again and directed his speech towards Chad, "See the thing is I would go back to fucking my boyfriend, except I kinda love this girl right here," he said pointing to me.

Chad just looked at him with a dumbfounded look.

"Yup, that one. And she loves me too," Johnny continued. "I've just been a really big dick lately. Looking at the size of the bulge in your underpants there, I'd say that you understand big dicks," Johnny gestured towards Chad's crotch then continued, "But I need you to leave."

Chad clearly felt uncomfortable having another man staring at his package. This whole situation was making me beyond embarrassed, except for one small thing. Johnny just said he loved me. Well he didn't say it to me. He said it to my attempted fuck boy of the night, which I oddly preferred.

I felt something in my chest, something I couldn't quite describe, like I swallowed a piece of metal or ate something that wasn't edible. I wanted to throw up.

"Is this your place, buddy?" Chad said grabbing his shirt off the floor and slowly moving towards Johnny.

"Okay you know what, Johnny, you should leave, Chad stay," I said.

"No, I think Chad should leave, I'll stay," said Johnny.

"Johnny," I pleaded.

"Whatever dude," Chad put on his shirt as he got ready to leave.

Seriously, he's not even going to put up a fight. In the movies there'd definitely be more action.

"Johnny, leave us alone," I said hoping for some privacy with Chad while knowing it was probably a failed mission.

Chad was already by the door.

"See yah, Ray," he said before shutting the front door in a hurry.

"I hate you," I said to Johnny looking him straight in the face.

"I love you," he said.

"Are you serious right now?! If you loved me you wouldn't take every opportunity you get to torture me."

"Torture you? I'm sorry it came out like this, but how have I tortured you?"

"I haven't had good sex since we broke up. I masturbated for three fucking hours yesterday," I yelled at him. "Over and over. I was like a hard core porn star after consuming a six pack of energy drinks, or like one of those bunnies that just keeps beating that drum..." I had one hand on my hip and the other mimicking the gesture a drummer makes when they're smashing their drum set.

"What?"

"You know that pink bunny with the black glasses and those big drumsticks and it just keeps beating and beating, and..." I let out a big sigh as my mind wandered off.

"What was I talking about again?" I asked.

"Your masturbation habits," he said calmly.

"Right." I looked at him for a moment without speaking. I wondered why I had just shared that information with Johnny. I used anger to cover up the excitement I felt deep down knowing that Johnny cared enough to screw up my planned orgasm for the night.

"I'm tired of having to manufacture my own orgasms. I want somebody else to do it for once," I said, sounding a lot whinier than I had intended. My voice started to linger off as my shoulders slumped over, and I sat down defeated and horny on my untainted bedspread.

"I'm sorry if I ruined your night...and your orgasm," said Johnny in the softest tone I had heard from him since we broke up. "But I think I can help you out with that." A large grin washed across his face, but I was so not in the mood anymore.

I could tell he was trying to de-escalate the situation, but I wasn't ready to let that happen. With a renewed source of energy, a furrowed brow and anger in my eye, I ignored his apology and continued yelling at him, "Did I get to step in when you were fucking Gigi or the other half of the women in LA? No!" I answered my own question then continued again. "I told you I was sorry, and I tried to be patient, and I tried to get you back and you not only resisted every time, but also did whatever you could to dig the knife in just a little bit more each and every fucking time, you mother fucking...UGH." I let out a huge angry grunt. I could feel it stemming from the pit of my stomach and reverberate through every nerve in my body. "Finally, after a painful string of meaningless sexual experiences, we finally mended fences. Why are you trying to hurt me again?"

Johnny wore a pair of dark washed jeans. I could see his grey boxers sticking out at the top. I hated how sexy he always looked. I forced myself to think about the way I felt when he was selfishly using me for his own satisfaction. I remembered him leaving right after we made love and pushing his date in my face. I had no tangible souvenir to remember how I felt in that moment, but the images in my brain and the memory of my soul sinking into its little cocoon was really all I needed to stay away from the guy I was afraid to admit I still loved.

With that I left. I walked passed Johnny into the

living room, slipped on my shoes and was out the door in two seconds. I hoped to find Chad.

"Chad, wait!" He walked outside my building. "I'm so sorry about that," I said.

"Johnny's just my roommate's friend. But his recent mission unfortunately has been depriving me of good sex," I laughed a nervous laugh that came out more as a pity-me chuckle.

"No worries baby, want to come to my place?"

It kind of surprised me that he didn't care another man just professed his love for me. His mind was still on the prize after all that. The beer stain on his shirt caught my attention. Looked like he may have also spilled some ketchup, or was that lipstick? I didn't know for sure. I looked up at him again and saw the harshness of the bright moon behind him.

"Actually, I think I'll just call it a night," I said.

"Okay baby, that's my ride. See yah," he said as he walked away without giving me so much as a kiss goodnight.

"See yah," I said.

When I entered my apartment, Johnny and Maksim were sitting on the couch. They both turned around to look at me. I shot them a two second angry glance then went to my room and slammed the door shut.

"So how do you think that went for you buddy?" Maksim asked Johnny.

"Not well," he replied.

"Yeah."

There was a moment of silence.

"Am I an asshole?" Johnny asked Maksim casually, staring straight ahead at the television as he sat slouched over on the couch.

"Yeah," said Maksim. "You are."

Johnny shook his head and took another sip of his beer.

38 THRESHOLD FOR HAPPINESS

Someone once told me, if you can't understand the world around you, you should just do what makes sense, even if that's just masturbation. I couldn't explain a lot recently. I couldn't decipher my feelings or my actions. I couldn't see the consequences of my choices; I just blindly felt them pushing me forward in a direction so unknown.

Without a map guiding my way, I focused on the small things: the things I could control. I applied to a whole bunch of writing jobs. They weren't exactly the kind of writing jobs I wanted, but at least I'd be getting paid to write instead of getting paid to pour shots. At the very least, they'd allow me to build some sort of portfolio.

I was surprised when I had inspiration to get out of bed this morning at six. I didn't even have a job yet. I had no security, no defined path, no boyfriend, and yet I was excited. For once I was finally excited to do something besides tequila shots. I was utterly fucking terrified, but excited.

I was a free agent. I was feigning confidence hoping it would one day turn into something genuine. I was learning to act the way I wanted to feel, hoping that fake would turn to real, ambition would turn into happiness, and persistence would turn into strength.

I started to realize that the writing process was actually quite selfish. I used it as an excuse to hide. I used it as a reason to explain my absence in anything I didn't want to do or was afraid to do. I decided to take one week off of writing. I decided to challenge myself to spend the week outside living, meeting, experiencing, and feeling the world instead of hiding from it and writing about the walls: those same four walls.

I went to a recreational dance class. I wore my tummy-baring top and my favorite Mary Jane pumps. I listened to every note and followed the instructor, adding in my own expressions as I saw fit. I felt the sweat drip down my body. I relished in that sober feeling of happiness I hadn't experienced in a while.

That night I went into work with a typed letter in hand. I walked into the back office. The owner had redecorated the office to match the new white and gold décor that the bar would soon unveil.

He looked up at me and I smiled.

"Hello there," he said.

"Hi."

"Ray, right?"

"Yes," I said, surprised he knew my name. My

manager was the one that hired me and worked with me. I had only ever seen the owner twice.

"It's nice to meet you. I'm really looking forward to meeting all of our staff both new and old as we transition into our new and improved bar. I've heard really great things about you."

That was surprising. I held the letter in my hand.

"I'm glad you came to see me today. How are you liking it here?"

I froze.

"It's great," I lied.

I clutched that letter. All I had to do was give it to him.

"That's great," he said. "How would you like to take on an assistant managerial position?"

Why was this happening now?

I was just seconds away from pursuing a better future.

"I would love that."

"Wonderful," he said with such enthusiasm.

"Do assistant managers have to wear the bathing suit?" I asked.

He paused for a moment.

"Do you not want to wear the bathing suit?" He asked as he looked me up and down. "I can't see why you wouldn't." He chuckled.

"I would prefer not to," I said, wondering if he would revoke my promotion.

"As assistant manager, you'll be the one setting the example." He paused to think for a moment. "Then again, we want our managerial team to be professional. So no. You can wear what you'd like."

"That's great," I said. "Thank you." I turned around to leave.

"Just no pant suits," he added.

"Excuse me?"

"No pant suits. Keep it elegant. Feminine. Classy, but alluring. We're here to impress remember," he said.

"I can't impress in a pant suit?"

"No. The way we dress shows who we are, what we stand for, you know?"

"Right," I said smiling. "Thank you."

"You're welcome."

"Here," I said, leaving the letter on his desk.

"What is this?" he asked as he reached for his glasses.

"My two weeks notice."

"But...why? I..."

"Because I look fucking hot in a pant suit."

"No woman looks hot in a pant suit."

"That's unfortunate you think that."

"So this is all about the dress code?" he asked.

"No...and yes. Well it's about me. If you took the time to notice, I'm actually a pretty shitty bartender and server. I don't really like people all that much. I mean I like some of them, but not particularly the ones that grace us with their presence at this establishment."

"Then why'd you work here for so long?"

"I needed to know what it felt like to hit rock bottom."

"Sweetie, I hate to tell you, but working here is not rock bottom. There's much worse out there."

"You're right," I said. "But this was my rock bottom."

I left his office with the greatest spark of hope I had felt in a long time. I wasn't nearly free, but there was one less strap holding me down.

39 A GUY NAMED SPIKE

When Maksim came home from work tonight, the apartment smelled like Thanksgiving. I made dinner: a huge dinner that Maksim and I would be snacking on for probably a week because there was only Maksim and I there to consume it. I restocked our fridge with enough beer to supply a frat party and there was every varietal of wine available. Tonight I wanted to celebrate.

I wore a long flippy skirt and a floral apron over my t-shirt. I put on that red lipstick that made me feel sexy, and curled my hair to look classy. If you didn't know any better you'd say I was a housewife from the fifties. I channeled my inner spirit, that of a woman born in the thirties and living out her life as an enthusiastic housewife.

"Hello dear," I said when Maksim walked through the front door of our apartment.

"Well, that's a bit creepy," he said.

"What's creepy?" I asked.

"That apron and you calling me 'dear,' and what's that incredible smell?" he asked.

"I made dinner," I said. "You are my best pal, and as my best pal who helps me out tremendously all the time, I thought you deserved a nice home-cooked meal."

"Well, that's extremely cool of you, Ray, but what's the occasion?"

"Well," I paused, "I have some news."

"Please tell me you're not leaving, converting to a different religion, getting a tattoo, questioning your sexuality, or becoming a nun?"

I looked at Maksim, smiled, and hesitated before saying, "Wait, why would I want to become a nun…or experiment with women?" I asked.

"I don't know, but quarter-life crises can be unpredictable," he said, half-joking I hope.

"Is this a quarter-life crisis that I'm having?" I joshed. "If it was, I would have thought my hair would be green, I'd have a nose ring, and I'd be dating a guy in a motorcycle club named Spike."

"Fine it's not a quarter life crisis, just tell me your news," Maksim said impatiently interrupting my banter.

"My second novel is done and it's now available to buy online. I also have six small bookstores around the LA area that have agreed to sell it," I paused. "I am officially a published author." I looked at Maksim smiling ear-to-ear and totally speechless.

"Holy shit!" Maksim ran up to me giving me the biggest hug and lifting me off the ground.

"And there's more," I said.

"Oh jeeze, what?" he asked.

"I got a job as an assistant editor for an online lifestyle magazine. It's nothing big or anything, but the website gets about 100,000 unique visitors every month, and it's been growing rapidly since it's conception two years ago. I figure that this could be a good stepping stone to maybe creating my own online magazine one day, or even just a good way to improve my writing portfolio so that I can get more writing jobs in the future," I said before finally taking a breath.

"Holy shit, Ray that's amazing," he said as he opened the fridge to grab himself a beer. There, sitting in front, was a twelve pack of Cold Breath, Johnny's favorite beer. I ordered some, just to keep our fridge stocked with a nice selection, or at least that's what I told myself. Maksim saw it and turned to me after he grabbed another brand of beer for himself.

"You sure I'm the one you want to celebrate with?" he asked me with those knowing eyes I loved and hated.

"Who else do I have?" I took a moment to feel bad; I took a moment to think about Johnny.

"I want to celebrate with you, my friend."

"Okay." He sighed. "We're gunna end tonight blacked out on the floor, just so you know," he said.

I chuckled even though I knew it was true. "Okay great, but before we black out, can we eat this meal I slaved over all day? I made cookies for dessert and I think this is the first time in my life I successfully baked something. I've eaten four already without gagging, and I actually remembered to add in the sugar...unlike last time."

"Huh, right, I forgot about your awful accidentally sugarless cookies," he said. "I believe you called them chocolate chip crackers."

"Yeah, I've been trying to forget that too."

"But yeah sure, let's eat first. Anything for my newly employed roomie," said Maksim.

"You make me sound like a vagabond. I've been employed this whole time...it just hasn't been good employment."

"You're right, my mistake. I forgot what an upstanding bartender you were," he said.

Halfway through devouring the roasted chicken, the candied vegetables, and the garlic avocado mashed potatoes Maksim and I were already drunk. We started out slow, but by the time we finished the salad appetizer, our beers turned into shots of tequila and trust me there's only one way to go after starting with beer, and that is down.

"Wine!" I said with over-the-top exuberance.

"What?"

"I forgot about the wine," I said. I bought some oaky, fruity, full-bodied, peppery concoction or some shit, but when the guy was describing it to me it was oddly turning me on so I assumed it would be good."

"Well lets open that horny thing up," said Maksim

drunk and loud like an impatient twenty-one year old.

"The wine is not horny," I said, "The wine was making me horny," I clarified, as I went over my own words trying to understand them myself.

"Oh. Ew, I don't want to open you up," he said.

"Okay you know what, stop. Don't finish that thought. Just open the wine and let's drink up," I said, stumbling slightly as I spoke with one word slurring into the next, drunk and delirious and loving every second of it.

A few hours passed and our drinking sped up. One bottle, two bottles, three bottles, I forget how many we finished, but I think it was a few because we were now lying on the floor staring at the ceiling fan.
"I think I've finally accepted the fact that my current mode of living is not conducive to a happy spirit," I said.

Maksim concentrated intently on a rip in our carpet.

"Maksim?" I said expecting him to respond.

"I'm sorry, I've finally accepted the fact that ignoring your sappy banter is most conducive for my happiness," he said.

"That's fair."

"You've made your path to happiness and fulfillment so fucking narrow, it'll always be impossible," he said.

"Fuck you," I said. "You're supposed to be the one encouraging me not to settle."

"Everyone's always searching for something better. The most valuable advice someone ever gave me was to settle," he said.

"That's not how I find happiness."

"You're the last person on this entire planet that should be giving advice on achieving happiness," he said.

"What about the moon?"

"What?" he asked.

"What if I lived on the moon? Could I give advice on happiness then?"

"Yes. But only if you lived on the moon."

"Okay," I said, content.

I suddenly worried that I'd be the loser at the end of the game with no coins in my pocket because I'd given back every mystery bag hoping that the next one would contain the jackpot.

40 TEN THOUSAND SLIPPERY GOATS

Maksim and I sat at the kitchen table drinking coffee, waiting for it to sync into our systems and help us feel alive after drinking ourselves into an oblivion last night.

"I think you just need to make up your mind and realize the steps it'll take to get what you want and then decide to go after it, or find another way to make yourself happy," said Maksim.

"And if I decide I want Johnny, then what?"

"I want you to be happy, and Johnny too," he said. "I think he's generally a good guy. He has his fair share of faults, but hey, we're all sons of bitches from time to time aren't we?"

"I love him," I said.

"Yeah no shit," said Maksim.

"But I'm mad at him for the way he treated me when I got back from Vermont," I said.

"Maybe you should be the bigger person and forgive him, the way you wanted him to forgive you when you got back?"

"Be the bigger person?" I asked myself the question.

"Seems strange, huh?"

"Totally," I said.

I looked at Maksim and smiled, one of those 'I just finished masturbating and eating chocolate chips out of the bag' kind of smiles.

"Go get him," he said. "I mean, finish your coffee first. But then go get him."

For once I believed I could. For once I felt like I was capable of deciding my future instead of leaving it up to the highest bidder. I wasn't sure if it was the combination of drugs in my system or whether it was just truly my heart's desire that I was starting to embrace.

"Okay, I need to take some time to formulate a plan: something strategic and effective. Can you call him and find out if he's got himself a new girl yet or if he's gone back to Gigi? I don't want to show up at his apartment when he's in the middle of…Or actually…"

"Ray, stop! Your plans suck. Just go get him."

"But."

"Ray, I will come down on you like the wrath of ten thousand slippery goats if you don't get your butt out of this apartment and over to Johnny's."

"What does that even mean?"

"I don't know, but it's bad."

"Okay." I grabbed my jean jacket off the coat hook, slipped on my flip-flops and put my navy ombré power pumps in a bag to take with me. I guzzled down the rest of my coffee.

"Why are you taking the pumps?" Maksim asked.

"To wear to Johnny's," I said.

"Why don't you just put them on now?"

"I need my flip-flops for the beach first."

"The beach? Why now?" he asked.

"I need to hear the waves. It'll help me think," I said.

"No thinking, Ray. Your thinking sucks. Act. Go. Do!" he said rather harshly.

I looked at him and smiled.

"Thanks, dude," I said.

I ran to the fridge and put some beer in a box. Then I left, escaping those four walls that nearly consumed me.

41 THE END OF LONGING

It took me a long time to realize that longing for something or someone who wasn't there was the most toxic force I could have in my life. For me, that never-ending sense of longing was just as bad as my binge drinking. I held on to both of them because of the good feelings they gave me, but I didn't realize how fast I was drowning in my own toxic sludge.

Now I stood there at his door still damp from the ocean waves, but ready to embrace the present because that's the only moment in time that could breed happiness. Although I hadn't planned on going in the water, the waves consumed me, heart and soul. So I let myself feel something all the way down the sandy shore into the cold salty water. I let myself feel the waves and let my feet collapse into the sand as my eyes got lost in the horizon. Then I walked out of the ocean with the free will to do so. I walked away remembering what I loved and who I loved.

In one single moment, I let myself be vulnerable standing there in ripped jeans and messy hair. I let the rain from the sun shower wash away the mask. I held my hand up, closed-fist, and took a deep breath before finally knocking on the door. My heart beat quickly. I felt my chest rise and fall. I still didn't know what I was going to say.

The door opened. I felt the drops of sweat forming on my fingertips. He looked so good standing there before me in his work pants and his button-down shirt.

Every time I opened my mouth nothing came out. I swallowed again and again. My mind went from running a mile a minute to blacking out every other second like the lights at a rave. He didn't say anything; I think he was waiting for me. I tore my gaze away from my shoes and looked up at him again.

Shit I forgot to change out of my flip-flops into my pumps.

I opened my mouth, but again no words were there.

By this point I should have been feeling more embarrassed; somehow I didn't.

Should I turn around and walk away?

I wasn't getting anywhere. I wasn't able to speak. He just stood there. I stood there. Nothing was happening. And then…

And then I swallowed. A big, loud swallow with my red lips pressed together.

"I'm a published author," I said. "Well, self-published author but…"

Johnny didn't say anything, but a smile slowly started to form across his face. I waited for the words that would resolve this turmoil between us; I waited to hear his reaction.

Then he stepped forward and embraced me with his whole body, one arm holding me tight around the waist and the other wrapped around me with his hand holding the back of my head.

I let my whole body melt into his with the greatest force like that of the ocean's waves crashing into a sandy shore.

"You did it, Ray," he said. You finally fucking did it."

There was a disconnect between my heart and my mind for just a second and in that second all I felt was the pure sweetness that reverberated off his every word like the juiciest strawberries in the middle of summer. His words gave me warmth. That feeling I was falling off the Brooklyn Bridge wasn't there. Instead, I flew high like a bird that just learned how to take flight. I rose higher and higher with every word he said.

As I stared straight ahead with my head resting on his shoulders seeing nothing but the light from the lamp in the hallway beaming forth towards us highlighting our embrace and solidifying our future, I couldn't help but feel like there was a reason I made it this far. The light was sharp and severe, but it was better than darkness. I grew to love what I never thought I would. I grew to love the light, to love the embrace, to love the feeling of revealing my wants and needs, and wanting something I believed myself to be capable of receiving. This feeling felt so good, but it still felt so foreign.

In that moment I wondered whether my imagination had grown so strong that I was able to create an image of myself that blended in with the image I had conjectured for my future self. For the first time in a long time, my body wasn't just a body. It had a soul. How did I know this? The only proof I had was the feeling in my limbs, the way my skin felt when I stroked it with my fingers, or the way my muscles hurt when I pushed too hard.

Although I was there in physical proximity to him, in some ways I knew I'd never be there. I'd always be in the future or the past looking backwards or forwards, wondering how the light in my eyes as a child somehow diminished so fiercely as I grew up. A candle's flame can be flickering one second and out the next. I stood there sharp and erect, waiting for the light to go out. I was a candle flickering in the wind; I was a portrait of nothing.

"I was hoping you'd want to celebrate with me," I said to Johnny as I pulled away from his embrace slightly.

He looked down at the package on his doorstep. "I assume you've got some celebratory fluids in your box."

I furrowed my eyebrows. He paused for a second.

"Eww, I think that's in the top ten list of things I said that didn't come out right."

"Yeah, it made me a little queasy to be honest."

"I was referring to some sort of alcoholic beverage, just to clarify," he said.

"I hope so."

"And I think instead of fluids, I should have said liquids."

"Probably," I said.

He let out an awkward laugh.

"It's not just any alcohol," I said as I pulled out a twelve pack of Cold Breath beer.

"My favorite beer," he said.

"Yeah, I had it shipped here all the way from Canada."

Like a bulldozer, the curvature of his lips broke down the concrete surrounding my heart.

"Well then, come in," he said.

I walked inside feeling the warmth of his arm around me.

"By the way, I'm gunna buy twenty-five copies of your book," he said nonchalantly.

"Twenty-five?" I paused. "Are you sure that's enough?"

"It's in case I lose a couple."

"In case you lose a couple, you'll have twenty-three left?"

"Yeah, you know, one for every surface in my apartment." He smiled so I smiled, like one wave crashing into the next.

"Maybe we'll try to recreate that scene from *The Wolf of Wall Street* where they fuck on the bed on top of all that money, but instead of money, we'll use your books."

I cringed. My eyebrows furrowed and my nose crinkled like when you get a whiff of your parent's bedroom and you wish you didn't know the smell of cum and sweaty ball sacks.

"Nah," I said.

"Sorry. Too much."

Every once in a while you meet someone who has such a profound effect on your life and you can't quite explain it. It could be someone you've known for a day or someone you've known for ten years. The lucky ones get to spend every day of their lives getting to know the one they loved from the first moments they spent together, and the unlucky ones get to think and reflect on where they went wrong in losing someone so special.

My fate has yet to be determined but I'm learning everyday. There was never going to be a magic ticket to happiness. There was no lifestyle I could lead that was perfect because perfect doesn't exist and I could only be happy if I chose to be happy with no fear and no hesitation.

The only thing stopping me from greatness were those four walls I hid behind, writing a lifeless work that couldn't be brought to life until I learned how to live. A wingless bird can only learn how to fly after feeling the sting of falling a few times. We learn to make our own wings through darkness or in light. By feeling everything deeply or feeling nothing at all, we open our eyes and illuminate the road to reaching our wildest desires.

And then we watch as we fuck it all up.

SUCCESS HAS NO PLACE HERE

ABOUT THE AUTHOR

Jaclyn works towards perfection because she thrives on failure.